Dear Reader,

From the time I started writing novels, romantic comedies have particularly appealed to me—especially those involving matchmakers and arranged marriages. These classic romance plots are longtime favorites of mine (and I know lots of other writers and readers like them, too). Here, in this volume, are two I think you'll enjoy.

First Comes Marriage was written in 1991 and features what you might call a "Grandfather knows best" scenario. *Wanted: Perfect Partner,* on the other hand, is a story about a single mother with a teenage daughter who's sure *she* knows best—or at least better than her mom. (If you've had or currently have teenaged children, you'll be familiar with this situation!)

As the title suggests, both stories take place in a city I know well, with streets I've often walked and places I've visited. Seattle is a setting I love for that reason.

Although I've gone on to write many romantic comedies, these two stories still bring me great pleasure and make me laugh—even after all these years. Everyone can use an excuse to smile, and I hope that's what you do when you read them.

I appreciate hearing from my readers. You can reach me at www.debbiemacomber.com or P.O. Box 1458, Port Orchard, Washington 98366.

Warmest regards,

Debbie Macomber

DEBBIE
MACOMBER

Married in Seattle

MIRA

MIRA

ISBN-13: 978-0-7783-2679-3
ISBN-10:   0-7783-2679-9

MARRIED IN SEATTLE

Copyright © 2009 by MIRA Books.

The publisher acknowledges the copyright holder
of the individual works as follows:

FIRST COMES MARRIAGE
Copyright © 1991 by Debbie Macomber.

WANTED: PERFECT PARTNER
Copyright © 1995 by Debbie Macomber.

www.MIRABooks.com

Printed in U.S.A.

CONTENTS

FIRST COMES MARRIAGE

To Anna and Anton Adler,
Russian immigrants and
my loving grandparents.
Thank you for the wonderful heritage
you gave me.

One

"You must be Zachary Thomas," Janine said breathlessly as she whirled into the office. "Sorry I'm late, but I got hung up in traffic on Fourth Avenue. I didn't realize they'd torn up the whole street." Still a little winded, she unfastened her coat, tossed it over the back of the visitor's chair and threw herself down, facing the large executive desk.

The man on the other side blinked twice as though he didn't know quite what to think.

"I'm Janine Hartman." She drew in a deep breath. "Gramps said if he wasn't back from his appointment, I should introduce myself."

"Yes," Zachary said after a moment of strained silence. "But he didn't tell me you'd be wearing—"

"Oh, the bandanna dress," Janine said, smoothing one hand over her lap. The dress had been constructed of red and blue bandannas; it featured a knee-length zigzag hemline and closely hugged her hips. "It was a gift. And since I'm meeting the girl who made it later, I thought I should wear it."

"And the necklace?"

Janine toyed with the colored Christmas-tree lights strung between large beads on a bootlace that dangled from her neck. "It's a bit outrageous, isn't it? That was a gift, too. I think it's kind of cute, don't you? Pamela is so clever."

"Pamela?"

"A teenager from the Friendship Club."

"I…see," Zach said.

"I do volunteer work there and the two of us hit it off as soon as we met. Pam's mother doesn't live in the area and she's at that awkward age and needs a friend. For some reason she took a liking to me, which was fine because I think she's wonderful."

"I see," he said again.

Janine doubted he did.

"The necklace is *different* I'll grant you," Zach was saying—which wasn't admitting to much. His dark eyes narrowed as he studied it.

Now that she'd met Zachary Thomas, Janine could understand why her grandfather was so impressed with him— if appearances were anything to judge by. In his well-tailored suit, he was the very picture of a high-powered executive, crisp, formal and in control. He was younger than she'd assumed, possibly in his early thirties, but it was difficult to tell. His facial features were attractive enough, but he wasn't strikingly handsome. Still, she found herself fascinated by the strength of character she saw in the uneve planes of his face. His dark hair was cut military short. His jaw was strong, his cheekbones high and his mouth full. That was the way she'd describe him physically, but there was apparently much more to this man than met the eye. At least, her grandfather was convinced of it.

Several months earlier Anton Hartman had merged his well-established business-supply firm with the fast-expanding company owned by Zachary Thomas. Together the two men had quickly dominated the market.

For weeks now, Gramps had wanted Janine to meet Zachary. His name had popped up in every conversation, no matter what they were discussing. To say her grandfather thought highly of his partner was an understatement.

"Gramps has spoken...well of you," she said next.

A hint of a smile—just the merest suggestion—touched his mouth, giving her the impression that he didn't smile often. "Your grandfather has one of the keenest business minds in the country."

"He's incredible, isn't he?"

Zachary's nod betrayed no hesitation.

There was a polite knock on the door and a tall middle-aged woman wearing a navy-blue pin-striped suit stepped into the room. "Mr. Hartman phoned," she announced primly. "He's been delayed and asked that you meet him at the restaurant."

Zach's lean dark face tightened briefly before he cast Janine an uneasy glance. "Did he say when he was going to get there?"

"I'm sorry, Mr. Thomas, but he didn't."

Janine looked at her watch. She was supposed to meet Pam at three. If they were delayed much longer, she'd be late.

She scowled at Zach's apparent reluctance to entertain her in Gramp's absence. "Maybe it would be best if we rescheduled for another day," she offered brightly. She wasn't any happier about the prospect of waiting in a restaurant, just the two of them, than he was. "Gramps is held up, I'm meeting Pam, and you're obviously a busy man."

An uncomfortable silence followed her remark. "Is it your habit not to show up when your grandfather's expecting you?" he asked sharply.

Janine bristled. "Of course not." She swallowed the words to defend herself. Her suggestion hadn't been unreasonable and he had no right to insinuate that she was inconsiderate and rude.

"Then I feel we should meet your grandfather at the restaurant as he requested," he finished stiffly.

"By all means," she said, forcing a smile. She stood and reached for her coat, watching Zach from the corner of her eye. He didn't like her. That realization had a peculiar effect on Janine. She felt disappointed and a little sad. Zach hadn't said much, and actually there hadn't been time for a real conversation, but she'd sensed his attitude almost from the first. He thought of her as spoiled and frivolous, probably because he knew she didn't hold a responsible job and loved to travel. Part of her longed to explain that there were good reasons she'd chosen the lifestyle she had. But from the looks he was sending her, it would be a waste of breath.

Besides, it was more important to maintain the peace

however strained, for Gramps's sake. She'd have enjoyed getting to know Zach, perhaps even becoming friends, but that didn't seem likely.

That morning, before Gramps had left the house, he'd been as excited as a little boy about their luncheon date. He'd come down the stairs whistling when he'd joined her for breakfast, his blue eyes sparkling. When she'd refused the use of the limousine, he'd spent the next fifteen minutes giving her detailed directions, as though she'd never driven in downtown Seattle.

Almost as an afterthought, he'd mentioned that he had a morning meeting with an important client. If he hadn't returned by the time she arrived, she was to go directly to Zach's office, introduce herself and wait for him there.

Shrugging into a raincoat, Zachary moved toward the door. "Are you ready?"

She nodded, burying her hands in her pockets.

Thankfully the restaurant her grandfather had chosen was close by. Without further discussion, they began to walk the few short blocks, although Janine had trouble matching her stride with Zach's much longer one.

Struggling to keep up with him, Janine studied Zachary Thomas, trying to determine exactly what disturbed her about the man. His height was a good example. He wasn't tall—under six feet, she guessed—and since she was almost five-eight there wasn't more than a few inches' difference between them. Why, then, did he make her feel much shorter?

He must have sensed her scrutiny because he turned and glared at her. Janine gave him a feeble smile, and felt the color rise in her cheeks. Zach's dismissive glance did nothing to boost her ego. She wasn't vain, but Janine knew she was attractive. Over the years, plenty of men had told her so, including Brian, the man who'd broken her heart. But she could have warts on her nose for all the notice Zachary Thomas gave her.

If he found the bandanna dress disconcerting, he was probably put off by her hairstyle as well. She wore it short, neatly trimmed in the back with extra-long bangs slanted across her forehead. For years Janine had kept her hair shoulder-length, parted in the middle. One afternoon a few weeks earlier, for no particular reason, she'd decided to have it cut. She was in the mood for something radical and the style she now sported seemed more appropriate to the pages of a fashion magazine. Pam had been crazy about the change, insisting she looked "phenomenal." Janine wasn't convinced. Her one comfort was that, given time, her hair would grow back.

Janine suspected Zach had characterized her as flamboyant, if not downright flashy. She, in turn, would describe him as austere and disciplined, perhaps solitary. Her grandfather saw all that, she knew, and a good deal more.

"Mr. Hartman is waiting for you," the maître d' informed them when they entered the plush waterfront restaurant. He led them across the thick carpet to a high semicircular booth upholstered in blue velvet.

"Janine, Zach." Anton Hartman smiled broadly as they approached. The years had been kind to her grandfather. His bearing was still straight and confident, although his hair had grown completely white. His deep blue eyes, only a little faded, were filled with warmth and wisdom. "I apologize for the inconvenience."

"It wasn't any problem," Zach answered for both of them before Janine could respond—as if he'd expected her to complain!

Ignoring him, Janine removed her coat and kissed her grandfather's leathery cheek.

"Janine," he began, then gasped. "Where did you get that…dress?"

"Do you like it?" She threw out her arms and whirled around once to give him the full effect. "I know it's a bit unconventional, but I didn't think you'd mind."

Gramps's gaze flickered to Zach, then back to her. "On anyone else it would be scandalous, but on you, my dear, it's a work of art."

"Honestly, Gramps," she said, laughing softly. "You never could lie very well." She slid into the booth next to her grandfather, forcing him into the center, between her and Zach. Gramps looked a bit disgruntled, but after her turbulent first encounter with Zach, she preferred to keep her distance. For that matter, he didn't seem all that eager to be close to her, either.

She glanced at him and noted, almost smugly, that he was already studying the menu. No doubt he found ordinary conversation a waste of time. Janine picked up her own menu. She was famished. At breakfast she'd only had time for coffee and a single piece of toast, and she had every intention of making up for it now.

When the waiter came to take their order, Janine asked for the seafood entrée and soup *and* salad. She'd decide about dessert later, she said. Once he'd left, Gramps leaned toward Zach. "Janine never has to worry about her weight." He made this sound as if it was a subject of profound and personal interest to them both. "Her grandmother was the same way. How my Anna could eat, and she never gained an ounce. Janine's just like her."

"Gramps," Janine whispered under her breath. "I'm sure Zach couldn't care less how much I weigh."

"Nonsense," Gramps said, gently patting her hand. "I hope you two had the chance to introduce yourselves."

"Oh, yes," Janine returned automatically.

"Your granddaughter is everything you claimed," Zachary said, but the inflection in his voice implied something completely different to Janine than it did to her grandfather. She guessed that to Anton, he seemed courteous and complimentary. But he was telling Janine he'd found her to be the spoiled darling he'd long suspected. He didn't openly dislike her, but he wasn't too impressed with her, either.

Unfortunately, that was probably due to more than just the dress and the lightbulb necklace.

Janine watched for her grandfather's reaction to Zach words and she knew she was right when his gaze warme and he nodded, obviously pleased by his partner's assess ment. Zachary Thomas was clever, Janine had to gra him that much.

"How did the meeting with Anderson go?" Zach ask

For a moment her grandfather stared at him blank

"Oh, Anderson... Fine, fine. Everything went just as I'd hoped." Then he cleared his throat and carefully spread the linen napkin across his lap. "As you both know," he said, "I've been wanting the two of you to meet for some time now. Janine is the joy of my life. She's kept me young and brought me much happiness over the years. I fear that, without her, I would have turned into a bitter old man."

His look was so full of tenderness that Janine had to lower her eyes and swallow back a rush of tears. Gramps had been her salvation, too. He'd taken her in after the sudden deaths of her parents, raised her with a gentle hand and loved her enough to allow her to be herself. It must've been difficult for him to have a six-year-old girl unexpectedly thrust into his life, but he'd never complained.

"My only son died far too young," Anton said slowly, painfully.

"I'm sorry," Zachary murmured.

The genuine compassion Janine heard in his voice surprised her. And it definitely pleased her. Zach's respect and affection for her grandfather won her immediate approval—even if the man didn't seem likely to ever feel anything so positive toward *her*.

"For many years I mourned the loss of my son and his wife," Anton continued, his voice gaining strength. "I've worked all my life, built an empire that stretches across these fifty states, and in the process have become a wealthy man."

Janine studied her grandfather closely. He was rarely his serious. He wasn't one to list his accomplishments, and he wondered at his strange mood.

"When Zach brought his business into the area, I saw in him a rare gift, one that comes along seldom in this life. It's said that there are men who make things happen, those who watch things happen and those who wonder what happened. Zachary is a man who makes things happen. In many ways, the two of us are alike. That's one of the primary reasons I decided to approach him with a proposal to merge our companies."

"I'm honored that you should think so, sir."

"Sir," Anton repeated softly and chuckled. He raised his hand, motioning for the waiter. "You haven't called me that in six months, and there's no reason to start again now."

The waiter returned with a bottle of expensive champagne. Soon glasses were poured and set before them.

"Now," Anton continued, "as I said earlier, I have the two people I love most in this world together with me for the first time, and I don't mind telling you, it feels good." He raised his glass. "To happiness."

"Happiness," Janine echoed, sipping her champagne.

Her eyes met Zach's above the crystal flute and she saw a glint of admiration. If she were dining on it, she'd starve—to quote a favorite expression of her grandfather's—but it was just enough for her to know that he'd think more kindly of her because of her love for Anton.

Her grandfather chuckled and whispered something in his native tongue, a German dialect from the old country. Over the years she'd picked up a smattering of the language, but when she'd repeated a few phrases to a college German professor, he'd barely recognized the words

Gramps paused and his smile lingered on Janine, then went to Zach. Whatever Gramps was muttering appeared to please him. His blue eyes fairly twinkled with delight.

"And now," he said, setting his glass aside, "I have an important announcement to make."

He turned to Janine and his face softened with affection. "I feel as though I've been an impossible burden to you, child, what with running this company." He shook his head. "Never in all my dreams did I expect to accumulate so much in a single lifetime. I've stayed in the business far longer than I should. It's time for me to retire and do a little traveling."

"It's past time," Janine said. For years, she'd been urging her grandfather to lessen his heavy work schedule. He'd often spoken of revisiting his birthplace and the surrounding countries. He talked at length of cousins and friends he'd left behind in the small German settlement. It was located in what was now part of Russia.

"This is where Zachary comes into the picture," Anton explained. "I know myself all too well. Full retirement would be impossible for me. If I stopped working, I'd shrivel up and die. That's just the way I am," he said simply.

Neither Janine nor Zachary disputed his words.

"I'll never be able to keep my fingers out of the business, yet I want to enjoy my travels. I couldn't do that if I was fretting about what was going on at the office." He paused as if he expected one of them to contradict him. "I believe I've come upon a solution. As of this afternoon, Zachary,

I'm handing the reins to you. You will assume my position as chairman of the board. I realize this is sooner than we discussed, but the time is right and I hope you'll agree."

"But, Anton—"

"Gramps—"

Anton held up his hand. "I've thought about this long and hard," he said confidently. "I find Zach's honesty unquestionable, his loyalty certain and his intelligence keen. He's shrewd, perceptive and insightful. I can think of no better man, and there's no better time."

Janine noticed that Zach seemed uncomfortable with the praise. "Thank you," was all he said.

"A share of this company will belong to you someday, Janine," Anton said next. "Do you have any objections to this appointment?"

She opened her mouth, but nothing came out. Of course she approved. What else could she do? "Whatever you decide is fine with me."

Anton turned his attention to the other man. "Zachary, do you accept?"

Although their acquaintance had been brief, Janine knew instinctively that it took a lot to fluster this man. But her grandfather had managed to do so.

Zachary continued to stare at him as though he couldn' quite believe what he was hearing. But when he spoke his voice was well modulated, revealing little emotior "I'm honored."

"For the next few months, we'll be working close! together, much as we have in the past, but with a diffe ence. No longer will I be showing you the ropes. I'll be handing them to you."

The first course of their lunch arrived, and after that, the conversation flowed smoothly. Her grandfather made sure of it. He was jubilant and entertaining, witty and charming. It would have been impossible not to be affected by his good humor.

When they'd finished the meal, Zachary looked at his watch. "I'm sorry to leave so soon, but I have an appointment."

Janine took a last sip of her coffee. "I should be leaving, too." She reached for her purse and coat, then slid out of the booth, waiting for her grandfather to join her.

"If neither of you objects, I'm going to linger over my coffee," Anton said, nodding toward his steaming cup.

"Of course." Janine leaned over to kiss him goodbye.

Zachary walked out to the street with her. Before he left, he shook her hand. "It's been a pleasure, Ms. Hartman."

"You're sure?" she teased, unable to stop herself.

"Yes." His eyes held hers and he smiled. She walked away feeling oddly excited about their meeting. Zach wasn't an easy person to know, but she suspected he was everything her grandfather claimed and more.

GRAMPS'S MOOD remained cheerful when he got home later that evening. Janine was in the library sipping herbal tea with her feet tucked under her as she watched the local news.

Sitting in the wingback leather chair next to her, Gramps crossed his legs and chose one of his Havana cigars. Janine shook her head affectionately as he lit it; she loved her grand-father dearly and wished he'd stop smoking, though she no longer bothered to express that wish. He was the kind of man who did exactly as he chose, got exactly what he wanted. He was obviously pleased with the way their luncheon had gone, and she wondered briefly if Zach had said anything about her afterward. Somehow she doubted it.

"Well," he said after a moment, "What do you think of Zachary Thomas?" He blew a steady stream of smoke at the ceiling while he awaited her answer.

All afternoon, Janine had prepared herself for his question. Several complicated answers had presented them-selves, clever replies that would sidestep her true feelings, but she used none of them now. Her grandfather expected the truth, and it was her duty to give it to him.

"I'm not sure. He's a very…reserved man, isn't he?"

Anton chuckled. "Yes, he is, but I've never known you to walk away from a challenge. The boy's a little rough around the edges, but on the inside, he's pure gold."

Janine hadn't thought of Zach in those terms—a chal-lenge. Frankly, she doubted there'd be much reason for her to have any future contact with him. Gramps and Zach would be working closely together, but she had almost nothing to do with the business.

"I've earned his trust, but it took time," Gramps was saying now.

"I'm glad you've decided to retire," she said absently, half listening to the weather report.

"Zachary will change," her grandfather added.

He had her full attention now. "Gramps," she said patiently, holding in a laugh. "Why should he? He's achieved considerable financial success. Everything's looking good for him. What possible reason could there be for him to change?"

Anton stood and poured himself a liberal dose of brandy, swirling it slowly in the bottom of the snifter. "You're going to change him," he said after a thoughtful moment.

"Me?" Janine laughed outright. "*I'm* going to change Zachary Thomas?" she repeated in wide-eyed disbelief. That would be the day!

"Before you argue with me, and I can see that's what you're dying to do, I have a story I want to tell you. A rather sad one as it happens."

Janine picked up the remote control and snapped off the television. She'd often listened to her grandfather's parables. "So tell me."

"It's about a boy, born on the wrong side of the tracks to an alcoholic father and a weak mother. He never had much of a chance in life. His father was abusive enough for the state to remove the lad and his younger sister. He was barely eight and subjected to a long series of foster homes, but he refused to be separated from his sister. He'd promised her he'd always take care of her.

"Once, there wasn't any alternative and the two were sent to separate homes. Beside himself with worry for his sister, the young boy ran away. The authorities were in a panic, but three days later, he turned up two hundred miles away at the home where they'd placed Beth Ann."

"He probably felt responsible for her."

"Yes. Which made matters much worse when she drowned in a swimming accident. He was twelve at the time."

"Oh, no." A pain squeezed Janine's heart at the agony the boy had suffered.

"He blamed himself, of course," Anton said softly.

"The poor kid."

"This lad never seemed to belong to anyone after that," Gramps said, staring into his brandy. "He never quite fit in, but that wasn't entirely his fault." He paused to take another puff of his cigar. "His mother died a month after his sister. They were the only ones who'd ever truly loved him. He lost contact with his father, which was probably for the best. So his family was gone and no one seemed to want this troubled, hurting boy."

"Did he turn into a juvenile delinquent?" It made sense to Janine that he would; she'd dealt with a number of troubled teenagers through her volunteer work and was familiar with the tragic patterns that so often evolved in cases like this.

"No, I can't say he did." Gramps dismissed her question with a shake of his head, more interested in continuing his tale than getting sidetracked by her questions. "He drifted through adolescence without an anchor and without ever being allowed to enjoy those formative years."

"Gramps—"

He raised his hand to stop her. "When he was eighteen he joined the military. He did well, which isn't surprising considering his intelligence and the fact that he had little regard for his own well-being. There was no one to mourn if he died. Because of his courage, he advanced quickly volunteering for the riskiest assignments. He traveled all over the world to some of the most dangerous political hot spots. His duties were often top secret. There's no telling how far he might have gone had he chosen to remain in the armed services, but for some reason, he resigned. No one understood why. I suspect he wanted to start his life over. This was when he opened a business-supply company. Within a year, he had my attention. His methods were aggressive and creative. I couldn't help admiring the way he handled himself and the company. Within five years, he'd become one of my most serious rivals. I saw a strength in him that age had stolen from me. We met. We talked. As a result of these talks we joined forces."

"Obviously you're telling me about Zachary's life."

Anton grinned and slowly sipped his brandy. "You noticed his remoteness quickly. I thought knowing all this would help you. Zach's never had the security that a caring home and family provide. He's never really experienced love, except what he shared with his sister, Beth Ann. His life has been a long progression of painful experiences. By sheer force of will, he's managed to overcome every obstacle placed in his path. I realize Zachary Thomas isn't going to win any Mr. Personality contests, but by heaven, he's earned my respect."

Janine had rarely heard such emotion in her grandfather's voice. "Zach told you all this?"

Anton's laughter echoed through the room. "You're joking, aren't you? Zach has never spoken of his past to me. I doubt that he has to anyone."

"You had him investigated?"

Gramps puffed on his cigar before answering. "It was necessary, although I'd guessed early on that his life hadn't been a bed of roses."

"It's all very sad, isn't it?"

"You're going to be very good for him, my dear."

Janine blinked. "Me?"

"Yes, you. You're going to teach him to laugh and enjoy life. But most important, you're going to teach him about love."

She hesitated, uncertain of her grandfather's meaning. "I don't think I understand. I realize Zach and I will probably see each other now and then since he's assuming your responsibilities with the company, but I don't see how I could have any great impact on his life."

Gramps smiled, a slow lazy smile that curved the corners of his mouth. "That's where you're wrong, my dear. You're going to play a very big role in Zach's life, and he in yours."

Janine was still confused. "Perhaps I missed something this afternoon. I thought you made Zach the chairman of the board."

"I did." A lazy swirl of smoke circled his head.

"I don't understand where I come into the picture."

"I don't suppose you do," he said softly. "You see Janine, I've chosen Zachary to be your husband."

Two

For a stunned moment, Janine said nothing. "You're teasing, aren't you, Gramps?"

"No," he said, lighting a second cigar. He paused to stare at the glowing tip, his eyes filled with mischief—and with something else, less easily defined. "I'm serious."

"But…" Janine's thoughts were so jumbled she couldn't make sense of them herself, let alone convey her feelings to her grandfather.

"I've been giving the matter serious consideration for some time now. Zach's perfect for you and you're the ideal complement to him. You're going to have beautiful blond-haired children."

"But…" Janine discovered she was absolutely speechless. One minute she was listening to a touching story, and the next her grandfather was telling her about the husband he'd arranged for her—and even the color of her children's hair.

"Once you think about it," Gramps said confidently,

"I'm sure you'll agree with me. Zach is a fine young man, and he'll make you an excellent husband."

"You…Zach talked…agreed?" The words stumbled over the end of her tongue.

"Do you mean have I suggested this arrangement to Zach?" Gramps asked. "Heavens, no. At least not yet." He chuckled as if he found the thought amusing. "Zach wouldn't appreciate my blatant interference in his personal affairs. With him, I'll need to be far more subtle. To be honest, I considered making this marriage part of my handing over the chairmanship, but after thinking it through, I changed my mind. Zach would never have agreed. There are other ways, I decided, better ways. But I don't want you to worry about it. That's between Zach and me."

"I…see." At this point, Janine wasn't sure *what* she saw, other than one determined old man caught between two worlds. In certain respects, the old ways continued to dominate his thinking, but his success in America allowed him to appreciate more modern outlooks.

Gramps inhaled deeply on his cigar, his blue eyes twinkling. "Now, I realize you probably find the idea of an arranged marriage slightly unorthodox, but you'll get used to it. I've made a fine choice for you, and I know you're smart enough to recognize that."

"Gramps, I don't think you fully understand what you're suggesting," she said, trying to gather her scattered wits, hoping she could explain the ridiculousness of this whole scheme without offending him.

"But I do, my child."

"In this country and in this age," she continued slowly, "men and women choose their own mates. We fall in love and then marry."

Gramps frowned. "Sadly, that doesn't work," he muttered.

"What do you mean, it doesn't work?" she cried, losing her patience. "It's been like this for years and years!"

"Look at the divorce rate. I read in the paper recently that almost fifty percent of all marriages in this country fail. In the old country, there was no divorce. Parents decided whom a son or daughter would marry, and their decision was accepted without question. First comes marriage, and then comes love."

"Gramps," Janine said softly, wanting to reason this out with him. Her grandfather was a logical man; surely, if she explained it properly, he'd understand. "Things are done differently now. First comes love, then comes marriage."

"What do you young people know about love?"

"A good deal, as it happens," she returned, lying smoothly. Her first venture into love had ended with a broken heart and a shattered ego, but she'd told Gramps little if anything about Brian.

"Pfft!" he spat. "What could you possibly know of love?"

"I realize," she said, thinking fast, "that your father arranged your marriage to Grandma, but that was years ago, and in America such customs don't exist. You and I live *here* now, in the land of the free. The land of opportunity."

Gramps gazed down into his brandy for a long moment, lost in thought. Janine doubted he'd even heard her.

"I'll never forget the first time I saw my Anna," he said

in a faraway voice. "She was sixteen and her hair was long and blond and fell in braids to her waist. My father spoke to her father and while they were talking, Anna and I sat at opposite ends of the room, too shy to look at each other. I wondered if she thought I was handsome. To me, she was the most beautiful girl in the world. Even now, after all these years, I can remember how my heart beat with excitement when I saw her. I knew—"

"But, Gramps, that was nearly sixty years ago! Marriages aren't decided by families anymore. A man and a woman discover each other without a father introducing them. Maybe the old ways were better back then, but it's simply not like that now." Gramps continued to stare into his glass, lost in a world long since enveloped by the passage of time.

"The next day, Anna's parents visited our farm and again our two fathers spoke. I tried to pretend I wasn't concerned, determined to accept whatever our families decided. But when I saw our fathers shake hands and slap each other on the back, I knew Anna would soon be mine."

"You loved her before you were married, didn't you?" Janine asked softly, hoping to prove her point.

"No," he returned flatly, without hesitation. "How could I love her when I'd only seen her twice before the wedding? We hadn't said more than a handful of words to each other. Love wasn't necessary for us to find happiness. Love came later, after we arrived in America."

"Wasn't it unusual for a marriage to be arranged even then? It wasn't *that* long ago." There had to be some point for her to contend, Janine mused.

"Perhaps it was unusual in other parts of the world, but not in Vibiskgrad. We were a small farming community. Our world had been ravaged by war and hate. We clung to each other, holding on to our own traditions and rituals. Soon our lives became impossible and we were forced to flee our homes."

"As I said before, I can understand how an arranged marriage—back then—might be the best for everyone involved. But I can't see it working in this day and age. I'm sorry to disappoint you, Gramps, but I'm not willing to accept Zachary Thomas as my husband, and I'm sure he'd be equally unwilling to marry me."

Briefly Gramps's face tensed with a rare display of disappointment and indignation, then quickly relaxed. Janine had seldom questioned his authority and had never openly defied him.

"I suppose this is a shock to you, isn't it?" he said.

If it astonished *her*, she couldn't wait to hear what Zachary Thomas thought! They'd only met once, but he hadn't disguised his opinion of her. He wouldn't take kindly to Gramps's plan of an arranged marriage—especially to a woman he viewed as spoiled and overindulged.

"All I'm asking is that you consider this, Janine," Gramps said. "Promise me you'll at least do that. Don't reject marriage to Zach simply because you think it's old-fashioned."

"Oh, Gramps…" Janine hated to refuse him anything. "It isn't just me. What about Zach? What about *his* plans? What if he—"

Gramps dismissed her questions with an abrupt shrug. "How often do I ask something of you?" he persisted.

Now he was going to use guilt. "Not often," she agreed, frowning at him for using unfair tactics.

"Then consider Zach for your husband!" His eyes brightened. "The two of you will have such beautiful children. A grandfather knows these things."

"I promise I'll think about it." But it wouldn't do any good! However, discretion was a virtue Janine was nurturing, and there'd never been a better time to employ it than now.

Gramps didn't mention Zach Thomas or even hint at the subject of her marrying his business partner again until the following evening. They'd just sat down to dinner, prepared to sample Mrs. McCormick's delicious fare, when Gramps looked anxiously at Janine. "So?" he asked breathlessly.

From the moment he'd walked into the house that afternoon, Gramps's mood had been light and humorous. Grinning, he handed her the platter of thinly sliced marinated and grilled flank steak. It happened to be one of Janine's favorite meals. "So?" he repeated, smiling at her. "What did you decide?"

Janine helped herself to a crisp dinner roll, buttering it slowly as her thoughts chased each other in frantic circles. "Nothing."

His smile collapsed into a frown. "You promised me you'd consider marrying Zach. I gave you more time than Anna's father gave her."

"You have to know now?"

"Now!"

"But, Gramps, a simple yes or no isn't an appropriate response to something as complex as this. You're asking me to decide on a lifelong commitment in less than twenty-four hours." She was stalling for time, and Gramps had probably guessed as much. Frankly, she didn't know what to tell him. She couldn't, wouldn't, marry Zach—even if he was willing to marry her—but she hated disappointing her grandfather.

"What's so difficult? Either you marry him or not!"

"I don't understand why you've decided to match me up with Zach Thomas," she cried. "What's wrong with Peter?" She'd been dating the other man casually for the last few months. Her heart was too bruised after what had happened with Brian for her to date anyone seriously.

"You're in love with that whitewashed weakling?"

Janine signed loudly, regretting the fact that she'd introduced Peter into their conversation. "He's very nice."

"So is chocolate mousse!" Gramps muttered. "Peter Donahue would make you a terrible husband. I'm shocked you'd even think about marrying him."

"I hadn't actually thought about him in those terms," she said. Peter was witty and fun, but Gramps was right; they weren't suited as husband and wife.

"I thank the good Lord you've been given some sense."

Janine took a deep breath and finally asked a question that had been nagging at her all afternoon. "Did—did you arrange my father's marriage?"

Gramps lowered his eyes, but not before he could disguise the pain there. "No. He fell in love with Patrice while

he was in college. I knew the match wasn't a good one, but
Anna reminded me that this was America and young people fell in love by themselves. She convinced me they
didn't need a father's guiding hand the way we did in the
old country."

"Do you think he would've listened if you'd wanted to
arrange a marriage?"

Her grandfather hesitated, and his hand tightened on
his water glass. "I don't know, but I'd like to believe he
would have."

"Instead he married my mother."

Neither spoke for a long moment. Janine remembered
little of her parents, only bits and pieces of memory, mostly
unconnected. What she did recall were terrible fights and
accusations, a house filled with strife. She could remember
hiding under her bed when the shouting started, pressing
her hands to her ears. It was her father who used to find
her, who comforted her. Always her father. Her memory
included almost nothing of her mother. Even pictures
didn't jar her recollection, although Janine had spent hour
upon hour looking at photographs, hoping to remember
something. But the woman who'd given birth to her had
remained a stranger to her in life and in death.

"You're the only consolation I have from Steven's marriage," Anton said hoarsely. "At least I had you after Steven
and Patrice died."

"Oh, Gramps. I love you so much and I hate to disappoint you, but I can't marry Zach and I can't see him agreeing to marry me."

Her grandfather was silent after that, apparently mulling over her words as he finished his dinner. "I suppose I seem like a feeble old man, still trying to live the old ways."

"Gramps, no, I don't think that at all."

He planted his elbows squarely on the table and linked his fingers, gazing at her. His brow was puckered in a contemplative frown. "Perhaps it would help if you told me what you want in a husband."

She hesitated, then glanced away, avoiding eye contact. Once she'd been so certain of what she wanted. "To be perfectly honest, I'm not sure. Romance, I suppose."

"Romance." Gramps rolled the word off his tongue as though he was tasting an expensive wine.

"Yes," she said with a nod of her head, gaining confidence.

"And what exactly is romance?"

"Well…" Now that she'd been called upon to define it, Janine couldn't quite put that magical feeling into words. "It's…it's an awareness that comes from the heart."

"The heart," her grandfather repeated, smacking his palm against his chest.

"Romance is the knowledge that a man would rather die than live his life without me," she said, warming to the subject.

"You want him to die?"

"No, just to be willing."

Gramps frowned. "I don't think I understand."

"Romance is forbidden trysts on lonely Scottish moors," she added, thinking of an historical romance she'd read as a teenager.

"There aren't any moors in the Seattle area."

"Don't distract me," she said, smiling, her thoughts gaining momentum. "Romance is desperate passion."

He snorted. "That sounds more like hormones to me."

"Gramps, please!"

"How can I understand when all you say is ridiculous things? You want romance. First you claim it's a feeling in the heart, then you say it's some kind of passion."

"It's more than that. It's walking hand in hand along the beach at twilight and gazing into each other's eyes. It's speaking of love without ever having to say the words." She paused, feeling a little foolish at getting so carried away. "I don't know if I can adequately describe it."

"That's because you haven't experienced it."

"Maybe not," she agreed reluctantly. "But I will someday."

"With Zach," he said with complete assurance and a wide grin.

Janine didn't bother to argue. Gramps was being obstinate and arguing with him was pointless. The only recourse she had was time itself. Soon enough he'd realize that neither she nor Zach was going to fall in with his scheme. Then, and only then, would he drop the subject.

A week passed and Gramps hadn't said another word about arranging a marriage between her and Zachary Thomas. It was a cold windy March evening and the rain was coming down in torrents. Janine loved nights like this and was curled up in her favorite chair with a mystery novel when the doorbell chimed. Gramps had gone out for the evening and she wasn't expecting anyone.

She turned on the porch light and looked out the peep-hole to discover Zach standing there, a briefcase in his hand. His shoulders were hunched against the pelting rain.

"Zach," she said in surprise, throwing open the door.

"Hello, Janine," he said politely, stepping inside. "Is your grandfather here?"

"No." She held the book against her chest, her heart pounding hard. "He went out."

Zach frowned, clearly confused. "He asked me to stop by. There were some business matters he wanted to discuss. Did he say when he'd be home?"

"No, but I'm sure if he asked you over, it'll be soon. Would you care to wait for him?"

"Please."

She took his raincoat, then led him into the library where she'd been reading. A fire was burning, and its warmth hugged the room. The three-story house, situated in Seattle's Mt. Baker district, was a typical turn-of-the-century home with high ceilings and spacious rooms. The third floor had once housed several servants. Charles was their only live-in help now, and his quarters had always been an apartment over the carriage house. He worked exclusively for Gramps, driving the limousine. Mrs. McCormick arrived early in the mornings and was responsible for housekeeping and meal preparation.

"Can I get you something to drink?" she asked, once he was comfortably seated.

"Coffee, if you have it."

"I made a fresh pot about twenty minutes ago."

Janine brought him a cup from the kitchen, then sat across from Zach, wondering what, if anything, she should say about Gramps and his idea of an arranged marriage.

She doubted that Gramps had broached the subject yet. Otherwise he wouldn't be sitting there so calmly sipping coffee. He'd be outraged and infuriated, and studying him now, she concluded that he wasn't even slightly ruffled. It was on the tip of her tongue to warn him about what was coming, but she decided against it. Better that he learn the same way she had.

Lacing her fingers together, she smiled, feeling awkward and a little gauche. "It's nice to see you again."

"You, too. I'll admit I'm a bit disappointed, though."

"You are?"

"On the drive over, I was trying to guess what you'd be wearing this time. A dress made from bread sacks? A blouse constructed out of men's socks?"

She muttered under her breath, annoyed by his teasing. He had the uncanny ability to make her feel fifteen all over again. So much for any possibility that they'd ever be compatible. And Gramps seemed to think he knew them both so well.

"I'll admit that an Irish cable-knit sweater and jeans are a pleasant surprise," he said.

A flicker of admiration sparked in his dark eyes, something that had been missing the first time they met.

In that instant, Janine knew.

She went stock-still, almost dizzy with the realization. Not only had Gramps approached Zach, but they'd apparently reached some sort of agreement. Otherwise Zach would never have been this friendly, this openly apprecia- tive. Nor would he arrive unannounced when Gramps had specifically stated that he'd be gone for the evening.

They were obviously plotting against her. Well, she had no intention of putting up with it. None. If Zach and Gramps thought they could lure her into marriage, they had a real shock coming.

Squaring her shoulders, she slid to the edge of her chair. "So you gave in to the pressure," she said, shooting him a scalding look. Unable to stay seated, she jumped to her feet and started pacing, rubbing her palms together as she cornered her thoughts. "Gramps got to you, didn't he?"

"I beg your pardon?" Zach stared up at her, his eyes curious.

"And you agreed?" She threw up her hands and groaned, "I don't believe it, I simply don't believe it. I thought better of you than this."

"What don't you believe?"

"Of all the men I've met over the years, I would've sworn you were the type who'd refuse to be bought. I'm disappointed in you, Zach."

He remained calm and unperturbed, which infuriated her more than anything he could have said or done.

"I haven't got the slightest idea what you're talking about," was all he said.

"Oh, sure, play the innocent," she snapped. She was so incensed that she continued to pace. Standing still was impossible.

In response, Zach merely glanced at his watch and drank his coffee. "Does your grandfather know you suffer from these bouts of hysteria?"

"Funny, Zach, very funny."

He exhaled an exaggerated sigh. "All right, I'll take the bait. What makes you think I've been bought? And what exactly am I getting in exchange?"

"Technically you're not getting anything, and I want that understood this very minute, because *I* refuse to be sold." Arms akimbo, she turned to glare down at him with the full force of her disdain. "What did he offer you? The entire company? Lots of money?"

Zach shrugged. "He's offered me nothing."

"Nothing," she repeated slowly, feeling unreasonably insulted. "He was just going to *give* me away." That was enough to deflate the billowing sails of her pride. Stunned, she sat down again. "I thought the bride's family was supposed to supply some kind of dowry. Gramps didn't even offer you money?"

"Dowry?" Zach repeated the word as if he'd never heard it before.

"Gramps's family received a cow and ten chickens from my grandmother's family," she said, as if that explained everything. "But apparently I'm not even worth a single hen."

Zach set his coffee aside and sat straight in his chair. "I think we'd better begin this conversation again. I'm afraid I lost you back there when you said something about cracking under pressure. Perhaps you should enlighten me about what I'm supposed to have done."

Janine just glared at him.

"Humor me."

"All right, if you insist. It's obvious that Gramps talked to you about the marriage."

"Marriage," he echoed in a shocked voice. His face went blank. "To whom?"

"Me, of course."

Zach flung himself out of the chair, bolting to his feet. "To you?"

"Don't look so horrified! My ego's taken about all it can for one evening. I'm not exactly the Wicked Witch of the West, you know. Some men would be more than happy to marry me." Not Brian, and certainly not Peter, but she felt it was important that Zach think she was sought after.

"Marriage between us is...would be impossible. It's completely out of the question. I don't ever plan to marry— I have no use for a wife or family."

"Tell that to Gramps."

"I have every intention of doing so." His face tightened and Janine guessed her grandfather was due for an earful when he got home. "What makes that crazy old man think he can order people's lives like this?" he asked angrily.

"His own marriage was arranged for him. Trust me, Zach, I argued until I was exhausted, but Gramps hasn't given up his old-country beliefs and he thinks the two of us—now this is really ridiculous—are perfect for each other."

"If you weren't serious, I'd find this highly amusing."

Janine noticed that he seemed rather pale. "I appear to

have jumped to the wrong conclusion earlier. I apologize for that but, well, I thought…I assumed Gramps had spoken to you already and you'd agreed."

"Was that when you started mumbling about a cow and a few chickens?"

She nodded and her long bangs fell over her eyes. Absently she pushed them aside. "For a moment there, I thought Gramps was offering me to you gratis. I know it's silly, but I felt insulted by that."

For the first time since they'd entered into this conversation, Zach's face softened and he granted her a faint smile. "Your grandfather loves you, no question."

"I know." Feeling self-conscious, she threaded her fingers through her hair. "I've used every argument I could come up with. I explained the importance of romance and told him how vital it is for men and women to fall in love with the person of their choice. However, he refused to accept any of it."

"He wouldn't listen to you?"

"He listened," she replied, feeling defeated, "but he disputed everything I said. Gramps says the modern version of love and marriage is a complete failure. With the divorce rate what it is, I'm afraid I don't have much of an argument."

"That's true enough," Zach said, looking frustrated.

"I told him men and women fall in love and then decide to get married, but Gramps insists it's better if marriage comes first."

Zach rubbed a hand over his face. "Now that I think

about it, your grandfather's been introducing you into every conversation, telling me how wonderful you are."

Janine gasped softly. "He's done the same to me about you. He started weeks before we even met."

Pressing his lips together, Zach nodded. "A lot of things are beginning to make sense."

"What should we do?" Janine wondered aloud. "It's perfectly obvious that we'll have to agree on a plan of action. I hate to disappoint Gramps, but I'm not willing to be married off like…like…" Words failed her.

"Especially to me."

Although his low words were devoid of emotion, Janine recognized the pain behind his statement. Knowing what she did about his past, the fact that he'd experienced only brief patches of love in his life and little or no approval tugged at her heart.

"I didn't mean it to sound like that," she insisted. "My grandfather wouldn't have chosen you if he didn't think you were pretty special. He prides himself on his ability to judge character, and he's always been impressed with you."

"Let's not kid ourselves, Janine," Zach returned, his voice hardening. "You're an uptown girl. We're totally unsuited."

"I agree with you there, but not for the reasons you assume. From the minute I stepped into your office, you made it clear that you thought of me as some kind of snob. I'm not, but I refuse to waste my breath arguing with you."

"Fine."

"Instead of hurling insults at each other," she suggested, crossing her arms in a show of indignation, "why don't we come up with a plan to deal with Gramps's preposterous idea?"

"That isn't necessary," he countered. "I want no part of it."

"And you think I do?"

Zach said nothing.

Janine expelled her breath loudly. "It seems to me the solution is for one of us to marry someone else. That would quickly put an end to this whole thing."

"I already told you I have no intention of marrying," he said emphatically. "You're the one who insinuated you had plenty of men hanging around just waiting for you to say 'I do.'"

"None that I'd consider marrying, for heaven's sake," she grumbled. "Besides, I'm not currently in love with anyone."

Zach laughed, if the sound that came from his throat could be called a laugh. "Then find a man who's current. If you fall in and out of love that easily, surely there's got to be at least one prospect on the horizon."

"There isn't. *You're* going to have to come up with someone! Why don't you go out there and sweep some sweet young thing off her feet," she muttered sarcastically.

"I'm not willing to sacrifice my life so you can get off scot-free." His words were low and furious.

"But it's perfectly all right for *me* to sabotage mine? That makes a lot of sense."

"Okay," he said after a tense moment. He paused, shaking his head. "That idea's obviously not going to work. I guess we'll have to come up with something better."

"Okay, then." Janine gestured toward him. "It's your turn."

He glared at her, seeming to dislike her even more. In all honesty, Janine wasn't too pleased with the way she was behaving, either. She'd been sarcastic and needlessly rude, but then, Zach had driven her to it. He could be the most unpleasant man.

Still, Janine was about to say something conciliatory when the sound of the front door opening distracted her. Her gaze flew to Zach and he nodded, reassuring her that he'd handle the situation.

They'd returned to their chairs and were seated by the time Gramps appeared in the library doorway.

"Zach, I'm sorry for the delay. I'm glad to see Janine entertained you." Her grandfather smiled brightly as if to tell her he approved and hoped she'd taken advantage of this hour alone with Zach.

"We did manage to have a stimulating conversation," Zach said, his eyes briefly meeting Janine's.

"Good. Good."

Zach stood and reached for his briefcase. "There were some figures you wanted to go over with me?"

"Yes." Looking satisfied with himself, Gramps led the way out of the room. Zach followed him, with a glance back at Janine that said he'd get in touch with her later.

Later turned out to be almost a week. She was puttering around outside, trimming back the rosebushes and deciding where to plant the geraniums this year, when Mrs. McCormick came to tell her she was wanted on the phone.

"Hello," Janine said cheerfully.

"We need to talk," Zach said without preamble.

"Why?" she demanded. If he was going to keep her hanging for six anxious days, then she wasn't going to give the impression that she was thrilled to hear from him.

"Your grandfather laid his cards on the table this afternoon. I thought you might be interested in hearing what he's offering me to take you off his hands."

Three

"All right," Janine said, bracing herself. "What's he offering you? Huge bonuses?"

"No," Zach said quickly.

"Cash? I want to know exactly how much."

"He didn't offer me money."

Janine frowned. "What then?"

"I think we should meet and talk about it."

If her grandfather had openly approached Zach with the arranged-marriage idea, Janine knew darn well that Gramps would've made it worth Zach's while. Despite his claims to the contrary, it wouldn't have surprised Janine to discover that the newly appointed chairman of the board of Hartman-Thomas Business Supply had taken the bait.

"You want us to meet?" she repeated in a faltering voice.

"There's a restaurant on University Way—Italian 642. Have you heard of it?"

"No, but I'll find it."

"Meet me there at seven." Zach paused, then added, "And listen, it might not be a good idea to tell your grandfather that we're getting together. He might misunderstand."

"I won't say anything," she promised.

Zach hesitated once more. "We have a lot to discuss."

Janine's heartbeat accelerated, and she felt the perspiration break out on her forehead. "Zach," she began, "you haven't changed your mind, have you? I mean, you're not actually considering this ridiculous idea of his? You can't… We agreed, remember?" She swiped at her forehead with the back of her free hand as she waited for him to answer.

"There's nothing to worry about," he finally said.

Replacing the receiver, Janine had the sudden horrible sensation of being completely at her grandfather's mercy. He was an unshakably stubborn man who almost always got what he wanted. Faced with a mountain, Anton Hartman either climbed it, tunneled through it or forged a path around it; failing such active alternatives, he settled down in the foothills and waited for the mountain to dissolve. He claimed he won a majority of his battles by simply displaying patience. Janine called it not knowing when to pack up and go home.

She knew her grandfather's methods, but then so did Zach. She hoped Anton's candidate for her husband would at least be able to withstand a few bribes, however tempting. Apparently he did, because he'd told her she had nothing to worry about. On the other hand, he sounded downright eager to discuss the subject with her.

"He *says* he never wants to get married," she muttered

aloud in an effort to reassure herself. Indeed, Zachary Thomas was the last man who'd be humming "The Wedding March"—especially when someone else was directing the band.

Janine was waiting in the library, coat draped over her arm, when her grandfather got home at six-thirty. He kissed her dutifully on the cheek and reached for the evening paper, scanning the headlines as he settled into his big leather chair.

"Zach called," she said without thinking. She hadn't intended to mention that to Gramps.

Anton nodded. "I thought he might. You meeting him for dinner?"

"Dinner? Zach and me?" she squeaked. "No, of course not! Why would you even think I'd agree to a dinner date with…him?" Darn, she'd nearly forgotten her promise to keep their meeting a secret. She detested lying to her grandfather, but there was no help for it.

"But you are dining out?"

"Yes." She couldn't very well deny that, dressed as she was and carrying her coat.

"Then you're seeing Peter Donahue again?"

"No. Not exactly," Janine said uncomfortably, "I'm meeting a…friend."

"I see." The corners of Gramps's mouth quirked into a knowing smile.

Janine could feel the telltale heat saturating her face. She was a terrible liar and always had been. Gramps knew as surely as if she'd spelled it out that she was meeting Zach.

And when she told Zach she'd let it slip, he'd be furious with her, and rightly so.

"What did Zach want?"

"What makes you think he wanted anything?" Janine asked fervently. Her heart was thundering as she edged toward the door. The sooner she escaped, the better.

"You just said Zach phoned."

"Oh. Yes, he did, earlier, but it wasn't important. Something about…something." Brilliant! She rushed out of the house before Gramps could question her further. What a fool she was. She'd blurted out the very thing she'd wanted to keep secret.

By the time Janine located the Italian restaurant in the University district and found a parking place, she was ten minutes late.

Zach was sitting in a booth in the farthest corner of the room. He frowned when he saw her and glanced at his watch, just so she'd know she'd kept him waiting.

Ignoring his disgruntled look, Janine slid onto the polished wooden bench, removed her coat and casually announced, "Gramps knows."

Zach's frown deepened. "What are you talking about?"

"He knows I'm having dinner with you," she explained. "The minute he walked in the door, I told him you'd called—I just wasn't thinking—and when he asked why, I told him it had to do with *something*. I'm sure you'll be able to make up an excuse when he asks you later."

"I thought we agreed not to say anything about our meeting."

"I know," she said, feeling guiltier than ever. "But Gramps asked if I was going out with Peter and he just looked so smug when I told him I wasn't." At Zach's sudden movement, she burst out, "Well, what was I supposed to do?"

He grunted, which wasn't much of an answer.

"If I wasn't going out with Peter, I'd have to come up with another man on the spot, and although I'm clever, I don't think *that* fast." She was breathless with frustration when she'd finished.

"Who's Peter?"

"This guy I've been seeing off and on for the past few months."

"And you're in love with him?"

"No, I'm not." Doubtless Zach would suggest she simply marry Peter and put an end to all of this annoyance.

Zach reached abruptly for the menu. "Let's order, and while we're eating we can go over what we need to discuss."

"All right," Janine said, grateful to leave the topic of her blunder. Besides, seven was later than she normally dined, and she was famished.

The waitress appeared then, and even as she filled Janine's water glass, her appreciative gaze never strayed from Zach. Once more Janine was struck by the knowledge that although he wasn't handsome in the traditional sense, he seemed to generate a good deal of female interest.

"I'll have the clam spaghetti," Janine said loudly, eyeing the attractive waitress, who seemed to be forgetting why she was there. The woman was obviously far more interested in studying Zach than in taking their order.

"I'll have the same," Zach said, smiling briefly at the waitress as he handed her his menu. "Now, what were you saying?" he asked, returning his attention to Janine.

"As I recall, you were the one who insisted we meet. Just tell me what my grandfather said and be done with it." No doubt the offer had been generous; otherwise Zach wouldn't have suggested this dinner.

Zach's hand closed around the water glass. "Anton called me into his office to ask me a series of leading questions."

"Such as?"

Zach shrugged. "What I thought of you and—"

"How'd you answer him?"

Zach took a deep breath. "I said I found you attractive, energetic, witty, a bit eccentric—"

"A bandanna dress and a string of Christmas-tree lights doesn't make me eccentric," Janine said, her voice rising despite herself.

"If the Christmas-tree lights are draped around your neck it does."

They were attracting attention, and after a few curious stares, Zach leaned closer and said, "If you're going to argue with everything I say, we'll be here all night."

"I'm sure our waitress would enjoy that," Janine snapped, then immediately regretted it. She sounded downright *jealous*—which, of course, was ridiculous.

"What are you talking about?"

"Never mind."

"Shall we return to the conversation between your grandfather and me?"

"Please," she said, properly chastised.

"Anton spent quite a long time telling me about your volunteer work at the Friendship Club and your various other community activities."

"And I'll bet his report was so glowing, I rank right up there with Joan of Arc and Florence Nightingale."

Zach grinned. "Something like that, but then he added that although you were constantly busy, he felt your life lacked contentment and purpose."

Janine could see it coming, as clearly as if she were standing on a track and a freight train was heading toward her. "Let me guess. He probably said I needed something meaningful in my life—like a husband and children."

"Exactly." Zach nodded, his grin barely restrained. "In his opinion, marriage is the only thing that will fulfill you as woman."

Janine groaned and sagged against the back of her seat. It was worse than she thought. And to her chagrin, Zach actually seemed amused.

"You wouldn't look so smug if he said marriage was the only thing that would fulfill you as a *man*," she muttered. "Honestly, Zach, do I look like I'm wasting away from lack of purpose?" She gestured dramatically with her hands. "I'm happy, I'm busy…in fact I'm completely delighted with my life." It wasn't until she'd finished that she realized she was clenching her teeth.

"Don't take it so personally."

Janine rolled her eyes, wondering what his reaction would be if he was on the receiving end of this discussion.

"In case you didn't know it, Anton's a terrible chauvinist," he remarked, still smiling. "An old-fashioned word, perhaps, for an old-fashioned man."

"That's true, but he *is* my grandfather," she said. "And he's so charming, it's easy to forgive him."

Zach picked up his wineglass and gazed at it thoughtfully. "What I can't figure out is why he's so keen on marrying you off now. Why not last year? Or next year?"

"Heavens, I don't know. I suppose he thinks it's time. My biological clock's ticking away and the noise is probably keeping him awake at night. By age twenty-four, most of the women from the old country had four or five children."

"He certainly seems intent on the idea of seeing you married soon."

"Tell me about it!" Janine cried. "I'd bet cold cash that when he brought up the subject he said you were the only suitable man he'd found for me."

"Anton also said you have a generous heart, and that he feared some fast-talker would show up one day and you'd fall for him."

"Really?" she asked weakly. Her heart stopped, then jolted to life again. Anton's scenario sounded exactly like her disastrous romance with Brian. She sighed deeply. "So then he told you he wants me to marry someone he respects, someone he loves like a son. A man of discretion and wisdom and honor. A man he trusts enough to merge companies with."

Zach arched his brows. "You know your grandfather well."

"I can just imagine what came next," Janine added scathingly and her stomach tensed at her grandfather's insidious cleverness. Zach wasn't someone who could be bought, at least not with offers of money or prestige. Instead, Gramps had used a far more subtle form of inducement. He'd addressed Zach's pride, complimented his achievements, flattered him. To hear Gramps tell it, Zachary Thomas was the only man alive capable of taking on the task of becoming Janine's husband.

"What did you tell him?" she asked, her voice low.

"I told him no way."

Janine blinked back surprise mingled with a fair amount of indignation. "Just like that? Couldn't you at least have mulled it over?" Zach was staring at her as though he thought someone should rush over and take her temperature. "Forget I said that," she mumbled, fussing with her napkin in order to avoid meeting his eyes.

"I didn't want to encourage him."

"That was wise." Janine picked up her water glass and downed half the contents.

"To your grandfather's credit, he seemed to accept my answer."

"Don't count on it," Janine warned.

"Don't worry, I know him, too. He isn't going to give up easily. That's the reason I suggested you and I meet to talk about this. If we keep in touch, we can anticipate Anton's strategy."

"Good idea."

Their salads arrived and Janine frowned when the

waitress tossed Zach another suggestive glance. "So," she began in a conversational tone once the woman had left, "Gramps was smart enough not to offer you a large incentive if you went along with his scheme."

"I didn't say that."

She stabbed viciously at her salad. "I hadn't expected him to stoop that low. Exactly what tactics did he use?"

"He said something about family members having use of the limousine."

Janine's fork made a clanging sound as it hit the side of her salad bowl. "He offered you the limousine if you married me? That's all?"

"Not even that," Zach explained, not bothering to disguise his amusement, "only the *use* of it."

"Why…why, that's insulting." She crammed some salad into her mouth and chewed the crisp lettuce as though it were leather.

"I considered it a step above the cow and ten chickens you suggested the first time we discussed this."

"Where he came from, a cow and ten chickens were worth a lot more than you seem to realize," Janine exclaimed, and immediately regretted raising her voice, because half the patrons in the restaurant turned to stare. She smiled blandly at those around her, then slouched forward over her salad.

She reached for a bread stick, broke it in half and glared at it. "The use of the limo," she repeated, indignant.

"Don't look so upset." He grinned. "I might have accepted."

Zach was deriving far too much pleasure from this to suit her. "Your attitude isn't helping any," she said, frowning righteously.

"I apologize."

But he didn't act the least bit apologetic. When she'd first met Zach, Janine had assumed he was a man who rarely smiled, yet in the short time they'd spent together today, he'd practically been laughing outright.

The waitress brought their entrées, but when Janine took her first bite, she realized that even the pretense of eating was more than she could manage. She felt too wretched. Tears sprang to her eyes, which embarrassed her even more, although she struggled to hide them.

"What's wrong?" Zach surprised her by asking.

Eyes averted, Janine shook her head, while she attempted to swallow. "Gramps believes I'm a poor judge of character," she finally said. And she was. Brian had proved it to her, but Gramps didn't know about Brian. "I feel like a failure."

"He didn't mean any of it," Zach said gently.

"But couldn't he have come up with something a little more flattering?"

"He needed an excuse to marry you off, otherwise his suggestion would have sounded crazy." Zach hesitated. "You know, the more we discuss this, the more ludicrous the whole thing seems." He chuckled softly and leaned forward to set his elbows on the table. "Who would've believed he'd come up with the idea of the two of us marrying?"

"Thank you very much," Janine muttered. He sat there

shredding her ego and apparently found the process just short of hilarious.

"Don't let it get to you. You're not interested in me as a husband, anyway."

"You're right about that—you're the last person I'd ever consider marrying," she lashed out, then regretted her reaction when she saw his face tighten.

"That's what I thought." He attacked his spaghetti as though the clams were scampering around his plate.

The tension between them mounted. When the waitress arrived to remove their plates, Janine had barely touched her meal. Zach hadn't eaten much, either.

After paying for their dinner, Zach walked her to her car, offering no further comment. As far as Janine was concerned, their meeting hadn't been at all productive. She felt certain that Zach was everything Gramps claimed—incisive, intelligent, intuitive. But that was at the office. As a potential husband and wife, they were completely ill-suited.

"Do you still want me to keep in touch?" she asked when she'd unlocked her car door. They stood awkwardly together in the street, and Janine realized they hardly knew what to say to each other.

"I suppose we should, since neither of us is interested in falling in with this plan of his," Zach said. "We need to set our differences aside and work together, otherwise we might unknowingly play into his hands."

"I won't be swayed and you won't, either." Janine found the thought oddly disappointing.

"If and when I do marry," Zach informed her, "which I sincerely doubt, I'll choose my own bride."

It went without saying that Janine was nothing like the woman he'd want to spend his life with.

"If and when *I* marry, I'll choose my own husband," she said, sounding equally firm. And it certainly wouldn't be a man her grandfather had chosen.

"I don't know if I like boys or not," thirteen-year-old Pam Hudson admitted over a cheeseburger and French fries. "They can be so dumb."

It'd been a week since Janine's dinner with Zach, and she was surprised that the teenager's assessment of the opposite sex should so closely match her own.

"I'm not even sure I like Charlie anymore," Pam said as she stirred her catsup with a French fry. Idly she smeared it around the edges of her plate in a haphazard pattern. "I used to be so crazy about him, remember?"

Janine smiled indulgently. "Every other word was Charlie this and Charlie that."

"He can be okay, though. Remember when he brought me that long-stemmed rose and left it on my porch?"

"I remember." Janine's mind flashed to the afternoon she'd met Zach. As they left the restaurant, he'd smiled at her. It wasn't much as smiles went, but for some reason, she couldn't seem to forget how he'd held her gaze, his dark eyes gentle, as he murmured polite nonsense. Funny how little things about this man tended to pop up in her mind at the strangest moments.

"But last week," Pam continued, "Charlie was playing basketball with the guys, and when I walked by, he pretended he didn't even know me."

"That hurt, didn't it?"

"Yeah, it did," Pam confessed. "And after I bought a T-shirt for him, too."

"Does he wear it?"

A gratified smile lit the girl's eyes. "All the time."

"By the way, I like how you're doing your hair."

Pam beamed. "I want it to look more like yours."

Actually, the style suited Pam far better than it did her, Janine thought. The sides were cut close to the head, but the long bangs flopped with a life of their own—at least on Janine they did. Lately she'd taken to pinning them back.

"How are things at home?" Janine asked, watching the girl carefully. Pam's father, Jerry Hudson, was divorced and had custody of his daughter. Pam's mother worked on the East Coast. With no family in the area, Jerry felt that his daughter needed a woman's influence. He'd contacted the Friendship Club about the same time Janine had applied to be a volunteer. Since Jerry worked odd hours as a short-order cook, she'd met him only once. He seemed a decent sort, working hard to make a good life for himself and his daughter.

Pam was a marvelous kid, Janine mused, and she possessed exceptional creative talent. Even before her father could afford to buy her a sewing machine, Pam had been designing and making clothes for her Barbie dolls. Janine's bandanna dress was one of the first projects she'd completed on her new machine. Pam had made several others since; they were popular with her friends, and she was ecstatic about the success of her ideas.

"I think I might forgive Charlie," she went on to say, her look contemplative. "I mean, he was with the guys and everything."

"It's not cool to let his friends know he's got a girl-friend, huh?"

"Yeah, I guess...."

Janine wasn't feeling nearly as forgiving toward Zach. He'd talked about their keeping in touch, but hadn't called her since. She didn't believe for an instant that Gramps had given up on his marriage campaign, but he'd apparently decided to let the matter rest. The pressure was off, yet Janine kept expecting some word from Zach. The least he could do was call, she grumbled to herself, although she made no attempt to analyze the reasons for her disappointment.

"Maybe Charlie isn't so bad, after all," Pam murmured, then added wisely, "This is an awkward age for boys, especially in their relationships with girls."

"Say," Janine teased, "who's supposed to be the adult here, anyway? That's my line."

"Oh, sorry."

Smiling, Janine stole a French fry from Pam's plate and popped it into her mouth.

"So when are you leaving for Scotland?" Pam wanted to know.

"Next week."

"How long are you going to be gone?"

"Ten days." The trip was an unexpected gift from her grandfather. One night shortly after she'd met Zach for dinner, Gramps had handed her a packet with airline tickets and hotel reservations. When she'd asked why, his reply had been vague, even cryptic—something about her needing to get away. Since she'd always dreamed of visiting Scotland, she'd leapt at the chance.

It wasn't until she'd driven Pam home that Janine thought she should let Zach know she was going to be out of the country. It probably wasn't important, but he'd made such a point of saying they should keep in touch....

Janine planned her visit to the office carefully, making sure Gramps would be occupied elsewhere. Since she'd been shopping for her trip, she was carrying several department and clothing store bags. She was doing this for a reason. She wanted her visit to appear unplanned, as if in the course of a busy day, she'd suddenly remembered their agreement. She felt that dropping in would seem more spontaneous than simply calling.

"Hello," she said to Zach's efficient secretary, smiling cheerfully. "Is Mr. Thomas available? I'll only need a moment of his time."

The older woman clearly disapproved of this intrusion, but although she pursed her lips, she didn't verbalize her objection. She pushed the intercom button and Janine felt a tingle of awareness at the sound of Zach's strong masculine voice.

"This is a pleasant surprise," he said, standing as Janine breezed into the room.

She set her bags on the floor and with an exaggerated sigh, eased herself into the chair opposite his desk and crossed her legs. "I'm sorry to drop in unannounced," she said casually, "but I have some news."

"No problem." His gaze fell to the bags heaped on the floor. "Looks like you had a busy afternoon."

"I was shopping."

"So I see. Any special reason?"

"It's my trousseau." Melodramatically, she pressed the back of her hand against her forehead. "I can't take the pressure anymore. I've come to tell you I told my grandfather to go ahead and arrange the wedding. Someday, somehow, we'll learn to love each other."

"This isn't amusing. Now what's so important that it can't—"

"Mr. Thomas," his secretary said crisply over the intercom, "Mr. Hartman is here to see you."

Janine's eyes widened in panic as her startled gaze flew to Zach, who looked equally alarmed. It would be the worst possible thing for Gramps to discover Janine alone with Zach in his office. She hated to think how he'd interpret that.

"Just a minute," Zach said, reading the hysteria in her eyes. She marveled at how composed he sounded. He pointed toward a closed door and ushered her into a small room—or a large closet—that was practically a home away from home. A bar, refrigerator, microwave, sink and other conveniences were neatly arranged inside.

No sooner was the door slammed shut behind her than it was jerked open again and three large shopping bags were tossed in.

Janine felt utterly ridiculous. She kept as still as she could, afraid to turn on the light and almost afraid to breathe for fear of being discovered.

With her ear against the door, she tried to listen to the conversation, hoping to discover just how long Gramps intended to plant himself in Zach's office.

Unfortunately, she could barely hear a thing. She risked opening the door a crack; a quick glance revealed that both men were facing away from her. That explained why she couldn't understand their conversation.

It was then that Janine spotted her purse. Strangling a gasp, she eased the door shut and staggered away from it. She covered her mouth as she took deep breaths. When she found the courage to edge open the door and peek again, she saw that all her grandfather had to do was glance downward.

If he shuffled his feet, his shoe would catch on the strap and he'd drag it out of the office with him.

Zach turned away from the window, and for the first time Janine could hear and see him clearly.

"I'll take care of that right away," he said evenly. He was so calm, so composed, as though he often kept women hidden in his closet. He must have noticed Janine's purse because he frowned and his gaze flew accusingly toward her.

Well, for heaven's sake, she hadn't purposely left it there for Gramps to trip over! He wasn't even supposed to be in the building. That very morning, he'd told her he was lunching at the Athletic Club with his longtime friend, Burt Coleman. Whenever Gramps ate lunch with his cronies, he spent the afternoon playing pinochle. Apparently he'd changed his habits, just so her hair would turn prematurely gray.

Several tortured minutes passed before Zach escorted Gramps to the door. The instant it was shut, Janine stepped into the office, blinking against the brightness after her wait in the dark. "My purse," she said in a strangled voice. "Do you think he saw it?"

"It would be a miracle if he didn't. Of all the stupid things to do!"

"I didn't purposely leave it out here!"

"I'm not talking about that," Zach growled. "I'm referring to your coming here in the first place. Are you crazy? You couldn't have called?"

"I…had something to tell you and I was in the neighborhood." So much for her suave, sophisticated facade. Zach was right, of course; she *could* have told him just as easily by phone.

He looked furious. "For the life of me I can't think of a solitary thing that's so important you'd do anything this foolish. If your grandfather saw the two of us together, he'd immediately jump to the wrong conclusion. Until this afternoon, everything's been peaceful. Anton hasn't mentioned your name once and, frankly, I appreciated that."

His words stung. "I…I won't make the mistake of coming again—ever," she vowed, trying to sound dignified and aloof. She gathered her purse and her bags as quickly as possible and hurried out of the office, not caring who saw her leave, including Gramps.

"Janine, you never did say why you came." Zach had followed her to the elevator.

Janine stared at the light above the elevator that indicated the floor number, as though it was a message of the utmost importance. Her hold on the bags was precarious and something was dragging against her feet, but she couldn't have cared less. "I'm sorry to have imposed on your valuable time. Now that I think about it, it wasn't even important."

"Janine," he coaxed, apparently regretting his earlier outburst. "I shouldn't have yelled."

"Yes, I know," she said smoothly. The elevator opened and with as little ceremony as possible, she slipped inside. It wasn't until she was over the threshold that she realized her purse strap was tangled around her feet.

So much for a dignified exit.

Four

"The castle of Cawdor was built in the fifteenth century and to this day remains the seat of the earl of Cawdor," the guide intoned as Janine and several other sightseers toured the famous landmark. "In William Shakespeare's *Macbeth*, the castle plays an important role. Macbeth becomes the thane of Cawdor…."

For the first few days of Janine's visit to Scotland, she'd been content to explore on her own. The tours, however, helped fill in the bits and pieces of history she might otherwise have missed.

The castle of Cawdor was in northeastern Scotland. The next day, she planned to rent a car and take a meandering route toward Edinburgh, the political heart of Scotland. From what she'd read, Edinburgh Castle was an ancient fortress, built on a huge rock, that dominated the city's skyline. Gramps had booked reservations for her at an inn on the outskirts of town.

The Bonnie Inn, with its red-tiled roof and black-trimmed gables, had all the charm she'd expected, and more. Janine's room offered more character than comfort, but she felt its welcome as if she were visiting an old friend. A vase filled with fresh flowers and dainty jars of bath salts awaited her.

Eager to explore, she strolled outside to investigate the extensive garden. There was a chill in the April air and she tucked her hands in her pockets, watching with amusement as the partridges fed on the lush green lawn.

"Janine?"

At the sound of her name, she turned, and to her astonishment discovered Zach standing not more than ten feet away. "What are you doing here?" she demanded.

"Me? I was about to ask you the same question."

"I'm on vacation. Gramps gave me the trip as a gift."

"I'm here on business," Zach explained, and his brow furrowed in a suspicious frown.

Janine was doing her own share of frowning. "This is all rather convenient, don't you think?"

Zach took immediate offense. "You don't believe I planned this, do you?"

"No," she agreed reluctantly.

Zach continued to stand there, stiff and wary. "I had absolutely nothing to do with this," he said.

"If you hadn't been so rude to me the last time we met," she felt obliged to inform him, with a righteous tilt to her chin, "you'd have known well in advance that Gramps was sending me here, and we could have avoided this unpleasant shock."

"If you hadn't been in such an all-fired hurry to leave my office, you'd have discovered I was traveling here myself."

"Oh, that's perfect! Go ahead and blame me for everything," she shrieked. "As I recall, you were furious at my being anywhere near your precious office."

"All right, I'll admit I might have handled the situation poorly," Zach said, and the muscles in his jaw hardened. "But as you'll also recall, I did apologize."

"Sure you did," she said, "after you'd trampled all over my ego. I've never felt like more of a fool in my life."

"You?" Zach shouted. "It may surprise you to know that I don't make a habit of hiding women in my office."

"Do you think I enjoyed being stuffed in that…closet like a bag of dirty laundry?"

"What was I supposed to do? Hide you under my desk?"

"It might've been better than a pitch-black closet."

"If you're so keen on casting blame, let me remind you I wasn't the one who left my purse in full view of your grandfather," Zach said. "I did everything but perform card tricks to draw his attention away from it."

"You make it sound like I'm at fault," Janine snapped.

"I'm not the one who popped in unexpectedly. If you had a job like everyone else—"

"If I had a job," she broke in, outraged. "You mean all the volunteer work I do doesn't count? Apparently the thirty hours a week I put in mean nothing. Sure, I've got a degree. Sure, I could probably have my pick of a dozen different jobs, but why take employment away from someone who really needs it when so many worthwhile organizations are hurting for volunteers?" She was breathless by the time she finished, and so angry she could feel the heat radiating from her face.

She refused to tolerate Zach's offensive insinuations any longer. From the moment they'd met, Zach had clearly viewed her as spoiled and frivolous, without a brain in her head. And it seemed that nothing had altered his opinion.

"Listen, I didn't mean—"

"It's obvious to me," she said bluntly, "that you and I are never going to agree on anything." She was so furious she couldn't keep her anger in check. "The best thing for us to do is completely ignore each other. It's obvious that you don't want anything to do with me and, frankly, I feel the same way about you. So, good day, Mr. Thomas." With that she walked away, her head high and her pride intact.

For the very first time with this man, she'd been able to make a grand exit. It should have felt good. But it didn't.

An hour later, after Janine had taken the tourist bus into Edinburgh, she was still brooding over her latest encounter with Zachary Thomas. If there was any humor at all in this situation, it had to be the fact that her usually sage grandfather could possibly believe she and Zach were in any way suited.

Determined to put the man out of her mind, Janine wandered down Princes Street, which was packed with shoppers, troupes of actors giving impromptu performances and strolling musicians. Her mood couldn't help but be influenced by the festive flavor, and she soon found herself smiling despite the unpleasant confrontation with her grandfather's business partner.

Several of the men who passed her in the street were dressed in kilts, and Janine felt as if she'd stepped into another time, another world. The air swirled with bagpipe music. The city itself seemed gray and gloomy, a dull background for the colorful sights and sounds, the excitement of ages past.

It was as Janine walked out of a dress shop that she bumped into Zach a second time. He stopped, his eyes registering surprise and what looked to Janine like a hint of regret—as though confronting her twice in the same day was enough to try anyone's patience.

"I know what you're thinking," he said, pinning her with his dark intense gaze.

"And I'm equally confident that you don't." She held her packages close and edged against the shop window to avoid hindering other pedestrians on the crowded sidewalk.

"I came here to do some shopping," Zach said gruffly. "I wasn't following you."

"You can rest assured I wasn't following *you*."

"Fine," he said.

"Fine," she repeated.

But neither of them moved for several nerve-racking seconds. Janine assumed Zach was going to say something else. Perhaps she secretly hoped he would. If they couldn't be friends, Janine would've preferred they remain allies. They should be uniting their forces instead of battling each other. Without a word, Zach gestured abruptly and wheeled around to join the stream of people hurrying down the sidewalk.

A half hour later, with more packages added to her collection, Janine strolled into a fabric store, wanting to purchase a sizable length of wool as a gift for Pam. She ran her fingertips along several thick bolts of material, marveling at the bold colors. The wool felt soft, but when she lifted a corner with her palm, she was surprised by how heavy it was.

"Each clan has its own tartan," the white-haired lady in the shop explained. Janine enjoyed listening to her voice, with its enthusiastic warmth and distinct Scottish burr. "Some of the best-known tartans come in three patterns that are to be worn for different occasions—everyday, dress and battle."

Intrigued, Janine watched as the congenial woman walked around the table to remove a blue-and-green plaid. Janine had already seen that pattern several times. The shop owner said that tourists were often interested in this particular tartan, called Black Watch, because it was assigned to no particular clan. In choosing Black Watch, they weren't aligning themselves with any one clan, but showing total impartiality.

Pleased, Janine purchased several yards of the fabric.

Walking down the narrow street, she was shuffling her packages in her arms when she caught sight of Zach watching a troupe of musicians. She started to move away, then for no reason she could name, paused to study him. Her impression of him really hadn't changed since that

first afternoon. She still thought Zach Thomas opinion-
ated, unreasonable and…fine, she was willing to admit it,
attractive. *Very* attractive, in a sort of rough-hewn way. He
lacked the polish, the superficial sophistication of a man
like Brian, but he had a vigor that seemed thoroughly
masculine. He also had the uncanny ability to set her teeth
on edge with a single look. No other man could irritate
her so quickly.

The musicians began a lively song and Zach laughed un-
selfconsciously. His rich husky tenor was smooth and
relaxed as it drifted across the street toward her. Janine
knew she should've left then, but she couldn't. Despite
everything, she was intrigued.

Zach must have felt her scrutiny because he suddenly
turned and their eyes locked before Janine could look away.
The color rose to her cheeks and for a long moment, neither
moved. Neither smiled.

It was in Janine's mind to cross the street, swallow her
pride and put an end to this pointless antagonism. During
the past several weeks her pride had become familiar fare;
serving it up once more shouldn't be all that difficult.

She was entertaining that thought when a bus drove past
her belching a thick cloud of black smoke, momentarily
blocking her view of Zach. When the bus had passed, Janine
noticed that he'd returned his attention to the musicians.

Disheartened, she headed in the opposite direction.
She hadn't gone more than a block when she heard him
call her name.

She stopped and waited for him to join her. With an inquiring lift of one eyebrow, he reached for some of her packages. She nodded, repressing a shiver of excitement as his hand brushed hers. Shifting his burden, he slowed his steps to match Janine's. Then he spoke. "We need to talk."

"I don't see how we can. Every time you open your mouth you say something insulting and offensive."

Only a few minutes earlier, Janine had been hoping to put an end to this foolish antagonism, yet here she was provoking an argument, acting just as unreasonable as she accused him of being. She stopped midstep, disgusted with herself. "I shouldn't have said that. I don't know what it is about us, but we seem to have a hard time being civil to each other."

"It might be the shock of finding each other here."

"Which brings up another subject," Janine added fervently. "If Gramps was going to arrange for us to meet, why send us halfway around the world to do it?"

"I used to think I knew your grandfather," Zach murmured. "But lately, I'm beginning to wonder. I haven't got a clue why he chose Scotland."

"He came to me with the tickets, reminding me it'd been almost a year since I'd traveled anywhere," Janine said. "He told me it was high time I took a vacation, that I needed to get away for a while. And I bought it hook, line and sinker."

"You?" Zach cried, shaking his head, clearly troubled. "Your grandfather sent me here on a wild-goose chase. Yes, there were contacts to make, but this was a trip any of our junior executives could've handled. It wasn't until I arrived at the inn and found you booked there that I realized what he was up to."

"If we hadn't been so distracted trying to figure out who was to blame for that fiasco at your office, we might've been able to prevent this. At least, we'd have guessed what Gramps was doing."

"Exactly," Zach said. "Forewarned is forearmed. Obviously, we have to put aside our differences and stay in communication. That's the key. Communication."

"Absolutely," Janine agreed, with a nod of her head.

"But letting him throw us together like this is only going to lead to trouble."

What kind of trouble, he didn't say, but Janine could guess all too easily. "I agree with you."

"The less time we spend together, the better." He paused when he noticed that she was standing in front of the bus stop.

"If we allow Gramps to throw us together, it'll just encourage him," she said. "We've got to be very firm about this, before things get completely out of hand."

"You're right." Without asking, he took the rest of the packages from her arms, adding them to the bags and parcels he already carried. "I rented a car. I don't suppose you'd accept a ride back to the inn?"

"Please." Janine was grateful for the offer. They'd started off badly, each blaming the other, but fortunately their relationship was beginning to improve. That relieved her. She'd much rather have Zachary for a friend than an enemy.

They spoke very little on the twenty-mile ride back to the Bonnie Inn. After an initial exchange of what sights

they'd seen and what they'd purchased, there didn't seem
to be much to say. They remained awkward and a little
uneasy with each other. And Janine was all too aware of
how intimate the confines of the small rented car were.
Her shoulder and her thigh were within scant inches of
brushing against Zach, something she was determined to
ignore.

The one time Janine chanced a look in his direction, she
saw how intent his features were, as if he was driving a
dangerous, twisting course instead of a straight, well-
maintained road with light traffic. His mouth was com-
pressed, bracketed by deep grooves, and his dark eyes had
narrowed. He glanced away from the road long enough for
their eyes to meet. Janine smiled and quickly looked down,
embarrassed that he'd caught her studying him so closely.
She wished she could sort out her feelings, analyze all her
contradictory emotions in a logical manner. She was attracted to Zach, but not in the same way she'd been attracted to Brian. Although Zach infuriated her, she admired
him. Respected him. But he didn't send her senses whirling
mindlessly, as Brian had. Then again, she didn't think of
him as a brother, either. Her only conclusion was that her
feelings for Zach were more confusing than ever.

After thanking him for the ride and collecting her
parcels, she left Zach in the lobby and tiredly climbed the
stairs to her room. She soaked in a hot scented bath, then
changed into a blue-and-gold plaid kilt she'd bought that
afternoon. With it, she wore a thin white sweater under her
navy-blue blazer. She tied a navy scarf at her neck, pleased

with the effect. A little blush, a dab of eye shadow and she was finished, by now more than ready for something to eat.

Zach was waiting to be seated in the dining room when she came downstairs. He wore a thick hand-knit sweater over black dress slacks and made such a virile sight she found it difficult not to stare.

The hostess greeted them with a warm smile. "Dinner for two?"

Janine reacted first, flustered and a little embarrassed. "We're not together," she said. "This gentleman was here before me." Anything else would negate the agreement they'd made earlier.

Zach frowned as he followed the hostess to a table set against the wall, close to the massive stone fireplace. The hostess returned and directed Janine to a table against the same wall, so close to Zach that she could practically read the menu over his shoulder. She was reading her own menu when Zach spoke. "Don't you think we're both being a little silly?"

"Yes," she admitted. "But earlier today we agreed that being thrown together like this could lead to trouble."

"I honestly don't think it would hurt either of us to have dinner together, do you?"

"No...I don't think it would." They'd spend the entire meal talking across the tables to each other, anyway.

He stood up, grinning. "May I join you?"

"Please." She couldn't help responding with a smile.

He pulled out the other chair, his gaze appreciative. "Those colors look good on you."

"Thanks." She had to admit he looked good—darkly

vibrant and masculine—himself. She was about to return his compliment when it dawned on her how senselessly they were challenging fate.

"It's happening already," she whispered, leaning toward him in order to avoid being overheard.

"What?" Zach glanced around as though he expected ghostly clansmen to emerge from behind the drapes.

"You're telling me how good I look in blue and I was about to tell you how nice *you* look and we're smiling at each other and forming a mutual admiration society. Next thing you know, we'll be married."

"That's ridiculous!"

"Sure, you say that now, but I can see a real problem here."

"Does this mean you want me to go back to my table and eat alone?"

"Of course not. I just think it would be best if we limited the compliments. All right?"

"I'll never say anything nice about you again."

Janine smiled. "Thank you."

"You might want to watch that, as well," he warned with a roguish grin. "If we're too formal and polite with each other, that could lead us straight to the jewelers. Before we know what's happening, we'll be choosing wedding bands."

Janine's lips quivered with a barely restrained smile. "I hadn't thought about that." They glanced at each other and before either could hold it in, they were laughing, attracting the attention of everyone in the dining room. As abruptly as they'd started, they stopped, burying their faces in the menus.

After they'd ordered, Janine shared her theory with

Zach, a theory that had come to her on their drive back to the inn. "I think I know why Gramps arranged for us to meet in Scotland."

"I'm dying to hear this."

"Actually, I'm afraid I'm the one responsible." She heaved a sigh of remorse. Every part of her seemed aware of Zach, which was exactly what she didn't want. She sighed again. "When Gramps first mentioned the idea of an arranged marriage, I tried to make him understand that love wasn't something one ordered like…like dinner from a menu. He genuinely didn't seem to grasp what I was saying and asked me what a woman needed to fall in love."

"And you told him a trip to Scotland?" Zach's eyes sparkled with the question.

"Of course not. I told him a woman needed romance."

Zach leaned forward. "I hate to appear dense, but I seem to have missed something."

Pretending to be annoyed with him, Janine explained, "Well, Gramps asked me to define romance…"

"I'd be interested in learning that myself." Zach wiped the edges of his mouth with his napkin. Janine suspected he did it to cover a growing need to smile.

"It isn't all that easy to explain, you know," Janine said. "And remember this was off the top of my head. I told Gramps romance was forbidden trysts on Scottish moors."

"With an enemy clan chieftain?"

"No, with the man I loved."

"What else did you tell him?"

"I don't remember exactly. I think I said something

about a moonlight stroll on the beach, and…and desperate passion."

"I wonder how he'll arrange that?"

"I don't think I want to find out," Janine murmured. Considering how seriously Gramps had taken her impromptu definition, she almost dreaded the thought of what he might do next.

When they'd finished, their plates were removed by the attentive waiter and their coffee served. To complicate her feelings, she was actually a little sad their dinner was about to end.

They left the dining room, and Zach escorted her up the stairs. "Thank you for being willing to take a risk and share dinner with me," he said, his voice deadpan. "I enjoyed it, despite the, uh, danger."

"I did, too," Janine said softly. More than she cared to admit. Against her better judgment, her mind spun with possible ways to delay their parting, but she decided against each one, not wanting to tempt fate any more than she already had.

Zach walked her to her room, pausing outside her door. Janine found herself searching for the right words. She longed to tell him she'd enjoyed spending the evening with him, talking and laughing together, but she didn't know how to say it without sounding like a woman in love.

Zach appeared to be having the same problem. He raised one hand as though to touch her face, then apparently changed his mind, dropping his hand abruptly. She felt strangely disappointed.

"Good night," he said curtly, stepping back.

"Good night," she echoed, turning to walk into her room. She closed the door and leaned against it, feeling unsettled but at a loss to understand why.

After ten restless minutes she ventured out again. The country garden was well lit, and a paved pathway led to rocky cliffs that fell off sharply. Even from where she stood, Janine could hear the sea roaring below. She could smell its salty tang, mixed with the scent of heath. Thrusting her hands into her blazer pockets, Janine strolled along a narrow path into the garden. The night air was cool and she had no intention of walking far, not more than a few hundred feet. She'd return in the morning when she planned to walk as far as the cliffs with their buffeting winds.

The moon was full and so large it seemed to take up the entire sky, sending streaks of silvery light across the horizon. With her arms wrapped around her middle, she gazed up at it, certain she'd never felt more peaceful or serene. She closed her eyes, savoring the luxurious silence of the moment.

Suddenly it was broken. "So we meet again," Zach said from behind her.

"This is getting ridiculous." Janine turned to him and smiled, her heart beating fast. "Meeting on the moors…"

"It isn't exactly a tryst," Zach said.

"Not technically."

They stood side by side, looking into the night sky, both of them silent. During their meal they'd talked nonstop, but now Janine felt tongue-tied and ill at ease. If they'd been worried about having dinner together, they were placing themselves at even greater risk here in the moonlight.

Janine knew it. Zach knew it. But neither suggested leaving.

"It's a beautiful night," Zach said at last, linking his hands behind his back.

"It is, isn't it?" Janine replied brightly, as if he'd introduced the most stimulating topic of her entire vacation.

"I don't think we should put any stock in this," he surprised her by saying next.

"In what?"

"In meeting here, as if we'd arranged a tryst. Of course you're a beautiful woman and it would be only natural if a man…any red-blooded man were to find himself charmed. I'd blame it on the moonlight, wouldn't you?"

"Oh, I agree completely. I mean, we've been thrust together in a very romantic setting and it would be normal to…find ourselves momentarily…attracted to each other. It doesn't mean anything, though."

Zach moved behind her. "You're right, of course." He hesitated, then murmured, "You should've worn a heavier jacket." Before she could assure him that she was perfectly comfortable, he ran his hands slowly down the length of her arms, as though to warm her. Unable to restrain herself, Janine sighed and leaned against him, soaking up his warmth and his strength.

"This presents a problem, doesn't it?" he whispered, his voice husky and close to her ear. "Isn't moonlight supposed to do something strange to people?"

"I...think it only affects werewolves."

He chuckled and his breath shot a series of incredible light-as-air sensations along her neck. Janine felt she was about to crumple at his feet. Then his chin brushed the side of her face and she sighed again.

His hands on her shoulders, Zach urged her around so that she faced him, but not for anything would Janine allow her gaze to meet his.

He didn't say a word.

She didn't, either.

Janine experienced one worry after another, afraid to voice any of them. Zach apparently felt the same way, because he didn't seem any more eager to explain things than she did. Or to stop them...

After a moment, Zach pressed his hands over her cheekbones. Leisurely, his thumbs stroked the line of her jaw, her chin. His eyes were dark, his expression unreadable. Janine's heart was churning over and over, dragging her emotions with it. She swallowed, then moistened her lips.

He seemed to find her mouth mesmerizing. Somewhere deep inside, she discovered the strength to warn him that her grandfather's plan was working. She opened her mouth to speak, but before she could utter a single word, Zach's arms came around her and drew her close against him. She felt his comforting warmth seep through her, smelled the faint muskiness of his skin. The sensations were unlike anything she'd ever known. Then he lowered his mouth to hers.

The immediate shock of pleasure was almost frightening. She couldn't keep from trembling.

He drew back slightly. "You're cold. You should've said something."

"No, that's not it." Even her voice was quivering.

"Then what is?"

In response she kissed him back. She hadn't meant to, but before she could stop herself, she slipped her arms around his neck and slanted her mouth over his.

Zach's shoulders were heaving when at last she pulled her mouth away and hid her face against his chest.

"What are we doing?" he whispered. He broke hastily away from her.

Janine was too stunned to react. In an effort to hide his effect on her, she rubbed her face as though struggling to wake up from a deep sleep.

"That shouldn't have happened," Zach said stiffly.

"You're telling me," she returned raggedly. "It certainly wasn't the smartest move we could've made."

Zach jerked his fingers roughly through his hair and frowned. "I don't know what came over me. Over us. We both know better."

"It's probably because we're both tired," Janine said soothingly, offering a convenient excuse. "When you stop to think about it, the whole thing's perfectly understandable. Gramps arranged for us to meet, hoping something like this would happen. Clearly the power of suggestion is stronger than either of us realized."

"Clearly." But he continued to frown.

"Oh, gee," Janine said glancing at her watch, unable to read the numbers in the dark. Her voice was high and wavering. "Will you look at the time? I can't believe it's so late. I really should be getting back inside."

"Janine, listen. I think we should talk about this."

"Sure, but not now." All she wanted was to escape and gather some perspective on what had happened. It had all started so innocently, almost a game, but quickly turned into something far more serious.

"All right, we'll discuss it in the morning." Zach didn't sound pleased. He walked through the garden with her, muttering under his breath. "Damn it!" he said, again shoving his fingers through his hair. "I knew I should never have come here."

"There's no need to be so angry. Blame the moonlight. It obviously disrupts the brain and interferes with wave patterns or something."

"Right," Zach said, his voice still gruff.

"Well, good night," Janine managed cheerfully when they reached the staircase.

"Good night." Zach's tone was equally nonchalant.

Once Janine was in her room, she threw herself on the bed and covered her eyes with one hand. *Oh, no,* she lamented silently. They'd crossed the line. Tempted fate. Spit in the eye of common sense.

They'd kissed.

Several minutes later, still shaking, Janine got up and undressed. She slid under the blankets and tried to find a relaxing position. But she didn't feel like sleeping. Tomorrow she'd have to make polite conversation with Zach and she didn't know if she could bear it. She was sure he'd feel just as uncomfortable with her. She'd seen how he could barely look at her when they entered the inn.

Tossing aside the blankets, Janine decided she had only one option. She'd leave Scotland, the sooner the better. Grabbing the phone, she called the airport, booked a seat on the earliest flight home and immediately set about packing her bags.

Not bothering to even try to sleep, she crept down the stairs a little before midnight and checked out.

"You're leaving sooner than you expected, aren't you, Miss Hartman?" the night manager asked after calling for a cab.

"Yes," she said.

"I hope everything was satisfactory?"

"It was wonderful." She pulled a folded piece of paper from her purse and placed it on the counter. "Would you see to it that Mr. Thomas receives this in the morning?"

"Of course." The young man tucked it in a small cubbyhole behind him.

Satisfied that Zach would know she was leaving and wouldn't be concerned by her hurried return to Seattle, she sat in a chair in the small lobby to wait for her cab.

About fifteen minutes later, Janine watched silently as the cabdriver stowed her luggage in the trunk. She paused before climbing in the backseat of the car and glanced one last time at the muted moonlit landscape, disappointed that she wouldn't have an opportunity to visit the cliffs.

The ride to the airport seemed to take an eternity. She felt a burning sense of regret at leaving Scotland. She'd fallen in love with the country during her short visit and hoped someday to return. Although the memory of her evening stroll through the garden would always bring with it a certain chagrin, she couldn't completely regret that time with Zach. In fact, she'd always remember the fleeting sense of contentment she'd felt in his arms.

Janine arrived at the airport long before her flight was scheduled to leave. She spent an hour drinking coffee and leafing through fashion magazines, several of which she took with her to give to Pam later.

A cup of coffee in one hand, she approached the airline counter with her passport in the other. The bag she had draped over her shoulder accidentally collided with the man standing next to her. An automatic apology formed on her lips, but before she could voice it, that same man turned to face her.

"Zach," she cried, nearly dropping her coffee in shock. "What are you doing here?"

Five

"You think this is intentional, don't you?" Zach demanded. "It's obvious *you're* the one running after me. You found the note I slipped under your door and—"

"I checked out just before midnight so I couldn't possibly have read your note," she said angrily. "And furthermore I left a message for you."

"I didn't get it."

"Then there's been a misunderstanding."

"To say the least," Zach muttered. "A misunderstanding…" His tone was doubtful, as if he suspected she'd purposely arranged to fly home with him. She launched into an indignant protest.

"Excuse me, please."

The interruption was from a uniformed airline employee who was leaning over the counter and waving in an effort to gain their attention.

"May I have your ticket and passport?" she asked Janine. "You're holding up the line."

"Of course. I'm sorry." The best thing to do, she decided, was to ignore Zach completely. Just because they were booked on the same flight didn't mean they had to have anything to do with each other. Evidently they'd both panicked after their encounter in the garden. He was as eager to escape as she was.

Okay, so she'd ignore him and he'd ignore her. She'd return to her life, and he'd return to his. From this point forward, they need never have contact with each other again. Then they'd both be satisfied.

The airline clerk punched something into her computer. "I can give you your seat assignment now," she remarked, concentrating on the screen.

Standing on tiptoe, Janine leaned toward the woman and lowered her voice to a whisper. "Could you make sure I'm as far from Mr. Thomas's seat as possible?"

"This flight is booked solid," the attendant said impatiently. "The only reason you and your...friend were able to get seats was because of a last-minute cancellation. I'll do the best I can, but I can't rearrange everyone's seat assignments just before the flight."

"I understand," Janine said, feeling foolish and petty. But the way her luck had been going, Zach would end up in the seat beside hers, believing she'd purposely arranged that, too.

They boarded the flight separately; in fact, Zach was one of the last passengers to step onto the plane.

By that time, Janine was settled in the second row of the

first-class section, flipping through the in-flight magazine. Zach strolled past her, intent on the boarding pass clutched in his hand.

Pretending she hadn't seen him seemed the best tactic, and she turned to gaze out the window.

"It seems I'm sitting here," Zach announced brusquely, loading his carry-on luggage in the compartment above the seats.

Janine had to bite her tongue to keep from insisting she'd had nothing to do with that. She'd even tried to prevent it, but she doubted Zach would believe her.

"Before you claim otherwise, I want you to know I didn't arrange this," he said, sitting down beside her.

"I know that."

"You do?"

"Of course," Janine told him. "The fates are against us. I don't know how my grandfather arranged our meeting at the airport or the adjoining seats, any more than I know why I stumbled on you my first day at the Bonnie Inn. We might never have crossed paths. But somehow, some way, Gramps is responsible." That didn't sound entirely reasonable, but she thought it best not to mention their stroll in the moonlight.

"So you're not ready to unleash the full force of your anger on me?"

"I don't see how I can be upset with you—or the reverse. Neither of us asked for this."

"Exactly."

Janine yawned loudly and covered her mouth. "Excuse me. I didn't sleep last night and now it's catching up with me."

Her yawn was contagous and soon Zach's hand was warding off his own admission of drowsiness. The flight attendant came by with coffee, which both Zach and Janine declined.

"Frankly, I'd be more interested in a pillow," Janine said, yawning again. The attendant handed her one, as well as a blanket, then offered the same to Zach. He refused both, intending to work on some papers he'd withdrawn from his briefcase. The minute the plane was safely in the air, Janine laid her head back and closed her eyes. Almost immediately she felt herself drifting into a peaceful slumber.

She stirred twice in the long hours that followed, but both times a gentle voice soothed her back to sleep. Sighing, she snuggled into the warmth, feeling more comfortable than she had in weeks.

She began to dream and could see herself walking across the moors, wearing traditional Scottish dress, while bagpipes wailed in the background.

Then, on the crest of a hill, Zach appeared, dressed in a Black Watch kilt and tam-o'-shanter; a set of bagpipes was draped over his shoulder. Their eyes met and the music ceased. Then, out of nowhere, her grandfather appeared, standing halfway between the two of them, looking distinctly pleased. He cupped his hands over his mouth and shouted to Janine. "Is this romance?"

"Yes," she shouted back.

"What else do you need?"

"Love."

"Love," Gramps repeated. He turned to Zach, apparently seeking some kind of assistance.

Zach started fiddling with his bagpipes, avoiding the question. He scowled as he concentrated on his task.

"Look at the pair of you," Gramps called. "You're perfect together. Zach, when are you going to wake up and realize what a wonderful girl my Janine is?"

"If I do get married, you can be sure I'll choose my own bride," Zach hollered.

"And I'd prefer to pick out my own husband!"

"You're falling in love with Zach!" Gramps declared, obviously elated.

"I—I—" Janine was so flustered she couldn't complete her thought, which only served to please her grandfather more.

"Look at her, boy," Gramps directed his attention to Zach again. "See how lovely she is. And think of what beautiful children you'll have."

"Gramps! Enough about babies! I'm not marrying Zach!"

"Janine." Zach's voice echoed in her ear.

"Keep out of this," she cried. He was the last person she wanted to hear from.

"You're having a dream."

Her eyes fluttered open and she saw Zach's face close to her own, her head nestled against his chest. "Oh…" she mumbled, bolting upright. "Oh, dear…I am sorry. I didn't realize I was leaning on you."

"I hated to wake you, but you seemed to be having a nightmare."

She blinked and tried to focus on him, but it was difficult, and to complicate matters her eyes started to water. She wiped her face with one sleeve. Then, straightening, she removed the pillow from behind her back and folded the blanket, trying to disguise how badly her hands were trembling.

"You're worried about what happened after dinner last night, aren't you?"

Janine released a pent-up breath and smiled brightly as she lied. "Nothing really happened."

"In the garden, when we kissed. Listen," Zach said in a low voice, glancing quickly around to ensure that no one could overhear their conversation, "I think it's time we talked about last night."

"I… You're right, of course." She didn't feel up to this, but she supposed it was best dealt with before she had to face her grandfather.

"Egos aside."

"By all means," Janine agreed. She braced herself, not knowing what to expect. Zach had made his views on the idea of an arranged marriage plain from the first; so had she. In fact, even her feelings about a marriage based on love weren't all that positive at the moment. Brian had taught her a valuable lesson, a painful lesson, one she wouldn't easily forget. She'd given him her heart and her trust, and he'd betrayed both. Falling in love had been the most shattering experience of her life, and she had no intention of repeating it anytime soon.

"I'd be a liar if I didn't admit how nice kissing you was," Zach said, "but I wish it had never happened. It created more problems than it solved."

Janine wasn't exactly flattered by his remark. Keeping egos out of this was harder than it sounded, she thought ruefully. Her expression must have revealed her thoughts because Zach elaborated. "Before I arrived in Scotland, we hardly knew each other. We met that first afternoon over lunch—with Anton—and talked a couple of times, but basically we were strangers."

"We had dinner one night," Janine reminded him, annoyed that he could so casually dismiss it.

"Right," he acknowledged. "Then we met at the Bonnie Inn and, bingo, we were having dinner together and walking in the moonlight, and before either of us knew how it happened, we were kissing."

Janine nodded, listening quietly.

"There are several factors we can take into account, but if we're going to place blame for that kiss, I'm the one at fault."

"You?"

"Me," he confirmed with a grimace. "Actually, I'm prepared to accept full responsibility. I doubt you were aware of what was going on. It didn't take me long to see how innocent you are, and—"

"Now just a minute," Janine snapped. Once again he was taking potshots at her dignity. "What do you mean by that?"

"It's obvious you haven't had a lot of sexual experience and—"

"In other words I'm so incredibly naive that I couldn't possibly be held accountable for a few kisses in the moonlight?"

"Something like that."

"Oh, brother," she muttered.

"There's no need to feel offended."

"I wasn't exactly raised in a convent, you know. And for your information, I've been kissed by more than one man."

"I'm sure you have. But we're getting sidetracked here—"

"I'm sorry you found me so inept. A man of your vast worldly experience must've been sorely disappointed by someone as unsophisticated as me, and—"

"Janine," he said firmly, stopping her. "You're putting words in my mouth. All I was saying is that we—*I*—let matters get out of hand and we can't blame your grandfather for what happened."

"I'm willing to accept my part in this. I can also see where this conversation is leading."

"Good," Zach said. It was clear that his composure was slipping. "Then you tell me."

"You think that because I enjoyed spending time with you and we shared this mildly romantic evening and—"

"*Mildly* romantic?"

"Yes, you did say egos aside, didn't you? I'm just being honest."

"Fine," he said, tight-lipped.

"You seem to think that because you have so much more experience than I do, there's a real danger I'll be *swooning* at your feet." She drew out the word, enjoying her silliness, and batted her eyelashes furiously.

"Janine, you're behaving like a child," he informed her coldly.

"Of course I am. That's exactly what you seem to expect of me."

Zach's fingers tightened on the armrest. "You're purposely misconstruing everything I said."

"Whatever you're trying to say isn't necessary. You figure we had a borderline interest in each other and now we've crossed that border. Right? Well, I'm telling you that you needn't worry." She sucked in a deep breath and glared at him. "I'm right, aren't I? That's what you think, isn't it?"

"Something like that, yes."

Janine nodded grimly. "And *now* you think that since you held me in your arms and you lost your control long enough to kiss me, I'm suddenly going to start entertaining thoughts of the M word."

"The…M word?"

"Marriage."

"That's ridiculous," Zach said, jamming the airline magazine back into the seat pocket in front of him.

"Well?"

"All I mean is that the temptation might be there and we should both beware of it."

"Oh, honestly, Zach," she said sarcastically, "you overestimate yourself."

"Listen, I wasn't the one mumbling about babies."

"I was having a dream! That has absolutely nothing to do with what we're talking about now."

"Could've fooled me." He reached for the same magazine he'd recently rejected and turned the pages hard enough to rip them in two. "I don't think this discussion is getting us anywhere."

Janine sighed. "You were right, though. We did need to clear the air."

Zach made a gruff indistinguishable reply.

"I'll try to keep out of your magnetic force field, but if I occasionally succumb to your overwhelming charm and forget myself, I can only beg your forgiveness."

"Enough, Janine."

He looked so annoyed with her that she couldn't help smiling. Zach Thomas was a man of such colossal ego it would serve him right if she pretended to faint every time he glanced in her direction. The image filled her mind with laughter.

Zach leaned his head back and closed his eyes, effectively concluding their conversation. Janine stared out the window at the first signs of sunrise, thinking about all kinds of things—except her chaotic feelings for the man beside her.

Some time later, the pilot announced that the plane was approaching Seattle-Tacoma International Airport. Home sounded good to Janine, although she fully intended to have a heart-to-heart talk with her grandfather about his matchmaking efforts.

Once they'd landed, she cleared customs quickly. She struggled with her two large pieces of luggage, pulling one by the handle and looping the long strap of her carry-on bag over her shoulder. Zach was still dealing with the customs agent when she maneuvered her way outside into the bright morning sunlight, joining the line of people waiting for cabs.

"Here," Zach said, from behind her, "I'll carry one of those for you." He'd managed to travel with only his brief-case and a garment bag, which was neatly folded and easily handled.

"Thank you," she said breathlessly.

"I thought we'd agreed to limit our expressions of grat-itude toward each other," he grumbled, frowning as he lifted the suitcase.

"I apologize. It slipped my mind."

Zach continued to grumble. "What'd you pack in here, anyway? Bricks?"

"If you're going to complain, I'll carry it myself."

He muttered something she couldn't hear and shook his head. "Once we get a cab—"

"We?"

"We're going to confront your grandfather."

"Together? Now?" She was exhausted, mentally and physically. They both were.

"The sooner the better, don't you think?"

The problem was, Janine hadn't given much thought to what she was going to say. Yes, she intended to challenge Gramps but she'd planned to wait for the most opportune time. And she'd hoped to speak to him privately. "He might not even be home," she argued, "and if he is, I'm not sure now would really be best."

"I want this settled once and for all."

"So do I," she said vehemently. "But I think we should

choose when and how we do this more carefully, don't you?"

"Perhaps…" His agreement seemed hesitant, even grudging. "All right, we'll do it your way."

"It isn't my way. It just makes sense to organize our thoughts first. Trust me, Zach, I want this cleared up as badly as you do."

His reply was little more than a grunt, but whether it was a comment on the weight of her suitcase or her tactics in dealing with Anton, she didn't know.

"And furthermore," she said, making a sweeping motion with her arm, "we've got to stop doubting each other. Nobody's following anyone and neither of us is in any danger of falling in love just because we were foolish enough to kiss."

"Fine," Zach murmured. He set her suitcase down as a cab arrived and the driver jumped out.

"How is it that we always seem to agree and yet we constantly find ourselves at odds?" she asked.

"I wish I knew," he said, looking weary in body and spirit. The cabdriver opened the trunk, storing her suitcases neatly inside. Zach threw his garment bag on top.

"We might as well still share this taxi," he said, holding the door for her.

"But isn't the Mt. Baker district out of your way?"

"I do need to talk to your grandfather. There're some estimates I need to give him."

"But can't it wait until tomorrow? Honestly, Zach, you're exhausted. One day isn't going to make any difference. And like I said, Gramps might not even be at the house."

Zach rubbed his eyes, then glanced irritably in her direction. "Honestly, Janine," he mocked, "you sound like a wife."

Biting her tongue to keep back her angry retort, Janine crossed her arms and glared out the side window. Indignation seeped through her with every breath she drew. Of its own accord, her foot started an impatient tapping. She could hardly wait to part company with this rude, unreasonable man.

Apparently Zach didn't know when to quit, because he added, "Now you even act like one."

She slowly turned to him and in a saccharine voice inquired, "And what's that supposed to mean?"

"Look at you, for heaven's sake. First you start nagging me and then—"

"Nagging you!" she exploded. "Let's get one thing straight, Zachary Thomas. I do *not* nag."

Zach rolled his eyes, then turned his head to gaze out the window on his side.

"Sir, sir," Janine said, sliding forward in the seat. She politely tapped the driver on the shoulder.

The middle-aged man glanced at her. "What is it, lady?"

"Sir," she said, offering him her warmest, most sincere smile. "Tell me, do I look like the kind of woman who'd nag?"

"Ah… Look, lady, all I do is drive a cab. You can ask me where a street is and I can tell you. If you want to go uptown, I can take you uptown. But when it comes to answering personal-type questions, I prefer to mind my own business."

"Are you satisfied?" Zach asked in a low voice.

"No, I'm not." She crossed her arms again and stared straight ahead.

The cabdriver's eyes met hers in the rearview mirror, and Janine tried to smile, but when she caught a glimpse of herself, she realized her effort looked more like a grimace.

"Me and the missus been married for near twenty years now," the driver said suddenly, stopping at a red light just off the James Street exit. "Me and the missus managed to stay married through the good times and the bad ones. Can't say that about a lot of folks."

"I don't suppose your wife is the type who nags, though, is she?" Zach made the question sound more like a statement, sending Janine a look that rankled.

"Betsy does her fair share. If you ask me, nagging's just part of a woman's nature."

"That's absurd," Janine countered stiffly. She should've known better than to draw a complete stranger into the discussion, especially another male who was sure to take Zach's side.

"I'll tell you the real reason me and the missus stayed together all these years," the cabbie continued in a confiding tone. "We never go to bed mad. I know I look like an easygoing guy, but I've got a temper on me. Over the years, me and Betsy have had our share of fights, but we always kiss and make up."

Janine smiled and nodded, sorry she'd ever gotten involved in this conversation.

"Go on," the cabbie urged.

Janine's puzzled gaze briefly met Zach's.

"Go on and do what?" Zach wanted to know.

"Kiss and make up." The cabbie turned for a moment

to smile at them and wink at Janine. "If my wife was as pretty as yours, mister, I wouldn't be hesitating."

Janine nearly swallowed her tongue. "We are *not* married."

"And have no intention whatsoever of marrying," Zach added quickly.

The driver chuckled. "That's what they all say. The harder they deny it, the more in love they are."

He turned off Broadway and a few minutes later pulled into the circular driveway that led to Janine's house. As the talkative cabbie leapt from the car and dashed for the trunk, Janine opened her door and climbed out.

Apparently, Zach had no intention of taking her advice, because he, too, got out of the cab. It was while they were tussling with the luggage that the front door opened and Mrs. McCormick hurried outside.

"Janine," she cried, her blue eyes lighting up with surprise. "What are you doing back so soon? We weren't expecting you for another two days."

"I missed your cooking so much, I couldn't bear to stay away any longer," Janine said, throwing her arms around the older woman in a warm hug. "Has Gramps been giving you any trouble?"

"Not a bit."

Zach paid the driver, who got back in his cab, but not before he'd winked at Janine again. "Remember what I told you," he yelled, speeding off.

"How much was the fare?" Janine asked, automatically opening her purse.

"I took care of it," Zach said, reaching for his garment

bag and the heavier of Janine's two suitcases. He said it as though he expected an argument from her, but if that was the case, Janine didn't plan to give him one.

"Is Gramps home?" Janine curved her arm affectionately around the housekeeper's waist as she spoke.

"He went out early this morning, but he should be back soon."

"Good," Zach mumbled, following them into the house.

"I imagine you're both starved," Mrs. McCormick said, heading toward the kitchen. "Let me whip up something for you that'll make you both glad you're home."

Left alone with Zach, Janine wasn't sure what to say to him. They'd spent almost twenty-four hours in each other's company. They'd argued. They'd talked. They'd laughed. They'd kissed.

"Janine—"

"Zach—"

They spoke simultaneously, then exchanged nervous smiles.

"You first," Zach said, gesturing toward her.

"I…I just wanted to say thanks for everything. I'll be in touch," she said. "By phone," she assured him. "So you don't need to worry about me dropping the office unannounced."

He grinned sheepishly. "Remember, communication is the key."

"I agree one hundred percent."

They stood facing each other in the foyer. "You wanted to say something?" she prompted after a moment.

"Yes." Zach exhaled sharply, then drew a hand along the side of his jaw. "What that cabbie said is true—even for us. I don't want us to part with any bad feelings. I shouldn't have said what I did back there, about nagging. You don't nag, and I had no right to say you did."

"I overreacted." The last thing she'd expected from Zach was an apology. His eyes, dark and tender, held hers, and without even realizing what she was doing, Janine took a step forward. Zach met her and she was about to slip into his arms when the sound of the front door opening drove them apart.

"Janine," Anton cried, delighted. "Zach. My, my, this is a pleasant surprise." He chuckled softly as he removed his coat. "Tell me, was your tryst on the moors as romantic as I hoped?"

Six

"**O**ur best bet is to present a united front," Janine said to Zach four days later. They'd met at her house early in the afternoon to outline their strategy. Gramps was gone for the day, but by the time he returned, Zach and Janine planned to be ready to talk him out of this marriage idea. The sooner Anton understood that his ploy wasn't working, the better. Then they could both get on with their lives and forget this unfortunate episode.

"It's important that we stand up to him together," Janine said when Zach didn't comment. From the moment he'd arrived, he'd given her the impression that he'd rather not be doing this. Well, she wasn't overjoyed about plotting against her grandfather, either, but in this instance it was necessary. "If we don't, I'm afraid Gramps will continue to play us against each other."

"I'm here, aren't I?" Zach grumbled. He certainly wasn't in one of his more charming moods.

"Listen, if you're going to act like this—"

"Like what?" he demanded, standing up. He walked over to the polished oak sideboard and poured himself a cup of coffee. When he'd finished, he ambled toward the fireplace and leaned against the mantel.

"Like you're doing me a big favor," Janine elaborated.

"You're the one who's left *me* dangling for three days. Do you realize what I've been forced to endure? Anton kept giving me these smug smiles, looking so pleased with himself and the way things worked out in Scotland. Yesterday he went so far as to mention the name of a good jeweler."

Before Janine could stop herself, she was on her feet, arms akimbo, glaring at Zach. "I thought you were going to call me! Weren't you the one who said communication is the key? Then it's as if you'd dropped off the face of the earth! And for your information, it hasn't exactly been a Sunday school picnic around here, either."

"It may surprise you to learn that I have other things on my mind besides dealing with you and your grandfather."

"Implying I don't have anything to do with *my* time?"

"No," he said slowly. "Damn it, Janine, we're arguing again."

She sighed regretfully. "I know. We've got to stop this squabbling. It's counterproductive."

Zach's nod was curt and she saw that he was frowning. "What bothers me most is the way your grandfather found us the other day. We were standing so close and you were staring up at me, practically begging me to kiss you."

"I most certainly was not," she denied, knowing Zach

was right. Her cheeks grew pink. She *had* wanted him to kiss her, but she hated having to admit that she would've walked into his arms without a second's hesitation. She decided to blame that unexpected longing on the exhausting flight home.

Zach shook his head and set his coffee cup carefully on the mantel. He thrust both hands into his pockets, still slouching against the fireplace wall. "The problem is, I was ready to do it. If your grandfather hadn't walked in when he did, I would've kissed you."

"You would?" she asked softly, feeling almost light-headed at his words.

Zach straightened, and a nerve in his jaw pulsed, calling her attention to the strong chiseled lines of his face. "I'm only human," he said drly. "I'm as susceptible to a beautiful woman as the next man, especially when she all but asks me to take her in my arms."

That was too much. Janine pinched her lips together to keep from crying out in anger. Taking a moment to compose herself, she closed her eyes and drew in a deep breath. "Instead of blaming each other for something that *didn't* happen, could we please return to the subject at hand, which is my grandfather?"

"All right," Zach agreed. "I'm sorry. I shouldn't have said anything." He went to the leather wingback chair and sat down. Leaning forward, he rested his elbows on his knees. "What are you going to say to him?"

"Me? I thought…I'd hoped…you'd want to do the talking."

Zach shook his head. "Tact doesn't seem to be my strong point lately."

"Okay, okay, I'll do it, if that's what you really want." She gazed silently down at the richly patterned carpet, collecting her thoughts. "I think we should tell him how much we both love and respect him and that we realize his actions have been motivated by his concern for us both and his desire for our happiness. We might even go so far as to thank him—" She stopped abruptly when Zach gave a snort of laughter. "All right, if you think you can do better, you do the talking."

"If it was up to me, I'd just tell that meddling old fool to stay out of our lives."

"Your sensitivity is really heartwarming," she muttered. "At first, this whole thing was one big joke to you and you really enjoyed tormenting me."

"You're exaggerating."

"As I recall, you played that cow-and-ten-chickens business for all it was worth, but I notice you're singing a different tune now and frankly—"

The library door opened, interrupting her tirade. Her grandfather and his longtime friend, veterinarian Dr. Burt Coleman, walked into the room.

"Zach. Janine," Gramps said, grinning broadly.

"Gramps," Janine burst out, rushing to her feet. They weren't prepared for this, and Zach was being impossible, so she said the first thing that came to mind. Pointing at Zach, she cried, "I don't know how you could possibly expect me to marry that man. He's stubborn and rude and we're completely wrong for each other." She was trembling by the time she finished, and collapsed gracelessly into the nearest chair.

"In case you haven't figured it out yet, you're no angel yourself," Zach said, scowling at Janine.

"Children, please," Gramps implored, advancing into the library, hands held out in supplication. "What seems to be the problem?"

"I want this settled," Zach said forcefully. "I'm not about to be saddled with Janine for a wife."

"As if I want to be *your* wife? In your dreams, Zachary Thomas!"

"We realize you mean well," Zach added, his face looking pinched. He completely ignored Janine. "But neither of us appreciates your matchmaking efforts."

Gramps walked over to the leather chair recently occupied by Zach and sat down. He smiled weakly at each of them, his shoulders sagging. "I thought…I'd hoped you two would grow fond of each other."

"I'm sorry to disappoint you, Gramps, I really am," Janine said, feeling guilty. "But Zach and I don't even like each other. We can barely carry on a civil conversation. He's argumentative and unreasonable—"

"And she's illogical and stubborn."

"I don't think we need to trade insults to get our message across," Janine said. Her face was so hot, she felt as if her cheeks were on fire.

"There's no hope?" Anton asked quietly.

"None whatsoever," Zach said. "Janine will make some

man a wonderful wife one day, but unfortunately, he won't be me."

Her grandfather slumped against the back of his chair. "You're sure?"

"Positive," Zach said, loudly enough to convince Mrs. McCormick who was working in the kitchen.

"I love you, Gramps," said Janine, "and I'd do almost anything you wanted, but I can't and won't marry Zach. We know you have our best interests at heart, but neither of us is romantically interested in the other."

Burt Coleman, who stood by the library doors, looked as if he'd rather be anyplace else. His discomfort at witnessing this family scene was obvious. "I think it'd be best if I came back another time," he murmured as he turned to leave.

"No," Anton said, gesturing his friend back. "Come in. You've met Zachary Thomas, haven't you?"

The two men nodded at each other, but Janine noticed how rigidly Zach held himself. This meeting with Gramps hadn't gone the way she'd planned. She'd wanted everything to be calm and rational, a discussion uncluttered by messy emotions. Instead they'd ended up practically attacking each other, and worse, Janine had been the one to throw the first punch.

Without asking, she walked over to the sideboard and poured Gramps and his friend a cup of coffee. Burt sat across from her grandfather, clearly ill at ease.

"I should be going," Zach said starkly. "Good to see you again, Dr. Coleman."

"You, too," Gramps's friend said, glancing briefly at Zach. His puzzled gaze quickly returned to Anton.

"I'll walk you to the front door," Janine offered, eager to make her own escape. She closed the library door behind her.

Both she and Zach paused in the entryway. Janine tried to smile, but Zach was studying her intently, and her heart clenched like a fist inside her chest. They'd done what they had to do; she should be experiencing relief that the confrontation she'd dreaded for days was finally over. Instead she felt a strange sadness, one she couldn't fully understand or explain.

"Do you think we convinced him?"

"I don't know," Zach answered, keeping his tone low. "Your grandfather's a difficult man to read. Maybe he'll never bring up the subject of our marrying again and we're home free. I'd like to believe that's the case. It's just as likely, though, that he'll give us a few days' peace while he regroups. I don't expect him to back off quite so easily."

"No, I don't suppose he will."

Zach looked at his watch. "I should be going," he said again.

Janine was reluctant to see him leave, but there was no reason to detain him. Her hand was on the doorknob when she suddenly hesitated and turned around. "I didn't mean what I said in there," she blurted in a frenzy of regret.

"You mean you do want us to get married?"

"No," she cried, aghast. "I'm talking about when I said you were stubborn and rude. That isn't really true, but I had to come up with some reason for finding you objectionable. I don't really believe it, though."

"It was the same with me. I don't think you're so intolerable, either. I was trusting that you knew it was all an act for your grandfather's sake."

"I did," she assured him, but her pride *had* been dented, although that wasn't anything new.

"The last four days have been difficult," Zach went on. "Not only was Anton gloating about Scotland, but like I told you, he's been giving me these amused looks and odd little smiles. A couple of times I heard him saying something in his native tongue—I'm afraid to guess what."

"Well, I know what he was saying, because he's been doing the same thing to me. He's talking about babies."

"Babies?" Zach echoed, his eyes startled.

"Ours in particular."

One corner of Zach's mouth lifted, as if he found the thought of them as parents amusing. Or unlikely.

"That was my reaction, too. Every time I've seen Gramps in the last few days, he's started talking about…well, you know."

Zach nodded. "I do know. The situation hasn't been pleasant for either of us."

"Setting Gramps straight was for the best." But if that was the case, why did she feel this terrible letdown? "If he accepts us at our word—and he just might—then I guess this is goodbye."

"Yes, I suppose it is," Zach responded, but he made no effort to leave.

Janine was glad, because these few moments gave her the opportunity to memorize his features. She stored them for the future, when there'd be no reason for her to have anything but the most infrequent and perfunctory contact with Zach.

"Unless, of course, your grandfather continues to throw us together."

"Of course," Janine added quickly, hating the way her heart soared at the prospect. "Naturally, we'd have to confront him again. We can't allow ourselves to be his pawns."

Zach was about to say something else when the library door flew open and Burt Coleman hurried out, the urgency on his face unmistakable. "Janine, I think we should call a doctor for your grandfather."

"What's wrong?"

"I'm not sure. He's very pale and he seems to be having trouble breathing. It might be his heart."

With Zach following, Janine ran into the library, her own heart in jeopardy. Dr. Coleman was right—she'd never seen her grandfather look worse. His breath came noisily and his eyes were closed as he rested his head against the back of the chair. He looked old, far older than she could ever remember seeing him. She felt a sense of panic as she raced across the room to the desk where there was a phone.

"I'm fine," Gramps said hoarsely, opening his eyes and slowly straightening. He raised his hand in an effort to stop Janine. "There's no need for everyone to go into a tizzy just because an old man wants to rest his eyes for a few minutes." His smile was weak, his complexion still pale. "Now don't go calling any doctor. I was in last week for a checkup and I'm fit as a fiddle."

"You don't look so fit," Zach countered and Janine noticed that his face seemed almost as ashen as her grandfather's. Kneeling beside him, Zach grasped his wrist and began to check his pulse.

"I'm fine," Gramps insisted again.

"Are you in any pain?"

Gramps's gaze moved from Zach to Janine. "None," he answered, dismissing their concern with a shake of his head.

"Dr. Coleman?" Janine turned to her grandfather's longtime friend. "Should I phone his doctor?"

"What does Burt know about an old man and his heart?" Gramps objected. "Burt's expertise is with horses."

"Call the doctor. Having him checked over isn't going to hurt," Burt said after a moment.

"Fiddlesticks," Gramps roared. "I'm in perfect health."

"Good," Janine said brightly. "But I'll just let Dr. Madison reassure me." She punched out the phone number and had to speak loudly in order to be heard over her grandfather's protests. A couple of minutes later, she replaced the receiver and told Zach, "Dr. Madison says we can bring him in now."

"I'm not going to waste valuable time traipsing downtown. Burt and I were going to play a few hands of cribbage."

"We can play tomorrow," Dr. Coleman said gruffly. "You keep forgetting, Anton, we're both retiring."

"I've got things to do at the office."

"No, you don't," Zach said firmly. "You've got a

doctor's appointment. Janine and I are going to escort you there and we're not going to listen to a single argument. Do you understand?"

Gramps's eyes narrowed as if he were preparing a loud rebuttal. But he apparently changed his mind, because he relaxed and nodded sluggishly, reluctantly. "All right, if it'll make you feel better. But I'm telling you right now, you're going to look like a fine pair of fools."

The next two hours felt like two years to Janine. While Dr. Madison examined Gramps, she and Zach paced the waiting room. Several patients came and went.

"What could be taking so long?" Janine asked, wringing her hands nervously. "Do you think we did the right thing bringing him here? I mean, should we have gone directly to the hospital emergency room instead?"

"I doubt he would have agreed to that," Zach said.

"Do you honestly believe I would've listened to him?" She sat on the edge of a chair, her hands clenched so tightly together her knuckles whitened. "It's ridiculous, but I've never thought of Gramps as old. He's always been so healthy, so alive. I've never once considered what would happen if he became ill."

"He's going to be fine, Janine."

"You saw him," she cried, struggling against the dread and horror that churned inside her.

Zach's hand clasped hers and the fears that had torn at her composure only seconds earlier seemed to abate with his touch. He lent her confidence and strength, and she was badly in need of both.

When the door leading to the doctor's office opened, they leapt to their feet. Zach's hand tightened around hers before he released it.

"Dr. Madison can talk to you now," the nurse told them briskly. She led them to a compact office and explained that the doctor would be with them in a few minutes. Janine sat in one of the cushioned chairs and studied the framed diplomas on the walls.

Dr. Madison came into the room moments later. He paused to shake hands with Janine and then with Zach. "So far, my tests don't show anything we need to be too concerned about," he said, shuffling through the papers on his desk.

"What happened? Why was he so pale? Why was he gasping like that?" Janine demanded.

Dr. Madison frowned and folded his hands. "I'm really not sure. He claims he hadn't been doing any strenuous exercise."

"No, he was drinking coffee and talking to a friend."

Dr. Madison nodded. "Did he recently receive any negative news regarding his business?"

"No," Janine replied, glancing at Zach. "If anything, the business is doing better than ever. Gramps is getting ready to retire. I hate the thought of anything happening to him now."

"I don't know what to tell you," Dr. Madison said thoughtfully. "He should take it easy for the next couple of days, but there's nothing to worry about that I can find."

Janine sighed and closed her eyes. "Thank God."

"Your grandfather's getting dressed now," Dr. Madison said. He stood, signaling the end of their interview. "He'll join you in a few minutes."

"Thank you, Doctor," Zach said fervently.

Relief washed through Janine like a tidal wave. She got up and smiled at Zach. It was a smile full of gratitude. A smile one might share with a good friend when something has gone unexpectedly right. The kind of smile a woman would share with her husband. The thought hit her full force and she quickly lowered her eyes to cover her reaction.

When Gramps joined them in the waiting room, he looked immeasurably better. His blue eyes were filled with indignation and his skin tone was a healthy pink. "I hope the two of you are satisfied," he said huskily, buttoning his coat. "Most of the afternoon was wasted with this nonsense."

"You were a hundred percent correct, Gramps," Janine said brightly. "You're as fit as a fiddle and we wasted valuable cribbage time dragging you down here."

"I should've been back at the office hours ago," Zach put in, sharing a smile with Janine.

"And whose fault is that?" Anton muttered. He brushed off his sleeves as though he'd been forced to pick himself up off the floor, thanks to them.

Once more Janine and Zach shared an intimate look. They both seemed to realize what they were doing at the same moment and abruptly glanced away.

Zach drove Gramps and Janine back to the house, Gramps protesting loudly all the while that they'd overreacted and ruined his afternoon. His first concern seemed to be rescheduling his cribbage game.

Afterward Janine walked Zach to his car. "Thanks for

everything," she said, folding her arms to repress the sudden urge to hug him.

"If you're worried about anything, give me a call," Zach said as he opened the car door. He hesitated fractionally, then lifted his head and gazed directly into her eyes. "Goodbye, Janine."

She raised her hand in farewell as a sadness settled over her. "Goodbye, Zach," she said forcing a lightness into her voice. "Thanks again."

For the longest moment, he said nothing, although his eyes still held hers. Finally he repeated, "Call me if you need anything, all right?"

"I will."

But they both knew she wouldn't. It was best to end this now. Make a clean break.

Janine stood in the driveway until Zach's car was well out of sight. Only then did she return to the house.

"This is really good of you," Patty St. John whispered, handing the sleeping infant to Janine. "I don't know what I would've done if I'd had to drag Michael to the interview. I need this job so badly."

"I'm happy to help." Janine peered down at the sweet face of the sleeping six-month-old baby. "I apologize if it was inconvenient for you to bring Michael here, but I've been sticking close to the house for the past few days. My grandfather hasn't been feeling well."

"It wasn't any problem," Patty whispered, setting the diaper bag on the floor. She glanced around the house.

"This place is really something. I didn't have any idea that you…well, you know, that you were so well off."

"This house belongs to my grandfather," Janine explained, gently rocking Michael in her arms. The warmth and tenderness she felt toward the baby was a revelation. She supposed it was understandable, though. Gramps had spent last week constantly telling her what remarkable babies she and Zach would have, and here she was with one in her arms. All the maternal instincts she didn't know she had came bubbling to the surface.

"I'll be back in about an hour," Patty said. She leaned over and kissed Michael's soft forehead. He didn't so much as stir.

Still carrying the baby, Janine walked to the door with her friend. "Good luck."

Patty gave a strained smile and crossed her fingers. "Thanks. Here's hoping."

No sooner had the door closed than Anton walked into the living room. He paused when he saw Janine rocking in the old chair that had once belonged to his wife. His face relaxed into a broad grin.

"Is that a baby you've got there?"

Janine smiled. "Nothing gets past you, does it, Gramps?"

He chuckled. "Who's he belong to?"

"Patty St. John. She's another volunteer at the Friendship Club. She quit her job when Michael was born, but now she'd like to find some part-time work."

"Are you volunteering to babysit for her?"

"Just for today," Janine explained. "Her regular sitter has the flu."

"I thought you were going out?" Gramps muttered with a slight frown. "You haven't left the house all week. Fact is, you're becoming a recluse."

"I've had other things to do," she returned, not raising her voice for fear of disturbing the baby.

"Right. The other things you had to do were keep an eye on your grandfather," he said. "You think I didn't notice? How long do you plan on being my shadow? You should be gadding about, doing the things you normally do, instead of worrying yourself sick over me. I'm fine, I tell you. When are you going to listen to me?"

"Dr. Madison said to watch you for a few days."

"It's been a week."

Janine was well aware of it. In fact, she was beginning to suffer from cabin fever. She'd hardly spoken to anyone all week. She hadn't heard from Zach, either. Not that she'd expected to. Perhaps Gramps had taken them at their word. Or else he was doing what Zach had suspected and simply regrouping for the next skirmish.

Michael stirred in her arms and she held him against her shoulder, rocking him back to sleep.

"I'm going to the office tomorrow," Gramps announced, eyeing her defiantly as though he anticipated a challenge.

"We'll see," she said, delaying the showdown.

Yawning, baby Michael raised his head and looked around. Gramps's weathered face broke into a tender smile. "All right," he agreed easily. "We'll see." He offered the little boy his finger and Michael gripped it firmly in his hand, then started to chew on it.

Janine laughed, enjoying her grandfather's reaction to the baby. After a couple of minutes, Michael grew tired of the game with Anton's finger and yawned again, arching his back. Janine decided it was time to check his diaper. She got up, reaching for the bag Patty had left.

"I'll be back in a minute," she told her grandfather.

She was halfway across the living room when Anton stopped her. "You look good with a baby in your arms. Natural."

Janine smiled. She didn't dare let him know it felt good, too.

While she was changing the baby, she heard the doorbell. Normally she would've answered it herself, but since she was busy, either Gramps or Mrs. McCormick would see to it.

Michael was happily investigating his toes and making cooing sounds as Janine pulled up his plastic pants. "You're going to have to be patient with me, kiddo," she told him, carefully untwisting the legs of his corduroy overalls and snapping them back in place. When she'd finished, she lifted him high above her head and laughed when Michael squealed delightedly. They were both smiling when she returned to the living room.

Gramps was sitting in the chair closest to the grand piano, and across from him sat Zach.

Janine's heart lurched as her eyes flew instantly to Zach's. "Hello, Zach," she said, striving to sound as nonchalant as possible, tucking Michael against her hip. She cast a suspicious glare at her grandfather, who smiled back, the picture of innocence.

"Zach brought some papers for me to sign," Gramps explained.

"I didn't mean to interrupt you," she apologized. Her eyes refused to leave Zach's. He smiled that slanted half-smile of his that wasn't really a smile at all. The one she'd always found so appealing. Something seemed to pass between them—a tenderness, a hunger.

"Janine's not interrupting anything, is she?" Gramps asked.

"No," Zach responded gruffly. He seemed to be taking in everything about her, from her worn jeans and oversize pink sweatshirt to the gurgling baby riding so casually on her hip.

Gramps cleared his throat. "If you'll excuse me a moment, I'll go get a pen," he said, leaving them alone together.

"How have you been?" Zach asked, his eyes riveted to her.

"Fine. Just fine."

"I see you haven't had any problems finding another admirer," he murmured, nodding at Michael.

Zach kept his tone light and teasing, and Janine followed his lead. "Michael St. John," she said, turning slightly to give Zach a better view of the baby, "meet Mr. Zachary Thomas."

"Hello," Zach said, holding up his palm. He seemed awkward around children. "I take it you're watching him for a friend."

"Yes, another volunteer. She's looking for a part-time job, but she's having a problem finding one with the right hours. She's at an interview."

"I see."

Janine sank down on the ottoman in front of Zach's chair and set Michael on her knee. She focused her attention on gently bouncing the baby. "Now that your life's back in order," she said playfully, glancing up at Zach, "have you discovered how much you miss me?"

He chuckled softly. "It's been how long since we last talked? Seven days? I'm telling you, Janine, I haven't had a single disagreement with anyone in all that time."

"That should make you happy."

"You're right. It should." He shook his head. "Unfortunately it doesn't. You know what, Janine? I was bored to death. So the answer is yes, I missed you."

Seven

Before Janine could respond, Gramps wandered back into the living room, pen in hand.

"So where are those papers you wanted me to sign?" he asked Zach.

With obvious reluctance, Zach tore his gaze from Janine's. He opened his briefcase and pulled out several papers. "Go ahead and read over these contracts."

"Do you need me to sign them or not?" her grandfather grumbled.

Once more Zach dragged his gaze away from Janine. "Please."

Muttering under his breath, Gramps took the documents to the small table, scanned them and quickly scrawled his name.

Janine knew she should leave; the two men probably had business to discuss. But she couldn't make herself stand up and walk away. Not when Zach had actually admitted that he'd missed her.

Gramps broke into her thoughts. "Janine, I—"

"I was just going," she said. She clambered to her feet, securing her hold on Michael.

But Gramps surprised her.

"I want you to stay," he declared. "I wanted to talk to you and Zach. Fact is, I owe you both an apology. Burt and I had a good long talk the other day and I told him how I'd tried to arrange a marriage between the two of you. He laughed and called me an old fool, said it was time I stepped out of the Dark Ages."

"Gramps," Janine began anxiously, unwilling to discuss the subject that had brought such contention, "Zach and I have already settled that issue. We understand why you did it and…and we've laid it to rest, so there's no need to apologize."

"I'm afraid there is," Gramps insisted. "Don't worry, Burt pointed out the error of my ways. Haven't got any new tricks up my sleeve." He rose to bring Zach the signed papers, then sat wearily in the chair across from them. He'd never looked so fragile, so old and beaten.

"Janine's a wonderful woman," Zach said unexpectedly. "I want you to know I realize that."

"She's got her faults," Gramps responded, pulling a cigar from his pocket, "but she's pretty enough to compensate."

"Thank you very much," Janine whispered sarcastically and was rewarded with a grin from Zach. Gramps didn't seem to hear her; if he had, he was ignoring her comment.

"I only want the best for my granddaughter, but when I approached her about marrying you, she made a big fuss. Fact is, it would've been easier to pluck a live chicken. She said she needed *romance*." Gramps pronounced the word as if it evoked instant amusement.

"There isn't a woman alive who doesn't need romance," she wailed, defending herself.

"I'm from the old country," Gramps continued. "Romance wasn't something I knew about from personal experience, and when I asked Janine to explain, she had some trouble defining it herself. Said it was a tryst on the moors and a bunch of other hogwash. That's the reason I sent you both to Scotland."

"We figured that out soon enough," Zach said dryly.

"As you'll recall," Janine found herself saying, "that definition was off the top of my head. Romance isn't easy to explain, especially to a man who scoffs at the entire idea."

Anton chuckled, moving the cigar to the side of his mouth. "It's unfortunate the two of you caught on to me so soon. I was looking forward to arranging the desperate passion part."

"Desperate passion?" Zach echoed.

"Yes. Janine said that was part of romance, too. I may be over seventy, but I know about passion. Oh, yes, Anna and I learned about that together." His blue eyes took on a faraway look and his lips curved in the gentlest of smiles. He glanced at Janine and his smile widened.

"I'm glad you find this so funny," Janine snapped.

Gramps dismissed her anger with a flick of his hand and

turned to Zach. "I suppose you've discovered she's got something of a temper?"

"From the start!" Zach declared.

"It may come as a surprise to you, Zachary Thomas," Janine said, "but you're not exactly Mr. Perfect."

"No," Zach countered smoothly. "I suspect your grandfather was thinking more along the lines of Mr. Right."

"Oh, brother!"

"Now, children, I don't see that arguing will do any good. I've willingly accepted defeat. Trying to interest you in each other was an old man's way of setting his world right before he passes on."

The doorbell chimed and, grateful for an excuse to leave the room, Janine hurried to answer it. Patty St. John stood there, her face cheerless, her posture forlorn.

"I wasn't expecting you back so soon."

"They'd already hired someone," Patty said, walking into the foyer and automatically taking her son from Janine. She held the infant close, as if his small warm body might absorb her disappointment. "I spent the whole day psyching myself up for this interview and it was all for nothing. Ah, well, who wants to be a receptionist at a dental clinic, anyway?"

"I'm so sorry," Janine murmured.

"Was Michael any problem?"

"None at all," Janine told her, wishing she could think of something encouraging to say. "I'll get his things for you."

It took Janine only a minute to collect Michael's diaper bag, but when she returned to the entryway, she discovered

Zach talking to Patty. Janine saw him hand her friend a business card and overheard him suggesting she report to the Human Resources department early the following week.

"Thanks again," Patty said enthusiastically. She lifted Michael's hand. "Say bye-bye," she coaxed the baby, then raised his arm and moved it for him.

Janine let her out, with Zach standing next to her. Gramps had gone into the library, and Zach glanced anxiously in that direction before lowering his voice to a whisper. "Can you meet me later?"

"When?"

"In an hour." He checked his watch, then mentioned the number of a pier along the waterfront. Janine had just managed to clarify the location when Gramps came back.

Zach left the house soon afterward and Janine was able to invent an excuse half an hour later. Gramps was reading and didn't bother to look up from his mystery novel, although Janine thought she saw the hint of a smile, as if he knew full well what she was doing. She didn't linger to investigate. The last time she'd agreed to a clandestine meeting with Zach had been the night they'd met at the Italian restaurant, when she'd all but blurted out the arrangements to her grandfather.

Zach was waiting for her, grim-faced. He stood against the pier railing, the wind whipping his raincoat against his legs.

"I hope there's a good reason for this, because I don't think Gramps was fooled," Janine said when she joined him. "He'll figure out that I'm meeting you if I'm not back soon." She buried her hands in her pockets, turning away from the wind. The afternoon sky was gray, threatening rain.

"Am I interrupting anything important?"

"Not really." Janine wouldn't have minded listing several pressing engagements, but she'd canceled everything for the next two weeks, wanting to stay close to home in case her grandfather needed her.

Zach clasped his hands behind his back and started strolling down the pier, the wind ruffling his neatly trimmed hair. Janine followed. "I'm worried about Anton," he said suddenly, stopping and facing Janine.

"Why?" Perhaps there was something she didn't know about his health, something Dr. Madison hadn't told her.

"He doesn't look good."

"What do you mean?" Although she asked, she already knew the answer. She'd felt the same thing during the past few days. Gramps was aging right before her eyes.

"I think you know."

"I do," she admitted reluctantly.

"Furthermore I'm worried about you."

"Me?" she asked, her voice rising. "Whatever for?"

"If, God forbid, anything should happen to Anton," Zach said, drawing in a ragged breath, "what will happen to you? You don't have any other family, do you?"

"No," she told him, her chest tightening at the thought. "But I'm not worried about it. There are several friends who are very close to the family, Burt Coleman for one, so I wouldn't be cast into the streets like an orphan. I'll have the house and more than enough money to live on. There's no need for you to be concerned. I'm not."

"I see." Zach frowned as he walked to the farthest end

of the pier, seeming to fix his gaze on the snow-capped peaks of the Olympic mountains far in the distance.

Janine hurried to catch up with him. "Why do you ask?" she demanded.

"He's always said he was concerned about your not having any other family. But it wasn't until recently that I really understood his motivation in trying to arrange a marriage between us."

"Good, then you can explain it to me, because frankly, I'm at a loss. He admitted he was wrong, but I don't think he's given up on the idea. He'd do just about anything to see the two of us together."

"I *know* he hasn't given up on us."

"What did he do? Up the ante?"

Zach chuckled and his features relaxed into a smile as he met her eyes. "Nothing so explicit. He simply told me that he's getting on in years and hates the thought of you being left so alone when he dies."

"I'll adjust. I'm not a child," she said, although her heart filled with dread at the thought of life without her cantankerous, generous, good-hearted grandfather.

"I don't doubt you would." Zach hesitated, then resumed strolling, apparently taking it for granted that she'd continue to follow him.

"I have plenty of friends."

Zach nodded, although Janine wasn't certain he'd heard her. He stopped abruptly and turned to look at her. "What I'm about to say is going to shock you."

Janine stared up at him, not knowing what to expect.

"When you think about it, our getting married does make an odd kind of sense."

"What?" Janine couldn't believe he was saying this.

"From a practical point of view," he added quickly. "Since the business is in both our names, and we're both alone. I realize I'm not exactly Prince Charming…" Zach paused as if waiting for her to contradict him. When she didn't, he frowned but went on. "The problem has more to do with whether we can get along. I don't even know if we're capable of going an entire day without arguing."

"What are you suggesting?" Janine asked, wondering if she was reading more into this conversation than he intended.

"Nothing yet. I'm trying to be as open and as honest as I can." He gripped the railing with both hands and braced himself, as though expecting a fierce wind to uproot him.

"Are you saying that our getting married wouldn't be such a bad idea after all?" Janine ventured. Initially he'd made a joke of the whole thing. Then he'd seen it as an annoyance. Now he seemed to have changed his mind again.

"I…don't know yet. I'm mulling over my thoughts, which I'm willing to confess are hopelessly tangled at the moment."

"Mine aren't much better."

"Does this mean you'd consider the possibility?"

"I don't know, either." Janine had been so sure she was in love with Brian. She remembered how he'd done everything a romantic hero should do. He'd sent her flowers, said all the things a woman longs to hear—and then he'd casually broken her heart. When she thought about it now, she couldn't really imagine herself married to Brian. But

Zach, who'd never made any romantic gestures, somehow seemed to fit almost naturally into her life. And yet...

As she pondered these contradictions, Zach started walking again. "I'm not the kind of husband you want," he was saying, "and not nearly as good as you deserve. I'd like to be the man of your dreams, but I'm not. Nor am I likely to change at this stage of my life." He paused, chancing a look in her direction. "What are you thinking?"

Janine sighed and concentrated as hard as she could, but her mind was filled with so many questions, so many doubts. "Would you mind kissing me?"

Shock widened his dark eyes. He glanced around, then scowled. "Now? Right here?"

"Yes."

"There are people everywhere. Is this really necessary?"

"Would I ask you to do it if it wasn't?"

As he searched her face, she moistened her lips and looked up at him, tilting her head slightly. Zach slipped one arm around her waist and drew her close. Her heart reacted immediately, leaping into a hard fast rhythm that made her feel breathless. He lifted her chin with his free hand and slowly lowered his mouth to hers.

The instant his lips grazed hers, Janine was flooded with a sensual languor. It was as if they'd returned to the moors of Scotland with the full moon overhead, pouring magic onto their small corner of earth. Everything around them faded. No longer did Janine hear the sound of water slapping against the wooden columns of the pier. The blustery day went calm.

She supported her hands on his chest, breathing erratically, when he stopped kissing her. Neither spoke. Janine wanted to, but none of her faculties seemed to be working. She parted her lips and Zach lowered his mouth to hers again. Only this time it was a full-fledged kiss, deep and probing. His hands slid up her back as his mouth abandoned hers to explore the sweep of her neck.

Several glorious moments passed before he shuddered, raised his head and drew back, although he continued to hold her. "Does that answer your question?"

"No," she answered, hating the way her voice trembled. "I'm afraid it only raised more."

"I know what you mean," Zach admitted, briefly closing his eyes. "This last week apart was an eye-opener for me. I thought I'd be glad to put this matter between your grandfather and us to rest. If you want the truth, I thought I'd be glad to be rid of you. I was convinced you felt the same way." He paused, waiting for a response.

"The days seemed so empty," she whispered.

His eyes burned into hers, and he nodded. "You were constantly on my mind, and I found myself wishing you were there to talk to." He groaned. "Heaven knows you deserve a different kind of husband than I could possibly be."

"What about you? I've heard you say a hundred times that when it comes to finding a wife, you'll choose your own."

He blinked, as though he didn't recognize his words. Then he shrugged. "Once I got to know you, I realized you're not so bad."

"Thanks." So much for wine and roses and sweet nothings whispered in her ear. But then again, she'd had those things and they hadn't brought her happiness.

"Like I said—and I hate to admit it—our getting married makes sense. We seem to like each other well enough, and there's a certain…attraction." Zach was frowning a little as he spoke. "It would be a smart move for both of us from a financial viewpoint, as well." He took her by the shoulders and gazed into her eyes. "The question is, Janine, can I make you happy?"

Her heart melted at the way he said it, at the simplicity and sincerity of his words. "What about you?" she asked. "Will you be content being married to me?"

The apprehension in his face eased. "I think so. We'll be good for each other. This isn't any grand passion. But I'm fond of you and you're fond of me."

"Fond?" Janine repeated, breaking away.

"What's wrong with that?"

"I hate that word," Janine said through gritted teeth. "*Fond* sounds so…watered down. So weak. I'm not looking for a grand passion, as you put it, but I want a whole lot more than *fond*." She gestured dramatically with her hands. "A man is fond of his dog or a favorite place to eat, not his wife." She spoke so vehemently that she was starting to attract attention from other walkers. "Would it be too much for you to come up with another word?"

"Stop looking at me as if it were a matter of life and death," he said.

"It's important," she insisted.

Zach looked distinctly uncomfortable. "I run a business.

There are more than three hundred outlets in fifty states. I know the office-supply business inside out, but I'm not good with words. If you don't like the word *fond,* you choose another one."

"All right," she said thoughtfully, biting the corner of one lip. Her eyes brightened. "How about *cherish?*"

"Cherish." Zach repeated it as if he'd never heard the word before. "Okay, it's a deal. I'll cherish you."

"And I'll cherish you," she said emphatically, nodding with satisfaction.

They walked along the pier until they came to a seafood stand, where Zach bought them each a cup of steaming clam chowder. They found an unoccupied picnic table and sat down, side by side.

Occasionally they stopped eating to smile at each other. An oddly exciting sensation attacked Janine's stomach whenever that happened. Finally, finishing her soup, she licked the back of her white plastic spoon. She kept her eyes carefully lowered as she said, "I want to make sure I understand. Did we or did we not just agree to get married?"

Zach hesitated, his spoon halfway between his cup and his mouth as an odd look crossed his face. He swallowed once. "We decided to go through with it, both accepting that this isn't the traditional love match, but one based on practical and financial advantages."

Janine dropped her spoon in the plastic cup. "If that's the case, the wedding is off."

Zach threw back his head and stared into the sky. "*Now* what did I say that was so terrible?"

"Financial and practical advantages! You make it sound about as appealing as a dentist appointment. There's got to be more of a reason than that for us to get married."

Shrugging, Zach gestured helplessly with his hands. "I already told you I wasn't any good at this. Perhaps we'd do better if you explained why you're willing to marry me."

Before she could prevent it, a smile tugged at her mouth. "You won't like my reason any better than I like yours." She looked around to ensure that no one could overhear, then leaned toward him. "When we kissed a few minutes ago, the earth moved. I know it's a dreadful cliché—the worst—but that's exactly what I felt."

"The earth moved," Zach repeated deadpan. "Well, we are in an earthquake zone."

Janine rolled her eyes. "It happened when we were in Scotland, too. I don't know what's going on between us or even if we're doing the right thing, but there's definitely... something. Something special."

She wasn't surprised when Zach scowled. "You mean to say you're willing to marry me because I'm good at kissing?"

"It makes more sense to me than that stuff about financial advantages."

"You were absolutely correct," he said evenly. "I don't like your reason. Is there anything else that makes the prospect appealing?"

Janine giggled. "You know," she reflected, "Gramps was right. We're going to be good for each other."

A flash of light warmed his eyes and his hand reached for hers. He entwined their fingers as their eyes met. "Yes, we are."

The wedding was arranged so fast that Janine barely had time to reconsider their decision. They applied for a license that same afternoon. When they returned to the house, Gramps shouted for joy, slapped Zach on the back and repeatedly hugged Janine, whispering that she'd made an old man very happy.

Janine was so busy, the days and nights soon blended together and she lost all track of time. There were so many things to do—fittings and organizing caterers and inviting guests—that for the next five days she didn't talk to Zach even once.

The day before the ceremony, the garden was bustling with activity. Mrs. McCormick was supervising the men who were assembling the wedding canopy and setting up tables and chairs.

Exhausted, Janine wandered outside and glanced up at the bold blue sky, praying the sunshine would hold for at least another day. The lawn was lush and green, and freshly mowed. The roses were in bloom, perfuming the air with their rich fragrance.

"Janine."

She recognized his voice immediately. She turned to discover Zach striding purposefully toward her, and her heart reacted of its own accord. Janine felt as though they'd been apart for a year instead of just a few days. She wore jeans and an old university sweatshirt and wished she'd chosen something less casual. In contrast, Zach was strikingly formal, dressed in a handsome pin-striped suit and dark tie. She was willing to admit she didn't know him as well as she should—as well as a woman who was about to become his wife. His habits, his likes and dislikes, were a mystery to her, yet those details seemed minor. It was the inner Zach she was coming to understand. Everything she'd learned assured her she'd made the right decision.

"Hello," she called, walking toward him. She saw that he looked as tired as she felt. Obviously he'd been busy, too, although the wedding preparations had been left to her.

They met halfway and stopped abruptly, gazing at each other. Zach didn't hug her or make any effort to touch her.

"How are you holding up?" he asked.

"Fine," she answered. "How about you?"

"I'll live." He glanced over at the activity near the rose garden and sighed. "Is there someplace we can talk privately?"

"Sure." Janine's heart leapt to her throat at his sober tone. "Is everything all right?"

He reassured her with a quick nod. "Of course."

"I don't think anyone's in the kitchen."

"Good." Hand at her elbow, he guided her toward the house. She pulled out a chair with trembling fingers and sat down at the oak table. As he lowered himself into a chair opposite her, she gripped the edge of the table. His eyes had never seemed darker. "Tomorrow's the day."

He said this as if he expected it to come as a shock to her. It didn't—but she understood what he was saying. Time was closing in on them, and if they wanted to back out, it would have to be now.

"Believe me, I know," she said, and her fingers tightened on the table. "Have you had a change of heart?"

"Have you?"

"No, but then again, I haven't had much time to think."

"I've done nothing *but* think about this wedding," Zach said, raking his hands through his hair.

"And?"

He shrugged. "We may both have been fools to agree to this."

"It all happened so fast," Janine said in a weak voice. "One minute we agreed on the word *cherish,* and the next thing I remember, we were deciding we'd be good for each other."

"Don't forget the kissing part," he added. "As I recall, that had quite a bit to do with this decision."

"If you're having second thoughts, I'd rather you said so now than after the ceremony."

His eyes narrowed fleetingly before he shook his head. "No."

"You're sure?"

He answered her by leaning forward, slipping his hand behind her neck and kissing her soundly. Tenderly. When they broke apart, they were silent. Not talking, not wanting to.

Janine stared into his dark warm eyes and suddenly she could hardly breathe.

"This is going to be a real marriage," he said forcefully.

She nodded. "I certainly hope so, Mr. Thomas." And her voice was strong and clear.

Less than twenty-four hours later, Janine stood at Zach's side, prepared to pledge her life to his. She'd never felt more uncertain—or, at the same time, more confident—of anything she'd ever done.

Zach seemed to grasp what she was feeling. His eyes held hers as she repeated the words that would bind them.

When she'd finished, Zach slid his arm around her waist and drew her close. The pastor smiled down on them, then looked to the fifty or so family friends who'd gathered on Anton's lawn and said, "I present to you Mr. and Mrs. Zachary Thomas."

A burst of applause followed his words.

Before Janine fully realized what was happening, they were mingling with their guests. One minute she was standing in front of the pastor, trembling but unafraid, and the next she was a wife.

"Janine, Janine!" Pam rushed to her side before anyone else could. "You look so gorgeous," she said softly, and bright tears shone in her eyes.

Janine hugged her young friend. "Thank you, sweetheart."

Pam gazed up at Zach and shook her head. "He sure is handsome."

"I think so, too."

Zach arched his brows, cocked his head toward her and murmured, "You never told me that."

"There's no need for you to be so smug."

"My children," Gramps said, rejoining them. He hugged Janine, and she saw that his eyes were as bright as Pam's. "You've never been more beautiful. I swear you look more like my Anna every year."

It was the highest compliment Gramps could have paid her. From the pictures Gramps kept of his wife, Janine knew her grandmother had been exceptionally beautiful.

"Thank you," she said, kissing his cheek.

"I have something for you." Pam thrust a neatly wrapped box into Janine's hands. "I made them myself," she announced proudly. "I think Zach will like them, too."

"Oh, Pam, you shouldn't have," Janine murmured. Sitting on a cushioned folding chair, she peeled away the paper and lifted the lid. The moment she did, her breath jammed in her throat. Inside were the sheerest white baby-doll pajamas Janine had ever seen. Her smile faltered as she glanced up to see half a dozen people staring at her.

Zach's hand, resting at the nape of Janine's neck, tightened as he spoke, though his voice was warm and amused. "You're right, Pam. I like them very much."

Eight

Janine sat next to Zach in the front seat of his car. Dressed in a pink suit and matching broad-brimmed hat, she clutched her small floral bouquet. Although the wedding had been arranged in seven short days, it had been a lovely affair.

Zach had taken care of planning the short honeymoon. All he could spare was three days, so instead of scheduling anything elaborate, he'd suggested they go to his summer place in Ocean Shores, a coastal town two and a half hours from Seattle by car. Janine had happily agreed.

"So you think I'm handsome?" Zach asked, keeping his eyes on the road. Neither of them had said much since they'd set off.

"I knew if I told you, it'd go straight to your head, and obviously I was right," she answered. Then, unable to hold back a wide yawn, she pressed one hand to her mouth.

"You're exhausted."

"Are you always this astute?"

"Testy, too."

"I don't mean to be," she apologized. She'd been up since before five that morning and in fact, hadn't slept well all week. This wasn't exactly the ideal way to start a marriage. There was an added stress, too, that had to do with the honeymoon. Zach had made it understood that he intended their marriage to be real, but surely he didn't expect them to share a bed so soon. Or did he?

Every now and then as they drove, she glanced in his direction, wondering what, if anything, she should say. Even if she did decide to broach this delicate subject, she wasn't sure how.

"Go ahead and rest," Zach suggested. "I'll wake you when we arrive."

"It should be soon, shouldn't it?"

"Another fifteen minutes or so."

"Then I'll stay awake." Nervously, she twisted the small floral bouquet. Unwrapping Pam's gift had made her all the more apprehensive, but delaying the subject any longer was impossible.

"Zach…are we going to…you know…" she stammered, feeling like a naive schoolgirl.

"If you're referring to what I think you're referring to, the answer is no. So relax."

"No?" He didn't need to sound so casual about it, as if it hardly mattered one way or the other.

"Why do you ask, Janine? Are you having second thoughts about…that?"

"No. Just some reservations."

"Don't worry. When it happens, it happens. The last thing we need is that kind of pressure."

"You're right," she answered, relieved.

"We need some time to feel comfortable. There's no reason to rush into the physical aspect of our marriage, is there?"

"None whatsoever," she agreed quickly, perhaps too quickly, because when she looked at him again, Zach was frowning. Yet he seemed so willing to wait, as though their lovemaking was of minor importance. But as he'd said, this marriage wasn't one of grand passion. Well, *that* was certainly true.

Before another five minutes had passed, Zach left the highway and drove into the resort town of Ocean Shores. He didn't stop in the business district, but headed down a side street toward the beach. The sun was setting as he pulled into a driveway and turned off the engine.

Janine was too enthralled with the house to say a word.

The wind whipped at them ferociously when they climbed out of the car. Janine held on to her hair with one hand, still clutching the flowers, and to Zach with the other. The sun cast a pink and gold reflection over the rolling hills of sand.

"Home, sweet home," Zach said, nudging her toward the house.

The front door opened before they reached it and a trim middle-aged man stepped onto the porch to greet them. He was grinning broadly. "Hello, Zach. I trust you had a safe trip."

"We did."

"Everything's ready. The cupboards are stocked. The firewood's stacked by the side of the house, and dinner's prepared."

"Wonderful, Harry, thanks." Zach placed his hand on Janine's shoulder. "This is my wife, Janine," he said. "We were married this afternoon."

"Your wife?" Harry repeated, looking more than a little surprised. "Why, that's fantastic. Congratulations to you both."

"Thank you," Janine said politely.

"Harry Gleason looks after the place for me when I'm not around."

"Pleased to meet you, Harry."

"So Zach got himself a wife," Harry said, rubbing his jaw in apparent disbelief. "I couldn't be more—"

"Delighted," a frowning Zach supplied for him, ushering Janine toward the front door.

"Right," Harry said. "I couldn't be more delighted."

Janine tilted back her head to survey the sprawling single-story house.

"Go on inside," Zach said. "I'll get the luggage."

Janine started to protest, suddenly wanting him to follow the traditional wedding custom of carrying her over the threshold. She paused, and Zach gave her a puzzled look. "Is something wrong?"

"No." She had no real grounds for complaint. She wasn't even sure why it mattered. Swallowing her disappointment, she made her way into the house. She stopped just inside the front door and gazed with wide-eyed wonder at the immense living room with its three long sofas and several upholstered chairs. A brick fireplace took up an entire wall; another was dominated by a floor-to-ceiling window that looked over the ocean. Drawn to it, Janine watched powerful waves crash against the shore.

Zach followed her inside, carrying their luggage, barely taking time to appreciate the scene before him. "Harry's putting the car away," he said.

"This place is incredible," Janine breathed, gesturing around her. She placed the flowers on the coffee table, then trailed after Zach into a hallway, off which were four bedrooms and an equal number of baths. At the back of the house, she found an exercise room, an office and an ultra-modern kitchen where a pot of coq au vin was simmering.

In the formal dining room, the polished mahogany table was set for two. On the deck, designed to take advantage of the ocean view, she discovered a steaming hot tub, along with a bottle of French champagne on ice.

Zach returned as she wandered back into the kitchen and a strained silence fell between them. He was the first to speak. "I put your suitcases in the master bedroom," he said brusquely. "I'm in the one across the hall."

She nodded, not taking time to question her growing sense of disappointment. They'd agreed to delay their wedding night, hadn't they?

"Are you hungry?" he asked, walking to the stove and lifting the pot's lid, as she'd done earlier.

"Only a little. I was thinking about slipping into the hot tub, unless you want to eat first."

"Sure. The hot tub's fine. Whatever you want."

Janine unpacked and located her swimsuit, then changed into it quickly. The warm water sounded appealing. And maybe it would help her relax. Draping a beach towel over her arm, she hurried into the kitchen, but Zach was nowhere to be seen. Not waiting for him, she walked out to the deck and stepped gingerly into the hot tub. The water felt like a soothing liquid blanket and she slid down, letting it lap just under her breasts.

Zach sauntered onto the deck a minute later, still in his suit. He stopped short when he saw her. "I...didn't realize you'd be out so soon," he said, staring at her with undisguised appreciation. He inhaled sharply and occupied himself by uncorking the bottle of champagne, then pouring a liberal glass. When he'd gulped it down, he reached for a second one and filled it for Janine.

"You're coming in, aren't you?" she asked, when he handed her the crystal flute.

"No," he said abruptly. "I won't join you, after all. There were several things I wasn't able to finish at the office this week, and I thought I'd look over some papers. You go ahead and enjoy yourself."

He was going to *work* on their wedding night! But she didn't feel she had any right to comment or complain. She was determined to conceal her bitter disappointment.

"The water's wonderful," she said, as cheerfully as she could manage, hoping her words would convince him to join her.

Zach nodded, but his eyes now avoided Janine. "It

looks…great." He strode to the end of the deck, ran his fingers through his hair, then twisted around to face her. He seemed about to say something, but evidently changed his mind.

Baffled by his odd behavior, Janine set aside her glass of champagne and stood up so abruptly that water sloshed over the edge of the tub. "You don't need to say it," she muttered, climbing out and grabbing her towel.

"Say what?"

"You warned me before the wedding, so I walked into this with my eyes wide open. Well, you needn't worry. I got the message the minute we arrived at the house."

"What message is that?"

"Never mind." Vigorously, she rubbed her arms with the towel.

"No," he said. "I want you to tell me."

Against her better judgment, she pointed a quaking finger at the front door. "You went out of your way to tell me how *fond* of me you were and how there wasn't going to be any grand passion. Great. Perfect. I agreed to those terms. That's all fine with me, but—"

"But what?"

Mutely, she shook her head.

He sighed. "Oh, great, we're fighting. I suppose you're going to ask for a divorce and make this the shortest marriage in Washington state history."

Janine paled. Divorce was such an ugly word, and it struck her as viciously as a slap. Despite her efforts, scalding tears spilled down her cheeks. With as much dignity as she could muster, which admittedly wasn't a lot, Janine went back inside the house, leaving a wet trail in her wake.

"Janine!" Zach shouted, following her into the kitchen. "Listen, Janine, I didn't intend to argue with you."

She turned abruptly. "This marriage doesn't mean anything to you, does it? You won't even interrupt your work long enough to…to act like a man who just got married."

With her head held high, she stared past him to a painting of yellow flowers on the dining room wall. When her tears blurred the flowers beyond recognition, she defiantly rubbed her eyes.

"I'm sorry," he whispered, reaching for her as if he needed to hold her. But then his arms fell to his sides. "I should've realized wedding traditions would be important to you. Like that carrying-you-over-the-threshold business. I'm sorry," he said again. "I completely forgot."

"It's not just that, it's everything. How many men bring a briefcase with them on their honeymoon? I feel like…like excess baggage in your life—and we haven't even been married for twenty-four hours."

Zach looked perplexed. "What does catching up on my reading have to do with any of this?"

His question only irritated her more. "You don't have the foggiest notion of how impossible you are, do you?"

He didn't answer right away, but seemed to be studying her, weighing his answer before he spoke. "I just thought I might have a chance to read over some papers," he said slowly. "Apparently that bothers you."

Janine placed her hands on her hips. "Yes, it bothers me."

Zach frowned. "Since we've agreed to delay the hon-eymoon part, what would you suggest we do for the next three days?"

"Couldn't we spend the time having fun? Becoming better acquainted?"

"I guess I do seem like a stranger to you," he said. "No wonder you're so nervous."

"I am *not* nervous. Just tired and trying hard not to say or do anything that'll make you think of me as a…a nag."

"A nag?" Zach repeated incredulously. "I don't think of you as anything but lovely. The truth is, I'm having one heck of a time keeping my eyes off you."

"You are?" The towel she was holding slipped unnoticed to the floor. "I thought you said you didn't know how to say anything romantic."

"That was romantic?"

"And very sweet. I was beginning to think you didn't find me…attractive."

Astonished, Zach stared at her. "You've got to be kidding!"

"I'm not."

"I can see that the next few days are going to be difficult," he said. "You'll just need to be patient with me, all right?"

"All right." She nodded, already feeling worlds better.

"How about if I dish up dinner while you're changing?"

"Thanks," she said, smiling.

By the time she got back to the kitchen, wearing gray slacks and a sweater that was the color of fresh cream, Zach had served their meal and poured the wine. He stood be-hind her chair, waiting politely.

"Before we sit down, there's something I need to do."

The last thing Janine expected was to be lifted in his strong arms. A gasp of surprise lodged in her throat as her startled gaze met his.

"What are you doing?"

"It's tradition to carry the bride over the threshold, isn't it?"

"Yes, but you're doing it all wrong! You're supposed to carry me from the outside in—not the other way around."

Zach shrugged, unconcerned. "There's nothing traditional about this marriage. Why start now?" He made a show of pretending his knees were buckling under her weight as he staggered through the living room.

"This is supposed to be serious," she chastised him, but no matter how hard she tried, she couldn't keep the laughter out of her voice.

With a great deal of feigned effort, he managed to open the front door and then ceremoniously step onto the porch. Slowly he released her, letting her feet drop first, holding her upper body close against his chest for a long moment. The humor left his eyes. "There," he said tenderly. "Am I forgetting anything?"

It wouldn't hurt to kiss me, Janine told him in her heart, but the words didn't make it to her lips. When Zach kissed her again, she wanted it to be *his* idea.

"Janine?"

"Everything's perfect. Thank you."

"Not quite," he muttered. He turned her to face him, then covered her mouth with his own. Janine trembled, slipping

her arms around his neck and giving herself completely to
the kiss. She quivered at the heat that began to warm her
from the inside out. This kiss was better than any they'd
ever shared, something she hadn't thought possible. And
what that meant, she had no idea.

Zach pulled his mouth abruptly from hers, but his eyes
remained closed. Almost visibly he composed himself, and
when he broke away he seemed in control of his emotions
once again. Janine sighed inwardly, unsure of what she'd
expected.

The next two days flew past. They took long walks on the
shore, collecting shells. They rented mopeds and raced
along the beach. They launched kites into the sky and delighted in their colorful dipping and soaring. The day before they were scheduled to return to Seattle, Zach declared
that he intended to cook dinner. With that announcement,
he informed her he had to go into town to buy the necessary groceries. After the first night, he'd given Harry a week
off, and Janine had been fixing simple meals for them.

"What are you serving?" she wanted to know when he
pulled into the parking lot of the town's only grocery store.
"Tell me so I can buy an appropriate wine."

"Wine," he muttered under his breath. "I don't normally
serve wine with this dish."

She followed him in, but when he discovered her trailing
down the aisle after him, he gripped her by the shoulders
and directed her back outside. "I am an artist, and I insist
upon working alone."

Janine had a difficult time not laughing outright.

"In order to make this dinner as perfect as possible, I must concentrate completely on the selection of ingredients. You, my dear wife," he said, pressing his index finger to the tip of her nose, "are too much of a distraction. A lovely one, but nevertheless a distraction."

Janine smiled, her heart singing. Zach wasn't free with his compliments, and she found herself prizing each one.

While Zach was busy in the grocery store, Janine wandered around town. She bought a lifelike ceramic sea gull, which she promptly named Chester, and a bag of saltwater taffy. Then on impulse, she purchased a bottle of sun lotion in case they decided to lie outside, tempting a tan.

When she returned to the car, Zach was already there, waiting for her. She was licking a double-decker chocolate ice-cream cone and feeling incredibly happy.

"Did the master chef find everything he needed?" she asked. Two brown paper bags were sitting on the floor and she restrained herself from peeking inside.

"Our meal tonight will be one you'll long remember, I promise you."

"I'm glad to hear it." Holding out her ice-cream cone, she asked. "Do you want a taste?"

"Please." He rejected the offer of the cone itself and instead bent forward and lowered his mouth to hers. As she gazed into his dark heavy-lidded eyes her heartbeat accelerated and she was filled with a sudden intense longing. Janine wasn't sure what was happening between them, but it felt, quite simply, right.

Although the kiss was fleeting, a shiver of awareness

twisted its way through her. Neither of them spoke or moved. He'd meant the kiss to be gentle and teasing, but it had quickly assumed another purpose. For a breathless second, the smile faded from his eyes. He continued to hold her, his breathing rapid.

After nearly two full days alone together, Janine found it amusing that when he finally chose to kiss her, he'd do it in a crowded parking lot.

"I don't remember chocolate being quite that rich," he murmured. He strove for a casual tone, but Janine wasn't fooled. He was as affected by their kiss as she was, and struggling just as hard to disguise it.

They were uncharacteristically quiet on the short drive back to the house. Until the kiss, they'd spent companionable days together, enjoying each other's company. Then, in the space of no more than a few seconds, all that had changed.

"Am I banished from the kitchen?" Janine asked once they were inside the house, forcing an airy note into her voice.

"Not entirely," Zach surprised her by saying. "I'll need you later to wash the dishes."

Janine laughed and pulled her suntan lotion out of her bag. While Zach puttered around inside, she put on her swimsuit, then dragged the lounge chair into the sun to soak up the last of the afternoon's rays.

Zach soon joined her, carrying a tall glass of iced tea. "You look like you could use this."

"Thanks. If I'd known how handy you were in the kitchen, I'd have let you take over long before now."

He set the glass down beside her and headed back to the kitchen. "You'd be amazed by the list of my talents," he threw over his shoulder.

Kissing was certainly one of them, she thought. The sample he'd given her earlier had created a sharp need for more. If she was a sophisticated, experienced kind of woman, she wouldn't have any problem finding her way back into his arms. It would all appear so effortless and casual. He'd kiss her, and she'd kiss him, and then... They'd truly be husband and wife.

Lying on her back with her eyes closed, Janine imagined how wonderful it would be if Zach were to take her in his arms and make love to her....

She awoke from her doze with a start. She hurried inside to change, and as soon as she was ready, Zach announced that dinner was about to be served. He'd set the patio table so they could eat on the deck.

"Do you need any help?" she asked, trying to peek inside the kitchen.

"None. Sit down before everything cools." He pointed to the chair and waited until she was comfortable.

"I only have a spoon," she said, after unfolding the napkin on her lap. He must have made a mistake.

"A spoon is all you need," he shouted to her from the kitchen.

Playfully she asked, "You went to all this trouble for soup?"

"Wait and see. I'll be there in a minute."

He sounded so serious, Janine had to smile. She was

running through a list of words to praise his efforts—"deliciously unique," "refreshingly different"—when Zach walked onto the deck, carrying a tin can with a pair of tongs.

"Good grief, what's that?" she asked in dismay.

"Dinner," he said. "The only real cooking I ever did was while I belonged to the Boy Scouts."

As though he was presenting lobster bisque, he set the steaming can in front of her. Janine leaned forward, almost afraid to examine its contents.

"Barbecued beans. With sliced hot dogs," he said proudly.

"And to think I doubted you."

Her reservations vanished, however, the moment she tasted his specialty. The beans were actually quite appetizing. He surprised her, too, by bringing out dessert, a concoction consisting of graham crackers covered with melted chocolate and marshmallows. He'd warmed them in the oven and served them on a cookie sheet.

Janine ate four of what Zach called "s'mores." He explained that once they'd been tasted, everyone asked for "some more."

"I don't know how you've managed to stay single all these years," she teased, forgetting for the moment that they were married. "If the news about your talent in the kitchen got out, women would be knocking at your door."

Zach chuckled, looking extraordinarily pleased with himself.

An unexpected thought entered Janine's mind, filling her with curiosity. She was astonished that she'd never asked Zach about other women in his life. It would be naive to assume there hadn't been any. She'd had her relationship with Brian; surely there were women in Zach's past.

She waited until later that night when they were sipping wine and listening to classical music in front of the fireplace. Zach seemed relaxed, sitting with one knee raised and the other leg stretched out. Janine lay on her stomach, staring into the fire.

"Have you ever been in love?" She was trying for a casual tone.

Zach didn't answer her right away. "Would you be jealous if I said I had?"

"No." She sounded more confident than she felt.

"I didn't think so. What about you?"

She took her time answering, too. She'd thought she was in love with Brian. It wasn't until later, after the pain of Brian's rejection had eased, that she realized she'd been in love with the *idea* of being in love.

"No," she said, completely honest in her response. What she felt for Zach, whom she was only beginning to know, was already a thousand times stronger than what she'd ever felt for any other man. She didn't know how to explain it, so she avoided the issue by reminding him, "I asked you first."

"I'm a married man. Naturally I'm in love."

"You're fond of me, remember?"

"I thought you detested that word."

"I do. Now stop tiptoeing around the subject. Have you ever *really* been in love—I mean head over heels in love? You don't need to go into any details—a simple yes or no will suffice."

"A desperate-passion kind of love?"

"Yes," she told him impatiently. "Don't make fun of me and please don't give me a list of all the women you've been *fond* of."

He grew so quiet and so intense that her smile began to fade. She pulled herself into a sitting position and looped her arms around her bent knees.

Zach stared at her. As she watched the harsh pain move into his eyes, Janine felt her chest tighten.

"Yes," he answered in a hoarse whisper. "I've been in love."

Nine

"Her name was Marie."

"Marie," Janine repeated the name as though she'd never heard it before.

"We met in Europe when I was on assignment with the armed forces. She spoke five languages fluently and helped me learn my way around two of them in the time we worked together."

"She was in the military with you?"

"I was army, she worked for the secret service. We were thrown together for a top-secret project that was only supposed to last a few days and instead dragged on for weeks."

"This was when you fell in love with her?" The ache inside her chest wouldn't go away. Her heart felt weighed down with the pain.

"We both were aware that the assignment was a dangerous one, and our working closely together was essential."

He paused, sighing deeply. "To make a long story short, I fell in love with her. But she didn't love me."

"Then what?"

"I wanted her to leave the secret service and marry me. She wasn't interested. If you insist on knowing the details, I'll give them to you."

"No."

Zach took a sip of his wine. "I left the army soon after that. I didn't have the heart for it anymore. Unlike Marie— her work, with all its risks, was her whole life. She was the bravest and most dedicated woman I've ever known. Although it was painful at the time, she was right to turn down my proposal. Marriage and a family would have bored her within a year. It *was* painful, don't misunderstand me. I loved her more than I thought possible."

They both were silent for a moment, then Janine asked, "What did you do once you left the army?"

"Over the years, I'd managed to put aside some money, make a few investments. Once I was on my own, I decided to go into business for myself. I read everything I could get my hands on about the business-supply field and modeled the way I dealt with my clients and accounts after your grandfather's enterprise. Within five years, I was his major competitor. We met at a conference last year, and decided that instead of competing with each other, we'd join forces. And as they say, the rest is history."

"Was she pretty?" Even as she asked the question, Janine knew it was ridiculous. What difference would it make if his Marie was a former Miss America or had a face like a gorilla? None. Zach had loved Marie. Loved her as he'd probably never love again. Loved her more than he'd thought possible. By comparison, what he felt for her, Janine, was indeed only fondness.

"She was blond and, yes, she was beautiful."

Janine made a feeble attempt at a smile. "Somehow I knew that."

Zach shook himself lightly as if dragging himself back to the present and away from the powerful lure of the past. "You don't need to worry. It was a long time ago."

"I wasn't worried," Janine muttered. She got to her feet and collected their wineglasses. "I'm a little tired. If you don't mind, I'll go to bed now."

Zach was still staring into the fire and Janine doubted he'd even heard her. She didn't need a crystal ball to know he was thinking of the beautiful Marie.

No more than ten minutes after she'd turned off her bedroom light, Janine heard Zach move down the hallway to his room. For a moment she thought he'd hesitated in front of her door, but Janine convinced herself that was just wishful thinking.

From the second Zach had told her about the one great love of his life, Janine had felt as if a lump were building inside her. A huge lump of disillusionment that seemed to be located somewhere between her heart and her stomach. With every breath she took, it grew larger. But why should she care about Marie? Zach had never confessed to any deep feeling for *her.* He hadn't cheated Janine out of anything that was her right.

An hour later, she lay on her side, wide awake, her hands pressed to her stomach. She didn't mind that Zach had loved another woman so deeply, but what did hurt was that he could never love her with the same intensity. Marrying her, he'd claimed, made practical and financial sense. He was *fond* of her.

Like a romantic idiot, Janine had been frolicking through their short marriage, confident that they'd soon be in love with each other and live happily ever after with their two-point-five children in their perfect little home with the white picket fence.

Zach had loved Marie, who'd dedicated herself to her country.

The most patriotic thing Janine had ever done was cast her vote at election time. She didn't think she should include the two occasions she'd made coffee at Red Cross meetings.

Marie was a linguist. After two years of high-school French, Janine wasn't bad at conjugating verbs, but got hopelessly lost in real conversations.

"I had to ask," she groaned to herself. She was almost certain that Zach would never have mentioned Marie if she hadn't forced the subject. How blissful her ignorance had been. How comfortable.

She could never be the great love of his life and would always remain in the background. Far in the background…

When Janine heard Zach moving around the house a few hours later, she rolled over and glanced at the clock, assuming it was the middle of the night. Then she noticed it was midmorning; they'd planned to be on the road before now. Tossing aside the blankets, she stumbled out of bed and reached blindly for her robe. But she wasn't paying attention. She collided with the wall and gave a shout of pain. She cupped her hand over her nose and closed her eyes. Tears rolled slowly down her cheeks.

"Janine." Zach pounded on the door. "Are you all right?"

"No," she cried, still holding her nose. She looked in the mirror and lowered her hand. Just as she'd suspected, her nose was bleeding.

"Can I come in?" Zach asked next.

"No…go away." She hurried to the adjoining bathroom, tilting back her head and clamping both hands over her nose.

"You sound funny. I'm coming in."

"No," she hollered again. "Go away." She groped for a washcloth. The tears rained down now, more from humiliation than pain.

"I'm coming in," Zach shouted, his voice distinctly irritated.

Before Janine could protest, the bedroom door flew open and Zach stalked inside. He stopped in the bathroom doorway. "What happened?"

Pressing the cold cloth over the lower half of her face with one hand, Janine gestured violently with the other, demanding that he leave.

"Let me look at that," he said, obviously determined to deal with her bloody nose, as well as her anger. He pushed gently against her shoulders, lowering her onto the edge of the tub, and carefully removed the cloth.

"What did you do? Meet up with a prizefighter?"

"Don't you dare make fun of me!" The tears ran down her cheeks again and plummeted on her silk collar.

It took only a minute or so to control the bleeding. Zach seemed to know exactly what to do. Janine no longer had any desire to fight, and she allowed him to do what he wanted.

Zach wiped the tears from her cheeks. "Do you want me to kiss it and make it better?"

Without waiting for an answer, Zach brought his mouth to hers. Janine felt herself go completely and utterly still. Her heart started to explode and before she realized what she was doing, she'd linked her arms around his neck and was clinging to him helplessly. Zach kissed her forehead and her eyes. His thumbs brushed the remaining tears from her cheeks. Then he nuzzled her neck. Trembling, she immersed herself in his tenderness. No matter what had happened in the past, Zach was hers for this minute, this day.

He lifted Janine to her feet and seemed to be leading her toward the bed. She might have been tempted to let him if she hadn't learned about his love for Marie. Knowing she'd always place a remote second in his affections was a crippling blow to her pride—and her heart. It would take time and effort to accept that she could never be the woman who evoked an all-consuming passion in him.

With that thought in mind, she pushed him away, needing to put some distance between them before it was too late.

Accepting Janine's decision, Zach dropped his arms and moved to lean against the doorjamb, as if he needed its support to remain upright.

Janine couldn't look at him, couldn't speak. She began fumbling with her clothes.

"I'll give you a few minutes to dress while I begin loading the car," Zach said a moment later, sounding oddly unlike himself.

Janine nodded miserably. There was nothing she could say. Nothing she could do. He'd wanted to make love to her, and she'd turned him away.

While he packed the car, Janine dressed. She met him fifteen minutes later, her suitcase in hand. She was determined to act cool toward him. But not too cool. Friendly, she decided, but not excessively so.

"I'm ready," she announced, with her most cheerful smile.

Zach locked the house, and they were on their way. Pretending there was nothing out of the ordinary, Janine chatted amicably during the drive home. If Zach noticed anything amiss, he didn't comment. For his part, he seemed as hesitant as she was to talk about what had happened. They seemed to be of one mind about the morning's incident. The whole thing was best forgotten.

Only once did Zach refer to it. He asked her if her nose was causing her any pain, but she quickly assured him she was fine. She flashed a smile bright enough to blind him and immediately changed the subject.

The Seattle sky was gray and drizzling rain when they pulled into the parking garage at the downtown condominium owned by Zach. Silently, she helped him unload the car. They were both unusually quiet as they rode the elevator to the tenth floor.

Zach paused outside his door and eyed her skeptically. "Am I obliged to haul you over the threshold again, or is once enough?"

"Once is enough."

"Good." He grinned and unlocked the door, then pushed it open for her to precede him. Curious, she quickened her pace as she walked inside. The living room was a warm mixture of leather and wood, and its wide window offered a breathtaking view of the Seattle skyline.

"It's lovely."

He nodded, seeming pleased at her reaction. "If you prefer, we can move. I suppose now that we're married, we should think about purchasing a house."

"Why?" she inquired innocently.

"I'm hoping we'll have children someday. Whenever you're ready, that is. There's no pressure, Janine."

"I...know that." She looked past him at the panoramic view, and wrapped her arms around herself, her heart speeding up at his words.

Walking to his desk, Zach listened to his voice mail messages; apparently there were a lot.

While he did that, Janine wandered from room to room, eager to see her new home. In the hallway, she noted that Zach had diplomatically left her luggage on the carpet between the two bedrooms. His was in the master. In his own way, he was telling her that where she slept would be her decision. If she wished to become his wife in the fullest sense, all she had to do was place her suitcase in the master bedroom. Nothing more needed to be said.

It didn't take Janine long to decide. She pulled her suitcase toward the guest room. When she looked up, Zach was standing in the hall, studying her, his expression aggrieved.

"Unless you need me for anything, I'm going to the office," he said gruffly.

"See you tonight."

His gaze moved past her and rested briefly on the bed in the guest room. He cocked one eyebrow questioningly, as though to give her the opportunity to reconsider. "Are you sure you'd rather sleep in here?" he asked.

"I'm sure."

Zach raked his fingers through his hair. "I was afraid of that."

A minute later, he was gone.

Zach didn't come home for dinner that night. Janine had been in the bathroom when the phone rang; Zach had left her a message saying he'd be late. So she ate by herself in front of the television, feeling abandoned and unloved. She was just putting the dishes in the dishwasher when he came home.

"Sorry I'm late."

"That's okay," she lied, never having felt more alone.

Zach glanced through the mail on his desk, although Janine was sure he'd looked at it earlier. "You got the message I wouldn't be home for dinner?"

"Yes. Did you want anything to eat? I could fix you something."

"I ate earlier. Thanks, anyway."

They watched an hour's worth of television and then decided to go to bed.

Janine changed into her pajamas—the same no-nonsense type she'd been wearing all week, since she couldn't bring herself to wear the baby-dolls Pam had given her—and had just finished washing her face. She was coming out of the bathroom, her toothbrush between her teeth, when she nearly collided with Zach in the hallway. She'd forgotten her slippers and was going to her bedroom to retrieve them. They'd already said their good-nights, and Janine hadn't expected to see him again until morning. She wasn't prepared for this encounter, and the air between them crackled with tension.

She had to force herself not to throw her toothbrush aside. Not to tell him that she longed for him to love her with the same passion he'd felt for Marie.

His hands reached out to steady her, and when she didn't immediately move away, he ran the tips of his fingers down her thick brown hair, edging her bangs to the side of her face so he could gaze into her eyes.

Janine lowered her head. "Esh-coo me," she managed, but it was difficult to speak with a toothbrush poking out of her mouth.

"Pardon?"

Janine hurried back to the bathroom and rinsed out her mouth. Turning, she braced her hands on the sink. "I said excuse me for bumping into you."

"Will you be comfortable in the guest room?"

"Yes, I'll be fine."

He held a blanket in his arms. "I thought you might need this."

"Thanks," she said as smoothly as possible, coming out of the bathroom to take the blanket from him. She wanted to be swept off her feet. She wanted love. She wanted passion.

He was offering a warm blanket.

"I…phoned Gramps," she said, looking for a way to delay their parting and cursing herself for her weakness.

"I intended to call him myself, but got sidetracked."

"He sounded good. Dr. Coleman and a couple of his other friends were at the house and the four of them were playing pinochle."

"I'm glad to hear he's enjoying his semi-retirement."

"I am, too."

A short silence followed.

"Good night, Janine," Zach said after a moment. He glanced, frowning, into the guest room.

"Good night," she said awkwardly.

Janine was sure neither of them slept a wink that night. They were across the hall from each other, but might as well have been on opposite sides of the state, so great was the emotional distance between them.

In the morning, Zach's alarm rang at seven, but Janine was already awake. She threw back her covers, dressed and had coffee waiting when he entered the kitchen.

Zach seemed surprised to see her. "Thanks," he murmured as she handed him a cup. "That's a very…wifely thing to do."

"What? Make coffee?"

"Get up to see your husband off to work."

"I happened to be awake and figured I should get out of bed and do something useful."

He opened the refrigerator, took out the orange juice and poured himself a glass. "I see." He replaced the carton and leaned against the counter. "You did agree that our marriage would be a real one."

"Yes, I did," she said somewhat defensively. But that agreement had been before she'd learned about the one great love of his life. Zach had warned her their marriage would be advantageous for a variety of reasons, the least of which was love. At the time, Janine had agreed, convinced their relationship would find a storybook ending nonetheless—convinced that one day they'd realize they were in love. Now she understood that would never happen. And she didn't know if she could stand it.

"Janine," Zach said, distracting her, "what's wrong?"

"What could possibly be wrong?"

"Obviously something's bothering you. You look like you've lost your best friend."

"You should've told me," she burst out, running from the kitchen.

"Told you what?" Zach shouted, following her down the hall.

Furious, she hurried into her room and sat on the end of the bed, her hands in tight fists at her sides.

"What are you talking about?" he demanded, blocking the doorway.

"About…this woman you loved."

"Marie? What about her? What's she got to do with you and me?"

"You loved her more than…more than you thought possible. She was brave and wonderful, and I'm none of those things. I don't deal with pain very well and…I'd like to be patriotic but all I do is vote and all I know in French are verbs."

"What's any of that got to do with you and me?" Zach repeated hoarsely, then threw his hands in the air. "What's it got to do with *anything?*"

Knowing she'd never be able to explain, Janine shook her head, sending her bangs fanning out in several directions. "All you are is *fond* of me."

"Correction," Zach said as he stepped into the bedroom. "I *cherish* you."

"It isn't enough," she said, feeling miserable and wretched and unworthy.

"What do you mean, it isn't enough? According to you the only reason you married me was that I was a good kisser, so you can't fault me for *my* reasons."

"I don't, it's just that you…you never told me about loving someone else. Not only that, you *admired* her—she was a hero. All you feel for me is fondness. Well, I don't want your fondness, Zachary Thomas!" She leapt to her feet, trying to collect her scattered thoughts. "If you cared for me, you would've told me about Marie before. Not mentioning her was a form of dishonesty. You were completely…unfair."

"And you weren't?" Zach's expression darkened and he

buried his hands in his pockets. "You didn't say one word to me about Brian."

Janine was so shocked she sank back onto the bed. Zach still glared at her, challenging her to contradict him. Slowly gathering her composure, she stood, her eyes narrowing as she studied her husband. "Who told you about Brian?"

"Your grandfather."

"How did he know? I never said a word to him about Brian. Not one solitary word."

"But obviously he knew."

"Obviously." Janine had never felt more like weeping. "I suppose he told you Brian lied to me and claimed to love me when all the while he was seeing someone else." Another, more troubling thought entered her mind. "I...bet Gramps told you that to make you feel sorry for me, sorry enough to marry me."

"Janine, no."

She hid her face in both hands, humiliation burning her cheeks. It was all so much worse than she'd imagined. "You felt sorry for me, didn't you?"

Zach paced the length of the bedroom. "I'm not going to lie to you, although I suspect it would be better if I did. Your grandfather didn't mention that you'd fallen in love with Brian until after the day we took him to the doctor."

"He waited until we got to know each other a little," Janine whispered, staggered by the realization that her grandfather had known about Brian all along.

"By then I'd discovered I liked you."

"The word *like* is possibly even worse than *fond*," she muttered.

"Just hear me out, would you?"

"All right," she sighed, fearing that nothing he said now mattered, anyway. Her pride had suffered another major blow. The one love of his life had been this marvelous patriot, while Janine had fallen for a weak-willed womanizer.

"It isn't as bad as it seems," Zach tried to assure her.

"I can just imagine what Gramps told you."

"All he said was that he was afraid you'd never learn to trust your own judgment again. For quite a while now, he's watched you avoid any hint of a relationship. It was as though you'd retreated from men and were content just to lick your wounds."

"That's not true! I was seeing Peter Donahue on a regular basis."

"Safe dates with safe men. There was never any likelihood that you'd fall in love with Peter, and you knew it. It was the only reason you went out with him."

"Is…is what happened with Brian why Gramps decided to play matchmaker?"

"I suspect that was part of it. Also his concern for your future. But I don't fully understand his intentions even now. I don't think it matters, though. He wanted you to be happy and secure. Anton knew I'd never purposely hurt you. And in his eyes, the two of us were perfect for each other." Zach sat down next to her and reached for her hand, lacing her fingers with his own. "*Does* it matter? We're married now."

She looked away from him and swallowed hard. "I…may not be blond and gorgeous or brave, but I deserve a husband who'll love me. You and Gramps both failed to take that into account. I don't want your pity, Zach."

"Good, because I don't pity you. You're my wife, and frankly, I'm happy about it. We can have a good life if you'll put this nonsense behind you."

"You'd never have chosen me on your own. I knew what you thought of me from the moment we met. You assumed I was a rich spoiled woman who'd never had anything real to worry about. I bet you thought I'd consider a broken nail a major disaster."

"All right, I'll admit I had the wrong impression, but that was before," Zach insisted.

"Before what?"

"Before I got to know you."

Janine's shoulders heaved with barely suppressed emotion. "As I recall, the reason you were willing to marry me was because I wasn't so bad. And let's not forget the financial benefits," she added sarcastically.

Zach's sigh was filled with frustration. "I told you I wasn't ever going to say the stuff you women like to hear. I don't know a thing about romance. But I care about you, Janine, I honestly care. Isn't that enough?"

"I need more than that," she said miserably. It was the promise of their future, the promise of learning about love together, that had intrigued her.

Zach frowned. "You told me even before we were married that you didn't need romantic words. You were content before I mentioned Marie. Why should my telling you change anything?"

She saw that Zach was losing his patience with her. She stared down at the thick carpet. "I really wish I could explain, but it does make a difference. I'm sorry, Zach, I really am."

A lifetime seemed to pass before he spoke again. "So am I," he whispered before turning away. A moment later the front door opened and almost immediately closed again. Zach had left.

"What did you expect?" she wailed, covering her face with both hands. "Did you think he was going to fall at your knees and declare his undying love?" The picture of the proud and mighty Zach Thomas playing the role of besotted husband was actually comical. If he'd done that for any woman, it would've been the brave and beautiful Marie. Not Janine.

After that disastrous morning, their relationship grew more strained than ever. Zach went to work early every day and returned late, usually past dinnertime. Janine never questioned where he was or who he was with, although she had to bite her tongue to keep from asking.

Zach proved to be a model housemate, if not a husband—cordial, courteous and remote. For her part, she threw herself into her volunteer work at the Friendship Club, spending hours each week with the children. She did her best to hide her unhappiness from her grandfather, although that was difficult.

"You look pale," he told her when she joined him for lunch one afternoon, several days after her return from Ocean Shores. "Are you losing weight?"

"I wish," she said, attempting to make a joke of it. They sat in the dining room, with Mrs. McCormick wandering in and out, casting Janine concerned glances. Janine resisted the urge to leap up and do aerobic exercises to demonstrate that she was in perfect health.

"You can't afford to get much thinner," Gramps said, eyeing her solemnly. He placed a dinner roll on the side of her plate and plunked the butter dish down in front of her.

"I'm not losing weight," she told him, spreading butter on the roll in order to please him.

"I took that sea gull you gave me into the office," Gramps said as he continued to study her. "Zach asked me where I got it. When I told him, he didn't say anything, but I could tell he wasn't pleased. Do you want it back?"

"No, of course not." Janine dropped her gaze. She'd never intended for Gramps to take Chester into the office. On impulse, she'd given him the ceramic bird, reluctant to have it around the condominium to remind her of those first glorious days with Zach.

"I wish I knew what was wrong with you two," Gramps blurted out in an uncharacteristic display of frustration. He tossed his napkin onto his dinner plate. "You should be happy! Instead, the pair of you look like you're recovering from a bad bout of flu. Zach's working so many hours it's a wonder he doesn't fall over from sheer exhaustion."

Janine carefully tore her roll into pieces. She toyed with

the idea of bringing up the subject of Brian, but in the end, she didn't.

"So you say you're fine, and there's nothing wrong between you and Zach," Gramps said sarcastically. "Funny, that's exactly what he said when I asked him. Except he also told me to mind my own business—not quite in those words, but I got the message. The thing is, he looks as pathetic as you do. I can't understand it—you're perfect for each other!"

Gramps reached into his pocket for a cigar. "I'll be seeing Zach this afternoon and I intend to give that boy a piece of my mind. By all rights, you should be a happy bride." He tapped one end of the cigar against the table.

"We'll be fine, Gramps. Please stay out of it."

For a long moment, he said nothing; he only stared at the cigar between his fingers. "You're sure you don't want me to talk some sense into the boy?" he finally asked.

The mental picture of him trying to do so brought a quivering smile to her lips. "I'm sure," she said, then glanced at her watch. Pam would be waiting for her. "But since you're seeing Zach, would you please let him know I'll probably be late for dinner? He…should go ahead and eat without me."

"Do you do this often?" His question was an accusation.

"No," she replied, shaking her head. "This is the first time. Pam needs my help with a school project and I don't know when we'll be finished."

Gramps glowered as he lit his cigar, puffing mightily before he spoke. "I'll tell him."

As it turned out, Janine spent longer with Pam than she'd expected. The homework assignment wasn't difficult, but Pam begged Janine to stay with her. Pam's father was working late and the girl seemed to need Janine more than ever. They made dinner together, then ate in the kitchen while Pam chatted about her friends and life in general.

It was almost nine by the time Janine pulled into the parking garage. The first thing she noticed was Zach's car. The atmosphere had been so falsely courteous between them that she dreaded each encounter, however brief. Since that first morning, Zach hadn't made any effort to talk about her role in his life. Janine wasn't looking for a long flowery declaration of love. Just a word or two more profound than *fond* or *like* to let her know she was important to him.

Drawing a deep breath, she headed for the condominium.

She'd just unlocked the door when Zach stormed into the room like a Minnesota blizzard. "Where the hell have you been?" he demanded.

Janine was so shocked by his fierce anger that she said nothing.

"I demand to know exactly where you were!"

She removed her sweater, hanging it carefully in the entry closet, along with her purse. Zach scowled at her silence, fists clenched at his sides. "Do you have any idea of the time? Did it even cross your mind that I might've been concerned about you? Your cell phone was off and you didn't return any calls."

"I'm sorry." Janine turned to face him. "But you knew where I was," she said calmly.

"All Anton said was that you'd be late. Not where you were going or who you were with. So naturally I was worried."

"I'm sorry. Next time I'll tell you myself." Janine yawned; the day had been exhausting. "If you don't mind, I think I'll go to bed now. Unless there's anything else you'd like to know?"

He glared at her, then shook his head. Wheeling around abruptly, he walked away.

Hours later, Janine was awakened by a gruff sobbing sound coming from the other room. It took her a moment to realize it was Zach. Was he having a nightmare?

Folding back the covers, she got out of bed and hurried into his room. The cries of anguish grew louder. In the light from the hallway, she could see him thrashing about, the bedding in disarray.

"Zach," she cried, rushing to his side. She sat on the edge of the bed and placed her hands gently on his shoulders. "Wake up. You're having a dream. Just a dream. It's okay...."

Zach's eyes slowly opened. "Janine." He ground out her name as though in torment and reached for her, hauling her into his arms with such force that he left her breathless. "Janine," he said, his voice so husky she could barely understand him. "I thought I'd lost you."

Ten

"Zach, I'm fine," Janine whispered. Emotion clogged her throat at the hungry way his eyes roamed her face. He seemed to have difficulty believing, even now, that she was unhurt.

"It was so real," he continued, his chest heaving. He hid his face as if to block out the vivid images the dream had induced. Making room in the large bed, he pulled her down beside him. His hands stroked her hair as he released several jagged breaths. "We were at the ocean," he told her, "and although I'd warned you against it, you decided to swim. A huge wave knocked you off your feet and you were drowning. Heaven help me, I tried, but I couldn't get to you fast enough." He shut his eyes briefly. "You kept calling out to me and I couldn't find you. I just couldn't get to you fast enough."

"Zach," she whispered, her mouth so close to his that their breath mingled, "I'm right here. It was only a dream. It wasn't real."

He nodded, but his eyes still seemed troubled, refusing to leave her face. Then ever so slowly, as though he expected her to object, he moved his mouth even closer to hers. "I couldn't bear to lose you. I'd rather die myself."

Helpless to deny him anything, Janine turned her face to receive his kiss.

His hands tangled in her thick dark hair, effectively holding her captive, while his mouth seized hers in a kiss that sent her senses swirling. Nothing mattered except his touch. Overcome for a moment by the fierce tenderness she felt in him, Janine eagerly fed his need.

"Janine, oh, my dear sweet Janine. I couldn't bear to lose you."

"I'm here...I'm here." Melting against him, she molded her body to the unyielding contours of his, offering her lips and her heart to his loving possession. Again and again, he kissed her. Janine slid her hands up his chest and twined them around his neck. This was what she'd longed for from the first, the knowledge that he needed her, and she gloried in the sensation.

With a groan, he reluctantly pulled his mouth from hers. He held her firmly to his chest, his breathing harsh and rapid. Peace combined with a delirious sense of happiness, and Janine released a deep sigh. Pressing her ear to his chest, she listened, content, to the heavy pounding of his heart.

"Did I frighten you?" he asked after a minute.

"No," she whispered.

He resumed stroking her hair as she nestled more

securely in his arms. Zach had made her feel wondrous, exciting things every time he kissed her, but the way he held and touched her now went far beyond those kisses. She'd experienced a bonding with Zach, a true joining of spirits that had been missing until now. He had told her he'd cherish her, but she hadn't believed it until this moment. Tears clouded her eyes and she struggled to restrain them.

For a long while neither of them spoke. But Janine didn't need words. Her eyes were closed as she savored this precious time.

When Zach did speak, his voice was little more than a hoarse whisper. "I had a sister who drowned. Her name was Beth Ann. I'd promised I'd always be there for her—but I failed her. I couldn't bear to lose you, too."

Janine tightened her hold, knowing how difficult it must be for him to speak of his sister.

"I never forgave myself." His body tensed and his fingers dug roughly into her shoulder. "Losing Beth Ann still haunts me. She wouldn't have drowned if I'd been with her. She—"

Lifting her head slightly, Janine's misty gaze met his. "It wasn't your fault. How could it have been?"

"But I was responsible for her," he returned harshly.

Janine suspected that Zach had rarely, if ever, shared his sorrow or his guilt over his sister's death with anyone. A low groan worked its way through him and he squeezed his eyes tightly shut. "For years, I've drummed out the memories of Beth Ann's death. The nightmare was so real, only this time it wasn't her—it was you."

"But I'm safe and sound. See?" She pressed her hands to both sides of his face, smiling down on him.

He sighed and smiled back, a little uncertainly. "I'm all right now. I shouldn't have burdened you with this."

"It wasn't a burden."

His arms tightened around her, and he inhaled deeply as if absorbing her scent. "Stay with me?"

She nodded, grateful that he needed her.

Within minutes, Janine felt herself drifting into drowsiness. From Zach's relaxed, even breathing, she knew he was already asleep.

When Janine next stirred, she was lying on her side, and Zach was cuddling her spoon fashion, his arm about her waist. At some point during the night, she'd slipped under the covers, but she had no recollection of doing so. A small satisfied smile touched the edges of her mouth. She rolled carefully onto her back so as not to disturb Zach, and wondered what she should do. When Zach woke and found her in bed with him, she was afraid he might regret what had happened, regret asking her to stay. He might feel embarrassed that he'd told her about his sister's death and the guilt he still felt.

Closing her eyes, Janine debated with herself. If she left his bed and returned to her own room, he might think she was rejecting him, shocked by his heart wrenching account of Beth Ann's death.

"Janine?" He whispered her name, his voice husky with sleep.

Her eyes flew open. "I…we fell asleep. What time is it?"

"Early. The alarm won't go off for another couple of hours."

She nodded, hoping to disguise any hint of disappointment in her voice. He didn't want her with him, she was sure of it. He was embarrassed to find her still in his bed. "I'll leave now if you want."

"No."

The single word was filled with such longing that Janine thought she'd misunderstood him. She tipped her head back to meet his gaze. The light from the hall allowed her to see the passion smoldering in his dark eyes. Turning onto her side, Janine lovingly traced the lines of his face.

"I'm sorry about the way I behaved over…Marie," she whispered. "I was jealous and I knew I was being ridiculous, but I couldn't help myself."

The corners of his eyes crinkled with his smile. "I'll forgive you if you're willing to overlook the way I behaved when you got home last night."

She answered him with a light kiss, and he hugged her to him. Janine surrendered to the sheer pleasure of being in Zach's arms, savoring the rush of warm sensations that sprang to life inside her.

"I don't know how to say all the words you deserve to hear, but I know one thing, Janine. I love you. It happened without my even being aware of it. One day I woke up and realized how important you'd become to me. It wasn't the grand passion you wanted, and I'm sorry for that. The love I feel for you is the quiet steady kind. It's buried deep in my heart, but trust me, it's there. You're the most important person in my life."

"Oh, Zach, I love you so much."

"You love me?"

"I have for weeks, even before we were married. That's what bothered me so much when I learned about Marie. I wanted you to love *me* with the same intensity that you felt for her…that I feel for you."

"It isn't like that. It never was. Marie was as brave as she was beautiful, but what we shared was never meant to last. And she was smart enough to understand that. I fell in love with her, but she was too much of a professional to involve her heart. She was the kind of person who thrives on excitement and danger. It wasn't until you and I met that I realized if I were ever to marry, it would be to someone like you."

"Someone like me?"

He kissed her briefly. "A woman who's warm and gentle and caring. Someone unselfish and—" he hesitated "—desirable."

Her throat tightened with emotion, and it was all she could do to meet his gaze. Zach found her desirable. He wanted to make love to her. He didn't need to say it; the message was there for her to read in his eyes. It wasn't the desperate passion she'd once craved, but his love, his need to have her in his life, was far more potent than any action he could have taken, any words he could have said.

"Love me, Zach," she whispered simply.

Zach's mouth touched hers with a sweet desperate ardor.

If she had any lingering doubts they vanished like mist in the sun as his lips took hers, twisting her into tight knots of desire.

His arms locked around her and he rolled onto his back, pulling her with him. His hands outlined her face as though he half expected her to stop him.

"Make me your wife," she said, bending forward to brush her moist mouth over his.

Zach groaned, and then he did the strangest, most wonderful thing. He laughed. The robust sound echoed across the room and was so infectious that it made Janine laugh, too.

"My sweet Janine," he said. "You've changed my life." And then he kissed her again, leaving her with no doubts at all.

For a long time afterward, their happiness could be heard in their sighs and gasps and whispered words of love....

The buzzing sound refused to go away. Janine moaned softly and flung out her hand, hoping to find the source of the distraction. But before she could locate it, the noise ceased abruptly.

"Good morning, wife," Zach whispered.

Her eyes remained closed as she smiled leisurely. "Good morning, husband." Rolling onto her back, she held her arms open to him. "I had the most marvelous dream last night."

Zach chuckled softly. "That wasn't any dream."

"But it must've been," she said, slipping her arms around his neck and smiling lazily. "Nothing could be that incredible in real life."

"I didn't think so, either, but you proved me wrong." He

kissed her tenderly, and then so thoroughly that by the time he lifted his head, Janine was breathless.

Slowly, almost against her will, her eyes drifted open. His were dark with desire. "You'll be late for work," she warned him.

His smile was sensuous. "Who cares?"

"Not me," she murmured. And with a small cry of pleasure, she willingly gave herself to her husband.

Zach was already an hour late for the office when he dragged himself out of bed and headed for the shower. Wearing her husband's pajama top, Janine wandered into the kitchen and prepared a pot of coffee. She leaned against the counter and smiled into space, hardly aware of the passage of time.

A few minutes later—or perhaps it was longer—Zach stepped behind her and slid his arms around her waist, nuzzling her neck.

"Zach," she protested, but not too strenuously. She closed her eyes and cradled her arms over his, leaning back against his solid strength. "You're already late."

"I know," he murmured. "If I didn't have an important meeting this morning, I'd skip work altogether."

Turning in his arms, Janine tilted back her head to gaze into his eyes. "You'll be home for dinner?"

"Keep looking at me like that and I'll be home for lunch."

Janine smiled. "It's almost that time now."

"I know," he growled, reluctantly pulling away from her. "We'll go out to dinner tonight," he said, kissing her again. His mouth was hot on her own, feverish with demand and passion and need. He raised his head, but his eyes remained shut. "Then we'll come home and celebrate."

Janine sighed. Married life was beginning to agree with her.

At precisely five, Zach was back. He stood by the door, loosening his tie, when Janine appeared. A smile traveled to his mouth as their eyes met. Neither moved. They stared at each other as if they'd spent years apart instead of a few short hours.

Janine was feeling distinctly light-headed. "Hi," she managed to say, shocked that her voice sounded more like a hoarse whisper than the cheery greeting she'd intended. "How'd the meeting go?"

"Bad."

"Bad?"

He nodded slowly and stepped forward, placing his briefcase on the desk. "I was supposed to be listening to an important financial report, but unfortunately all I could do was wonder how much longer the thing would take so I could get home to my wife."

"Oh." That wasn't the most intelligent bit of conversation she'd ever delivered, but just looking at Zach was enough to wipe out all her normal thought processes.

"It got to be almost embarrassing." His look was intimate and loving as he advanced two more steps toward her. "In the middle of it, I started smiling, and then I embarrassed myself further by laughing outright."

"Laughing? Something was funny?"

"I was thinking about your definition of romance. The

tryst on the moors was supplied by your grandfather. The walk along the beach, hand in hand, was supplied by me after the wedding. But the desperate passion, my dear sweet wife, was something we found together."

Her eyes filled with tears.

"I love you."

They moved toward each other then, but stopped abruptly when the doorbell chimed. Zach's questioning eyes met hers. Janine shrugged, not knowing who it could possibly be.

The second Zach answered the door, Anton flew into the room, looking more determined than Janine had ever seen him.

"All right, you two, sit down," he ordered, waving them in the direction of the sofa.

"Gramps?"

"Anton?"

Janine glanced at Zach, but he looked as mystified as she did. So she just shrugged and complied with her grandfather's demand. Zach sat down next to her.

Gramps paced the carpet directly in front of them. "Janine and I had lunch the other day," he said, speaking to Zach. "Two things became clear to me then. First and foremost, she's crazy in love with you, but I doubt she's told you that."

"Gramps—" Janine began, but her grandfather silenced her with a single look.

"The next thing I realized is that she's unhappy. Terribly unhappy. Being in love is difficult enough but—"

"Anton," Zach broke in, "if you'd—"

Gramps cut him off with the same laser-eyed look he'd sent Janine.

"Don't interrupt me, boy. I'm on a roll and I'm not about to stop now. If I noticed Janine was a little melancholy at lunch, it was nothing compared to what I've been noticing about you." Suddenly he ceased his pacing and planted himself squarely in front of Zach. "All week I've been hearing complaints and rumors about you. Folks in the office claim you're there all hours of the day and night, working until you're ready to drop." He paused. "I know you, Zach, probably better than anyone else does. You're in love with my granddaughter, and it's got you all tangled up inside."

"Gramps—"

"Shh." He dismissed Janine with a shake of his head. "Now, I may be an old man, but I'm not stupid. Maybe the way I went about bringing the two of you together wasn't the smartest, or the most conventional, but by golly it worked." He hesitated long enough to smile proudly. "In the beginning I had my doubts. Janine put up a bit of a fuss."

"I believe you said something about how it's easier to pluck a live chicken," Zach inserted, slanting a secret smile at Janine.

"True enough. I never knew that girl had so much spunk. But the fact is, Zachary, as you'll recall, you weren't all that keen on the idea yourself. You both think because I'm an old man, I don't see things. But I do. You were two lonely people, filling up your lives with unimportant relationships, avoiding love, avoiding life. I care about you. Too much to sit back and do nothing."

"It worked out," Janine said, wanting to reassure him.

"At first I thought it had. I arranged the trip to Scotland and it looked like everything was falling neatly into place, like in one of those old movies. I couldn't have been more pleased when you announced that you were going to get married. It was sooner than I'd expected, but I assumed that meant things were progressing nicely. Apparently I was wrong. Now I'm worried."

"You don't need to be."

"That's not the way I see it," Gramps said with a fierce glare. "Tell him you love him, Janine. Look Zach in the eye and put aside that silly pride of yours. He needs to know it. He needs to hear it. I told you from the first that he wasn't going to be an easy man to know, and that you'd have to be patient with him. What I didn't count on was that damnable pride of yours."

"You want me to tell Zach I love him? Here? Now?"

"Yes!"

Janine turned to her husband and, feeling a little self-conscious, lowered her eyes.

"Tell him," Gramps barked.

"I love you, Zach," she said softly. "I really do."

Gramps gave a loud satisfied sigh. "Good, good. Okay, Zach, it's your turn."

"My turn?"

"Tell Janine what you feel and don't go all arrogant on me."

Zach reached for Janine's hand. He lifted her palm to his mouth and brushed his lips against it. "I love you," he whispered.

"Add something else," Gramps instructed, gesturing toward him. "Something like…you'd be a lost and lonely soul without her. Women are impressed by that sort of thing. Damn foolishness, I know, but necessary."

"I'd be a lost and lonely soul without you," Zach repeated, then looked back at Janine's grandfather. "How'd I do?"

"Better than most. Is there anything else you'd like him to say, Janine?"

She gave an expressive sigh. "I don't think so."

"Good. Now I want the two of you to kiss."

"Here? In front of you?"

"Yes," Gramps insisted.

Janine slipped into Zach's arms. The smile he shared with her was so devastating that she felt her heart race with anticipation. Her eyes fluttered closed as his mouth settled on hers, thrilling her with promises for all the years to come.

Gently, provocatively, Zach moved his mouth over hers, ending his kiss far too soon to suit Janine. From the shudder that coursed through him, Janine knew it was too soon for him, too. Reluctantly they drew apart. Zach gazed into her eyes, and Janine responded with a soft smile.

"Excellent, excellent."

Janine had all but forgotten her grandfather's presence. When she turned away from Zach, she discovered Gramps sitting across from them, his hands on the arms of the leather chair. He looked exceedingly proud of himself. "Are you two going to be all right now?"

"Yes, sir," Zach answered for them both, his eyes hazy with

desire as he smiled at Janine. She could feel herself blushing, and knew her eyes were foggy with the same longing.

"Good!" Gramps declared, nodding once for emphasis. A slow grin overtook his mouth. "I knew all the two of you needed was a little assistance from me." He inhaled deeply. "Since you're getting along so well, maybe now would be the time to bring up the subject of children."

"Anton," Zach said, rising to his feet. He strode across the room and opened the door. "If you don't mind, I'll take care of that myself."

"Soon?" Gramps wanted to know.

Zach's eyes met Janine's. "Soon," he promised.

WANTED:
PERFECT PARTNER

For Arlene Tresness, a grandma like me,
a lover of books, a devoted reader of mine.
Thank you for your unfailing support and enthusiasm.
(Your grandchildren think the world of you!)

Prologue

"Is our ad there?" Fifteen-year-old Lindsey Remington whispered to her best friend. She glanced nervously at her bedroom door. Lindsey's biggest fear was that her mother would find her and Brenda scanning the Dateline section of the Wednesday paper and discover what they'd done.

Okay, so it was a bit…dishonest to write an ad on Meg Remington's behalf, but it was clear to Lindsey that her mom needed help. She was convinced that Meg *wanted* to remarry, whether she knew it or not.

It wasn't as if Lindsey could pull a potential husband out of nowhere. So she wrote the ad, with her best friend advising her.

"Here," Brenda said excitedly, pointing to the middle of the page. "It's here. Oh, my goodness! It's really here, just the way we wrote it."

Lindsey found the ad. She read aloud:

"Wanted: Perfect partner. I'm dating-shy, divorced

and seeking a man with marriage in mind. I look like a beauty queen, cook like a mom, kiss like a woman in love. Box 1234."

"It sounds even better in print," Brenda said.

"Do you think anyone will actually respond?" Lindsey asked.

"I bet we get lots of letters."

"I still think we should've said her kisses taste better than chocolate."

"It didn't fit. Remember?" They'd worked long and hard on the wording. Lindsey had wanted to describe her mother as "stunning," and Brenda was afraid it might not meet the truth-in-advertising rules.

All right, so her mother wasn't fashion model material, but she was very pretty. Or she could be, with a little assistance from the magazines Lindsey had been reading lately. Luckily Meg had a daughter who knew the ropes.

"Don't worry, Linds," Brenda said with a romantic sigh. "This is the best thing you could ever have done for your mother."

Lindsey hoped her mom appreciated her efforts. "Just remember, this guy has to be *perfect*. We'll need to be careful who we pick."

"No problem. If we don't like the sound of one guy, we'll choose someone else," Brenda said, as if they were guaranteed to have tons of applicants. "That's the beauty of our plan. We'll screen all the applicants before your mother has a chance to date them. How many teenagers get to choose their own stepfathers? Not many, I bet."

Lindsey returned her attention to the ad, gnawing on the corner of her lip. She was experiencing a twinge of pride along with a mild case of guilt.

Her mother wasn't going to like this. When Meg learned what she and Brenda had done, she'd probably get all bent out of shape.

As for the ad, Lindsey figured if she were a man inclined to read the Dateline section, the ad would intrigue her.

"Some men will write just because your mom's pretty, but it's the part about her being a good cook that'll really work," Brenda assured her. "My grandma says Grandpa married her because her German potato salad was so good. Can you believe it?"

Brenda brought up a good point. "How will we know if a man is marrying her for her looks or her meat loaf or 'cause he loves her?"

"We won't," Brenda said, "but by then we'll be out of the picture. Your mother will be on her own."

Lindsey wished she knew more about men. Unfortunately her experience was limited. She'd only gone on two real dates, both times to school dances. And her mother had been a chaperone.

"The day will come when Mom will appreciate what we've done for her," Lindsey said. "She's the one who's always saying how important it is to go after your dreams. Well, this is my dream for her. She wants a man. She just doesn't know it yet."

"All she needs is a little help from us."

"And she's got it," Lindsey said, smiling broadly.

One

Those girls were up to something. Meg Remington peeked in her fifteen-year-old daughter's bedroom to see Lindsey and her best friend, Brenda, crouched on the floor beside the bed. They were speaking in heated whispers.

Meg cleared her throat and instantly both girls were silent.

"Hi, Mom," Lindsey said, her bright blue eyes flashing.

Meg knew the look, which generally spelled trouble. "What are you two doing?"

"Nothing."

"Nothing," Brenda echoed with angelic innocence.

Meg crossed her arms and leaned her shoulder against the doorjamb. She had all the time in the world, and she wanted them to know it. "Tell me why I don't believe that. You two have the *look*."

"What look?" Lindsey repeated, turning to Brenda.

"The one every mother recognizes. You're up to something, and I want to know what." She crossed her ankles, indicating that she'd make herself comfortable until they were ready to let her in on their little secret. She could outwait them if need be.

"All right, if you *must* know," Lindsey said with a shrug of defeat. She leapt to her feet and Brenda followed suit. "But we haven't finished planning everything yet."

"I must know." Meg was struck by how beautiful her daughter had become over the past few years. She'd gone from the gangly, awkward, big-teeth stage to real beauty almost overnight. Meg's ex-husband, Dave, had commented on the changes in Lindsey when she'd flown from Seattle to Los Angeles to visit over spring break. Their little girl was growing up.

"We've been doing some heavy-duty planning," Brenda explained.

"And exactly what are the two of you working on? I haven't seen you all evening." Generally, when Brenda stayed over, which was at least one night of every weekend, the two of them were up until all hours playing music, watching television or DVDs. The house had been suspiciously quiet all evening. Come to think of it, they'd been spending a lot of time in Lindsey's bedroom of late. Far too much time.

The girls glanced at each other before answering.

"You tell her," Brenda urged, "she's your mother."

"I know." Lindsey brushed back the long strands of hair. "But it might be a little easier coming from you."

"Lindsey?" Meg was more curious than ever now.

"You'd better sit down, Mom." Lindsey took Meg by the hand and guided her to the bed.

Meg sat on the edge. Both girls stood in front of her and each seemed to be waiting for the other to speak first.

"You're such an attractive woman," Lindsey began.

Meg frowned. This sounded like a setup to her, and the best way to handle that was to get straight to the point. "You need money? How much, and for what?"

With her usual flair for the dramatic, Lindsey rolled her eyes. "I don't need any money. I meant what I said—you're beautiful."

"It's true," Brenda piped up. "And you're only thirty-seven."

"I am?" Meg had to think about that. "Yeah, I guess I am."

"You're still so young."

"I wouldn't go that far…"

"You've still got it, Mrs. Remington," Brenda cut in, her voice intense. "You're young and pretty and single, and you've got *it*." Her fist flew through the air and punctuated the comment.

"Got what?" Meg was beginning to feel a bit confused.

"You're not in bad shape, either," Lindsey commented, resting her chin on one hand.

Meg sucked in her stomach, feeling pleased with the girls' assessment.

"Of course you'd look even better if you lost ten pounds," her daughter said thoughtfully.

Ten pounds. Meg breathed again and her stomach pouched out. Those ten pounds had first made their appearance when Meg was pregnant with Lindsey nearly sixteen years earlier. She was downright proud of having maintained her post-pregnancy weight for all these years.

"Ten pounds isn't too much to lose," Brenda said confidently.

"It won't be hard at all—especially with the two of us helping you."

Meg stared into their eager, expectant faces. "Why is it so important for me to lose ten pounds? I happen to like the way I look."

"There's more."

Meg glanced from one girl to the other. "More? What is that supposed to mean?"

"You need to be physically fit. Think about it, Mom. When's the last time you ran an eight-minute mile?"

Meg didn't need to consider that at all—she already knew the answer. "Never." She'd jogged around the track during high school, only because it was required of her. The lowest grade she'd ever received was in phys ed.

"See?" Lindsey said to Brenda.

"We'll work with her," Brenda answered. "But we'll have to start soon."

Lindsey crossed her arms and carefully scrutinized Meg. "About your clothes, Mom."

"My clothes?" Meg cried, still astonished that her daughter wanted her to run an eight-minute mile. She owned a bookstore, for heaven's sake. In the eight years since she'd bought out Mr. Olsen, not once had she been required to run for anything.

"I want to know what's going on here," Meg said. "Now."

"I promise we'll answer all your questions in a minute," Brenda explained. "Please be patient, Mrs. Remington."

Lindsey sighed. "Mom, I don't mean to be rude or anything, but when it comes to your clothes, well…you need help."

"Help?" And to think Meg had been dressing herself for the past thirty-some years. Until now, no one had bothered to tell her what a poor job she'd done.

"I'm here to see you don't ever wear high-waisted jeans again," Lindsey said, as though pledging her life to a crusade. "They're called mom jeans," she whispered.

"So you two are official members of the fashion police?" Meg asked. Apparently they'd issued an APB on her!

Lindsey and Brenda giggled.

"That's what it sounds like."

"We're here to help you," Brenda said in loving tones.

"We're here to keep you from committing those fashion sins."

"What sins?" Meg should've known. "Do you mind telling me what this little heart-to-heart is all about?"

"*You*, Mom," Lindsey said, in a voice that suggested the answer should've been obvious.

"Why now? Why me?"

"Why not?" Lindsey responded.

Meg started to get up, but Lindsey directed her back onto the bed. "We aren't finished yet. We're just getting to the good part."

"Honey, I appreciate what you're doing, but…"

"Sit down, Mom," Lindsey said in stern tones. "I haven't told you the most important thing yet."

Meg held up both hands. "Okay, okay."

"Like we already said, you're still young," Brenda began.

Lindsey smiled sweetly. "You could have more children if you wanted and—"

"Now wait a minute!" Meg cried.

"What we're really saying is that you're quite attractive."

"Or I could be," Meg amended, "with a little assistance from the two of you."

"Not all that much," Brenda added sympathetically. "We just want to get you started on the right track."

"I see," Meg muttered.

"Together," Lindsey said, slipping her arm around Brenda's waist and beaming a proud smile, "we're going to find you a husband."

"A husband." Meg's feet went out from under her and she slipped off the bed and landed with a solid whack on the carpet.

Lindsey and Brenda each grabbed one arm and pulled her off the floor. "Are you all right?" Lindsey asked, sounding genuinely concerned.

"You should've been more subtle," Brenda said accusingly. "There was no need to blurt it out like that."

Meg rubbed her rear end and sat back down on the bed. "What makes either of you think I want a husband?" she demanded angrily. She'd already been through one bad marriage and she wasn't eager to repeat the experience.

"When's the last time you went out on a date?" Lindsey asked.

"I don't remember," Meg snapped. "What does it matter, anyway?"

"Mother, it's clear to me you aren't thinking about the future."

"The future? What are you talking about?"

"Do you realize that in three years I'll be in college?"

"Three years," Meg repeated. "No-o, I guess I hadn't given it much thought." Although at the moment sending her daughter away actually seemed appealing.

"You'll be all alone."

"Alone isn't such a bad thing," Meg told them.

"At forty it is," Lindsey said dramatically. "I'll worry myself sick about you," she continued.

"She will," Brenda confirmed, nodding twice.

Meg figured it was a good thing she was sitting down.

"Tell me, Mother," Lindsey said, "what would it hurt to start dating again?"

"Honey, has it ever occurred to you that I'm happy just the way I am?"

"No," Lindsey returned. "You aren't happy. You're letting life pass you by. It's time to take action. I don't know what went wrong between you and Dad, but whatever it was must've been traumatic. You haven't had a relationship since—have you?"

Meg didn't answer that question, but wanted to reassure Lindsey about the break-up of her marriage. "It was a friendly divorce." In fact, Meg got along better with Dave now than she had when they were married.

Brenda shook her head. "There's no such thing as a friendly divorce. My dad's an attorney and he should know."

"I don't want to talk about the divorce," Meg said in her sternest voice. "It happened a long time ago and bringing it up now isn't going to help anyone."

"It might help *you,*" Lindsey said, her eyes intense, "but I can understand why you don't want to talk about it. Don't worry," she said, and a bright smile transformed her face, "because you're going to get all the help you need from Brenda and me."

"That's what I was afraid of." Meg stood up and moved toward the door.

"Your diet starts tomorrow," Lindsey called after her.

"And your exercise regime," Brenda added. "You haven't got a thing to worry about, Mrs. Remington. We're going to find you a man before you know it."

Meg closed her eyes. If thirty-seven was so young, why didn't she have the energy to stand up to these two? She wasn't going on any diet, nor did she have time for exercising.

As for having Lindsey as a wardrobe consultant… That was ridiculous, and Meg intended to tell her daughter and Brenda exactly that.

First thing in the morning.

Meg soon learned exactly how serious Lindsey and Brenda were about finding her a husband. She woke Saturday morning to the sound of a workout DVD playing loudly on the television in her bedroom.

She lay facedown, awakened from a pleasant dream about a sunny beach. Her arm hung over the side of the bed, her fingertips dangling an inch or so above the carpet.

"You ready, Mrs. Remington?" Brenda called from the doorway.

She tried to ignore the girl, but that didn't work.

"You ready?" Brenda called a second time. She seemed to be jogging in place. "Don't worry, we'll go nice and slow in the beginning."

"I'm not doing anything without speaking to my attorney first," Meg muttered. She stuck out her arm and searched blindly for the phone.

"Forget it, Mom. That isn't going to work." Lindsey walked into the bedroom and set a coffee mug on the nightstand.

"Bless you, my child," Meg said. "Ah, coffee." She'd struggled into a sitting position before she realized caffeine had nothing to do with whatever Lindsey had brought her. "What *is* this?" she barked.

"It's a protein supplement. The lady at the health food store recommends it for toning skin in women over thirty."

"Are you sure you're supposed to drink it?" Meg asked.

Lindsey and Brenda looked at each other blankly.

"I'd better check the instructions again," Lindsey said and carried it away.

"Don't worry, Mrs. Remington, we'll have you whipped into shape in no time."

"Coffee," she pleaded. She couldn't be expected to do anything, let alone exercise, without caffeine.

"You can have your coffee," Brenda promised her, "but first…"

Meg didn't bother to listen to the rest. She slithered back under the covers and pulled a pillow over her head. Although it did block out some of the noise, she had no trouble hearing the girls. They weren't accepting defeat lightly. They launched into a lively discussion about the pros and cons of allowing Meg to drink coffee. She had news for these two dictators. Let either one of them try to stand between her and her first cup of coffee.

The conversation moved to the topic of the divorce; Brenda apparently believed Meg had suffered psychological damage that had prevented her from pursuing another relationship.

It was all Meg could do not to shove the pillow aside and put in her two cents' worth. What she should've done was order them out of the bedroom, but she was actually curious to hear what they had to say.

Her divorce hadn't been as bad as all that. She and Dave had made the mistake of marrying far too young. Meg had been twenty-two when she'd had Lindsey, and Dave was fresh out of college. In the five years of their marriage there hadn't been any ugly fights or bitter disagreements. Maybe it would've helped if there had been.

By the time Lindsey was four, Dave had decided he didn't love Meg anymore and wanted a divorce. It shouldn't have come as a surprise, but it did—and it hurt. Meg suspected he'd found someone else.

She was right.

For a long time after the divorce was final, Meg tried

to convince herself that her failed marriage didn't matter. She and her husband had parted on friendly terms. For Lindsey's sake, Meg had made sure they maintained an amicable relationship.

Dave had hurt her, though, and Meg had denied that pain for too long. Eventually she'd recovered. It was over now, and she was perfectly content with her life.

She'd started working at Book Ends, an independent bookstore, and then, with a loan from her parents she'd managed to buy it.

Between the bookstore and a fifteen-year-old daughter, Meg had little time for seeking out new relationships. The first few years after the divorce she'd had a number of opportunities to get involved with other men. She hadn't. At the time, Meg simply wasn't interested, and as the years went on, she'd stopped thinking about it.

"Mother, would you please get out of this bed," Lindsey said, standing over her. Then in enticing tones, she murmured, "I have coffee."

"You tricked me before."

"This one's real coffee. The other stuff, well, I apologize about that. I guess I misunderstood the lady at the health food store. You were right. According to the directions, you're supposed to use it in the bath, not drink it. Sorry about that."

Meg could see it wasn't going to do the least bit of good to hide her face under a pillow. "I can't buy my way out of this?" she asked.

"Nope."

"You'll feel much better after you exercise," Brenda promised her. "Really, you will."

An hour later, Meg didn't feel any such thing. She couldn't move without some part of her anatomy protesting.

"You did great, Mrs. Remington," Brenda praised.

Meg limped into her kitchen and slowly lowered herself into a chair. Who would've believed a workout DVD, followed by a short—this was the term the girls used—one-mile run, would reduce her to this. In the past hour she'd been poked, prodded, pushed and punished.

"I've got your meals all planned out for you," Lindsey informed her. She opened the refrigerator door and took out a sandwich bag. She held it up for Meg's inspection. "This is your lunch."

Meg would've asked her about the meager contents if she'd had the breath to do so. All she could see was one radish, a square of cheese—low-fat, she presumed—and a small bunch of seedless grapes.

"Don't have any more than the nonfat yogurt for breakfast, okay?"

Meg nodded, rather than dredge up the energy to argue.

"Are you going to tell her about dinner?" Brenda asked.

"Oh, yeah. Listen, Mom, you've been a real trooper about this and we thought we should reward you. Tonight for dinner you can have a baked potato."

She managed a weak smile. Visions of butter and sour cream waltzed through her head.

"With fresh grilled fish."

"You like fish don't you, Mrs. Remington?"

Meg nodded. At this point she would've agreed to anything just to get the girls out of her kitchen, so she could recover enough to cook herself a decent breakfast.

"Brenda and I are going shopping," Lindsey announced. "We're going to pick out a whole new wardrobe for you, Mom."

"It's the craziest thing," Meg told her best friend, Laura Harrison, that same afternoon. They were unpacking boxes of books in the back room. "All of a sudden, Lindsey said she wants me to remarry."

"Really?"

Laura found this far too humorous to suit Meg. "But she wants me to lose ten pounds and run an eight-minute mile first."

"Oh, I get it now," Laura muttered, taking paperbacks from the shipping carton and placing them on a cart.

"What?"

"Lindsey was in the store a couple of weeks ago looking for a book that explained carbs and fat grams."

"I'm allowed thirty fat grams a day," Meg informed her. "And one hundred grams of carbohydrates." Not that her fifteen-year-old daughter was going to dictate what she did and didn't eat.

"I hope Lindsey doesn't find out about that submarine sandwich you had for lunch."

"I couldn't help it," Meg said. "I haven't been that hungry in years. I don't think anyone bothered to tell

Lindsey and Brenda that one of the effects of a workout is a voracious appetite."

"What was that phone call about earlier?" Laura asked.

Meg frowned as she moved books onto the cart. "Lindsey wanted my credit card number for a slinky black dress with a scoop neckline." Lindsey had sounded rapturous over the dress, describing it in detail, especially the deep cuts up the sides that would reveal plenty of thigh. "She said she found it on sale—and it was a deal too good to pass up." She paused. "Needless to say, I told her no."

"What would Lindsey want with a slinky black dress?"

"She wanted it for me," Meg said, under her breath.

"You?"

"Apparently once I fit the proper image, they plan to dress me up and escort me around town."

Laura laughed.

"I'm beginning to think you might not be such a good friend after all," Meg told her employee. "I expected sympathy and advice, not laughter."

"I'm sorry, Meg. Really."

She sounded far more amused than she did sorry.

Meg cast her a disgruntled look. "You know what your problem is, don't you?"

"Yes," Laura was quick to tell her. "I'm married, with college-age children. I don't have to put up with any of this nonsense and you do. Wait, my dear, until Lindsey gets her driver's license. *Then* you'll know what real fear is."

"One disaster at a time, thank you." Meg sat on a stool and reached for her coffee cup. "I don't mind telling you I'm worried about all this."

"Why?" Laura straightened and picked up her own cup, refilling it from the freshly brewed pot. "It's a stage Lindsey's going through. Trust me, it'll pass."

"Lindsey keeps insisting I'll be lonely when she leaves for college, which she reminded me is in three years."

"Will you be?"

Meg had to think about that. "I don't know. I suppose in some ways I will be. The house will feel empty without her." The two weeks Lindsey spent with her father every year seemed interminable. Meg wandered around the house like a lost puppy.

"So, why *not* get involved in another relationship?" Laura asked.

"With whom?" was Meg's first question. "I don't know any single men."

"Sure you do," Laura countered. "There's Ed, who has the insurance office two doors down."

"Ed's single?" She rather liked Ed. He seemed like a decent guy, but she'd never thought of him in terms of dating.

"The fact that you didn't know Ed was single says a lot. You've got to keep your eyes and ears open."

"Who else?"

"Buck's divorced."

Buck was a regular customer, and although she couldn't quite understand why, Meg had never cared for him. "I wouldn't go out with Buck."

"I didn't say you had to go out with him, I just said he was single."

Meg couldn't see herself kissing either man. "Anyone else?"

"There are lots of men out there."

"Oh, really, and I'm blind?"

"Yes," Laura said. "If you want the truth, I don't think Lindsey's idea is so bad. True, she may be going about it the wrong way, but it wouldn't hurt you to test the waters. You might be surprised at what you find."

Meg sighed. She'd expected support from her best friend, and instead Laura had turned traitor.

By the time Meg had closed the bookstore and headed home, she was exhausted. So much for all those claims about exercise generating energy. In her experience, it did the reverse.

"Lindsey," she called out, "are you home?"

"I'm in my room," came the muffled reply from the bedroom at the top of the stairs.

Something she couldn't put her finger on prompted Meg to hurry upstairs to her daughter's bedroom despite her aching muscles. She knocked once and opened the door to see Lindsey and Brenda sitting on the bed, leafing through a stack of letters.

Lindsey hid the one she was reading behind her back. "Mom?" she said, her eyes wide. "Hi."

"Hello."

"Hello, Mrs. Remington," Brenda said, looking decidedly guilty.

It was then that Meg saw the black dress hanging from

the closet door. It was the most provocative thing she'd seen in years.

"How'd you get the dress?" Meg demanded, angry that Lindsey had gone against her wishes and wondering how she'd managed to do it.

The two girls stared at each other, neither one eager to give her an answer. "Brenda phoned her mother and she put it on her credit card," Lindsey said at last.

"What?" Meg felt ready to explode.

"It was only a small lie," Brenda said quickly. "I told my mom it was perfect and on sale and too cheap to resist. What I didn't tell her was that the dress wasn't for me."

"It's going back right this minute, and then the three of us are paying Brenda's parents a visit."

"Mom!" Lindsey flew off the bed. "Wait, please." She had a panicked look in her eyes. "What we did was wrong, but when you wouldn't agree to buy the dress yourself, we didn't know what to do. You just don't have anything appropriate for Chez Michelle."

Chez Michelle was one of the most exclusive restaurants in Seattle, with a reputation for excellent French cuisine. Meg had never eaten there herself, but Laura and her husband had celebrated their silver wedding anniversary at Chez Michelle and raved about it for weeks afterward.

"You're not making any sense," Meg told her daughter.

Lindsey bit her lip and nodded.

"You have to tell her," Brenda insisted.

"Tell me what?"

"You're the one who wrote the last letter," Lindsey said. "The least you could've done was get the dates right."

"It's tonight."

"I know," Lindsey snapped.

"Would someone tell me what's going on here?" Meg asked, her patience at its end.

"You need that dress, Mom," Lindsey said in a voice so low Meg had to strain to hear her.

"And why would that be?"

"You have a dinner date."

"I do? And just who am I going out with?" She assumed this had something to do with Chez Michelle.

"Steve Conlan."

"Steve Conlan?" Meg repeated. She said it again, looking for something remotely familiar about the name and finding nothing,

"You don't know him," Lindsey told her. "But he's really nice. Brenda and I both like him." She glanced at her friend for confirmation and Brenda nodded eagerly.

"You've met him?" Meg didn't like the sound of this.

"Not really. We exchanged a couple of letters and then we e-mailed back and forth and he seems like a really great guy." The last part was said with forced enthusiasm.

"You've been writing a strange man."

"He's not so strange, Mom, not really. He sounds just like one of us."

"He wants to meet you," Brenda put in.

"Me?" Meg brought her hand to her throat. "Why would he want to do that?"

The girls shared a look, reminiscent of the one she'd caught the night before.

"Lindsey?" Meg asked. "Why would this man want to meet me?"

Her daughter lowered her eyes, refusing to meet Meg's. "Because when we wrote Steve…"

"Yes?"

"Brenda and I told him we were you."

Two

Steve Conlan glanced at his watch. The time hadn't changed since he'd looked before. He could tell it was going to be one of those nights. He had the distinct feeling it would drag by, one interminable minute after another.

He still hadn't figured how he'd gotten himself into this mess. He was minding his own business and the next thing he knew… He didn't want to think about it, because whenever he did his blood pressure rose.

Nancy was going to pay for this.

He was early, not because he was so eager for tonight. No, he was only eager to get it over with.

He tried not to check the time and failed. A minute had passed. Or was it a lifetime?

His necktie felt as if it would strangle him. A tie. He couldn't believe he'd let Nancy talk him into wearing a stupid tie.

Because he needed something to occupy his time, he took the snapshot out of his shirt pocket.

Meg Remington.

She had a nice face, he decided. Nothing spectacular. She certainly wasn't drop-dead gorgeous, but she wasn't plain, either. Her eyes were her best feature. Clear. Bright. Expressive. She had a cute mouth, too. Very kissable. Sensuous.

What was he supposed to say to the woman? The hell if he knew. He'd read her letters and e-mails a dozen times. She sounded—he hated to say it—immature, as if she felt the need to impress him. She seemed to think that because she ran an eight-minute mile it qualified her for the Olympics. Frankly, he wondered what their dinner would be like, with her being so food conscious and all. She'd actually bragged about how few fat grams and carbs she consumed. Clearly she wasn't familiar with the menu at Chez Michelle. He couldn't see a single low-fat or low-carb entrée.

That was another thing. The woman had expensive tastes. Dinner at Chez Michelle would set him back three hundred bucks—if he was lucky. So far he'd been anything but...

Involuntarily his gaze fell to his watch again, and he groaned inwardly. His sister owed him for this.

Big time.

"I refuse to meet a strange man for dinner," Meg insisted coldly. There were some things even a mother wouldn't do.

"But you have to," Brenda pleaded. "I'm sorry, Mrs. Remington, I feel really bad springing this on you, but

Steve didn't do anything wrong. You've just *got* to show up. You have to…otherwise he might lose faith in all women."

"So?"

"But he's your date," Lindsey said. "It would've worked out great if…" she paused and scowled at her best friend "…if one of us hadn't gotten the days mixed up."

"Exactly when did you plan on telling me you've been communicating with a strange man, using *my* name?"

"Soon," Lindsey said with conviction. "We had to… He started asking about meeting you almost right away. We did everything we could to hold him off. Oh, by the way, if he asks about your appendix, you've made a full recovery."

Meg groaned. The time frame of their deception wasn't what interested her. She was stalling, looking for a way out of this. She could leave a message for Steve at the restaurant, explaining that she couldn't make it, but that seemed like such a cowardly thing to do.

Unfortunately no escape plan presented itself. Brenda was right; it wasn't Steve's fault that he'd been duped by a pair of teenagers. It wasn't her fault, either, but then Lindsey was her daughter.

"He's very nice-looking," Brenda said. She reached behind her and pulled out a picture from one of the envelopes scattered across Lindsey's bed. "Here, see what I mean?" Meg swore she heard the girl sigh. "He's got blue eyes and check out his smile."

Meg took the photo from Brenda and studied it. Her daughter's friend was right. Steve Conlan was pleasant-looking. His hair was a little long, but that didn't bother

her. He wore a cowboy hat and boots and had his thumbs tucked into his hip pockets as he stared into the camera.

"He's tall, dark and *lonesome,*" Lindsey said wistfully.

"Has he ever been married?" Meg asked, curiosity getting the better of her.

"Nope." This time it was Brenda who supplied the information. "He's got his own business, same as you, Mrs. Remington. He owns a body shop and he's been sinking every penny into it."

"What made him place the ad?" she asked the girls. A sudden thought came to her. "He *is* the one who advertised, isn't he?"

Both girls looked away and Meg's heart froze. "You mean to say you two advertised for a husband for me?" She spoke slowly, each word distinct.

"We got lots of letters, too," Brenda said proudly. "We went through them all and chose Steve Conlan."

"Don't you want to know why?" Lindsey prodded.

Meg gestured weakly, still too shocked to react.

"Steve says he decided to answer your ad because one day he woke up and realized life was passing him by. All his friends were married, and he felt like something important was missing in his life. Then he knew it wasn't *something* but someone."

"What about female friends?" Meg asked, thinking he didn't look like a man who'd have to find companionship in the classifieds.

"He said in his letter that…" Lindsey paused and rustled through a sheaf of papers, searching for the right envelope.

"Here it is," she muttered. "He doesn't have much opportunity to meet single women unless they've been in an accident, and generally they're not in the mood for romance when they're dealing with a body shop and an insurance company." Lindsey grinned. "He's kind of witty. I like that about him."

"He said a lot of women his age have already been married and divorced and had a passel of kids."

This didn't sound too promising to Meg. "You did happen to mention that I'm divorced, too, didn't you?"

"Of course," Lindsey insisted. "We'd never lie."

Meg bit her tongue to keep from saying the obvious.

"Just think," Brenda said, "out of all the women who advertised, Steve chose you and we chose him. It's destiny."

The girls thought she'd feel complimented, but Meg was suspicious. "Surely there was someone younger and prettier, without children, who interested him."

The two girls exchanged a smile. "He liked the fact that you count carbs and fat grams," Brenda said proudly.

So much for their unwillingness to stretch the truth. "You actually told him that?" She closed her eyes and groaned. "What else did you say?"

"Just that you're really wonderful."

"Heroic," Brenda added. "And you are."

Oh, great. They'd made her sound like a thin Joan of Arc.

"You will meet him, won't you?" Lindsey's dark eyes pleaded with Meg.

"What I should do is march the two of you down to that

fancy restaurant and have you personally apologize to him. You both deserve to be grounded until you're forty."

The girls blinked in unison. "But, Mom…"

"Mrs. Remington…"

Meg raised her hand and stopped them. "I won't take you to Chez Michelle, and as for the grounding part…we'll discuss it later."

Two pairs of shoulders sagged with relief.

"But I won't have dinner with Steve Conlan," she said emphatically. "I'll go to the restaurant, introduce myself and explain what happened. I'm sure he'll agree that the best thing to do is skip dinner altogether."

"You'll wear the dress, won't you?" Lindsey asked, eyeing the slinky black concoction hanging outside her closet door.

"Absolutely not," Meg said. She refused to even consider it.

"But you don't have anything special enough for Chez Michelle. Just try it on, Mom."

"No. Well…"

"Come on, Mom. Brenda and I want to see how it looks."

An hour later Meg pulled up at Chez Michelle in the very dress she'd sworn she'd never wear. It fit as if it'd been designed just for her, enhancing her figure and camouflaging those stubborn ten pounds. At least that was what Lindsey and Brenda told her.

"Hello." The hostess greeted her with a wide smile. "Table for one?"

"I'm…meeting someone," Meg said, glancing around

the waiting area looking for a man who resembled "tall, dark and lonesome" in the photo. No one did. Nor was there a single male wearing a cowboy hat.

The only man who looked vaguely like the one in the photograph stood in the corner of the room, leaning indolently against the wall as if he had all the time in the world.

He straightened and stared at her.

Meg stared back.

He reached inside his suit pocket and took out a picture.

Meg opened the clasp of her purse and removed the photo the girls had given her. She looked down at it and then up again.

He appeared to be doing the same thing.

"Meg Remington?" he asked uncertainly.

She nodded. "Steve Conlan?"

He nodded, too.

He wore a suit and tie. A suit and tie. The guy had really gone all out for her. Meg swallowed uncomfortably. He'd invited her to this ultrafancy restaurant expecting to meet the woman who'd exchanged those letters and messages with him. Meg felt her heart settle somewhere in the vicinity of her knees. She couldn't very well introduce herself and immediately say it had all been a mistake and cancel dinner. Not when he'd gone to so much trouble.

"I believe our table is ready," Steve said, holding out his arm to her. His hand touched her elbow and he addressed the hostess. "We can be seated now."

The woman gave him an odd look, then picked up two huge menus. "This way."

Meg might've been wrong, but she thought she heard some reluctance in his voice. Perhaps she was a disappointment to Steve Conlan. After the fitness drill Lindsey and Brenda had put her through, Meg was feeling her advancing age.

Pride stiffened Meg's shoulders. So she hadn't signed any modeling contracts lately. What did he expect from a thirty-seven-year-old woman? If he wanted to date a woman in her twenties, he shouldn't have answered her ad. Lindsey's ad, she corrected. It was all Meg could do not to stop Steve Conlan right then and there and tell him this was as good as it got.

Especially in this dress. It was simply gorgeous. Meg knew now the girls had made the perfect choice. She was glad she'd given in to them on this one. Besides, Lindsey was right; she didn't own anything fancy enough for Chez Michelle. Before she could stop herself she'd agreed to wear it. Soon both girls were offering her fashion advice.

They were escorted to a linen-covered table next to the window, which overlooked Elliot Bay and Puget Sound. The moon's reflection on the water sent gilded light across the surface, and the restaurant's interior was dimly lit.

Meg squinted, barely able to read her menu. She wondered if Steve was having the same problem. Originally she hadn't intended to have dinner with him. Wouldn't even now, if he hadn't gone to so much trouble on her behalf. It seemed crass to drop in, announce it had all been a misguided attempt by her daughter to play matchmaker, ask his forgiveness and speedily disappear.

"I believe I'll have the chicken cordon bleu," she said, deciding on the least expensive item on the menu. "And please, I insist on paying for my own meal." It would be unforgivable to gouge him for that as well.

"Dinner's on me," Steve insisted, setting his menu aside. He smiled for the first time and it transformed his face. He studied her, as if he wasn't sure what to make of her.

"But…" Meg lowered her gaze and closed her mouth. She didn't know where to start and yet she didn't know how much longer she could maintain the pretense. "This is all very elegant…."

"Yes," he agreed, spinning the stem of his water glass between his thumb and index finger.

"You look different than your picture." Meg had no idea why she'd told him that. What she *should* be doing was explaining about Lindsey and Brenda.

"How's that?"

"Your eyes are much bluer and you've cut your hair."

He gave a slight grin. "And your picture didn't do you justice."

Meg hadn't thought to ask Lindsey which one she'd mailed Steve. "Can I see?"

"Sure." He pulled it out of his pocket and handed it over.

Meg took one look and rolled her eyes. She couldn't believe Lindsey had sent this particular photograph to anyone. It'd been taken just before Christmas a year earlier. She was standing in front of the Christmas tree wearing a white dress that drained all the color from her face. The flash from the camera made her eyes appear red. She looked like she was recovering from a serious ailment.

"This is one of the worst pictures ever taken of me," she said impatiently. "The one of me at the bookstore is *much* better."

Steve's brow creased with a frown. "I see. You should've sent that one."

Meg realized what she'd said too late. "You're right, I should have.... How silly of me."

The waitress came and they placed their orders, both declining a drink, Meg to keep down the cost and Steve, no doubt, to hurry the meal along.

Once the server had left the table, Meg carefully smoothed the napkin across her lap. "Listen, Steve…"

"Meg…"

They both stopped.

"You go first," he said, gesturing toward her.

"All right." She cocked her head to one side and then the other, going over the words in her mind. "This isn't easy…."

Steve frowned. "It's been a pleasure to meet me, but the chemistry just isn't there and you'd like to let me down gently and be done with it."

"No!" she hurried to assure him.

"Oh."

The disappointment in his tone came as a mild shock. Then she understood. "You…expected a different kind of woman and—"

"Not in the least. If the truth be known, I'm pleasantly surprised."

She swallowed. "I wish you hadn't said that."

"Why not?"

"Because..." She dragged in a deep breath. "Because I'm not the person you think I am. I mean..." This was proving even more difficult than it should have. "I didn't write those letters."

Steve's eyes narrowed. "Then who did?"

"My daughter and her friend."

"I...see."

Meg's fingers crushed the linen napkin in her lap. "You have every reason to be upset. It was an underhanded thing to do to us both."

"You didn't know anything about this?"

"I swear I didn't. I would've put a stop to it immediately if I had."

Steve reached for his water and drank thirstily. "I would have, too."

"I want you to know I intend to discipline Lindsey for this. I can only apologize..." She stopped midsentence when she saw his shoulders moving with suppressed laughter. "Steve?"

"I didn't write those letters, either. The ones from me."

"What?" Disbelief settled over Meg. "You mean to say you didn't respond to the ad in Dateline?"

"Nope. My romantic little sister did. Nancy's on this kick about seeing me married. I don't understand it, but—"

"Just a minute," Meg said, raising her hand. "Let me see if I've got this straight. You didn't place the ad in Dateline."

"You've got it."

"Then why are you here?"

He shrugged. "Probably for the same reason you are. I figured you were some lonely heart seeking companionship and frankly I felt bad that Nancy had led you on like this. It isn't your fault my crazy sister thinks it's time I got married."

He paused when their meals were delivered.

Meg dug into her chicken with gusto. Irritation usually made her hungry. She stabbed a carrot slice with her fork.

"So you felt sorry for me?" she said, chewing the carrot vigorously.

He looked up, apparently sensing her irritation. "No sorrier than you felt for me."

He had her there.

"It's the reason you showed up, isn't it?" he pressed.

She agreed with a nod. "When did you find out about this dinner date?"

"This morning. You?"

She glanced at her watch. "About two hours ago."

Steve chuckled. "They didn't give you much opportunity to object, did they?"

"Actually they got the days mixed up and went into a panic. I don't suppose you happened to read any of the letters or e-mails they wrote?"

"As a matter of fact I did. Interesting stuff."

"I'll bet." She stabbed one of the potato pieces with her fork. "You should know that not everything they said was the truth." She put the potato in her mouth and chewed.

"So you don't actually run an eight-minute mile."

"No…"

"Nine minutes?"

"I don't exactly run, and before you ask me about carbs and fat grams, you can forget everything Lindsey told you about those, too. And for the record, my appendix is in great shape."

Steve chuckled. "What did Nancy tell you about me?"

"Since I've only read tidbits of your letters and e-mails, I can't really say."

"Oh?" His voice fell noticeably.

"As I recall, your sister did suggest that your life's quite empty and you're looking for something to fill your lonely nights—" she paused for effect "—until you realized it wasn't *something* you were searching for but *someone*."

His jaw tightened. "She said that?"

"Yup." Meg took some pleasure in telling him that.

"Well, that's a crock of bull. I certainly hope you didn't believe it."

Meg smiled. "Not really. Lindsey didn't mean any harm, you know."

"Nancy, either, although I'd like to throttle her. The kid's nineteen and she's got romance and marriage on her mind. Unfortunately, it's me she's trying to marry off."

"Lindsey thinks I'm lost and lonely, but I'm perfectly content with my life."

"Me, too."

"Why ruin everything now?"

"Exactly," Steve agreed with conviction. "A woman would want to change everything about me."

"A man would string me along until he found someone prettier and sexier. Besides," Meg added, "I have no intention of becoming a pawn in some ploy of my daughter's."

"Nancy can take a flying leap into Green Lake before I'll let her arrange my love life," Steve told her adamantly. "I certainly intend to marry, but on *my* time—not when my kid sister ropes me into a lonely-hearts-club relationship."

"I feel the same way."

"Great." Steve grinned at her, and Meg had to admit he had a wonderful smile. It lit up his eyes and softened his features. "Shall we drink to our agreement?"

"Definitely."

Steve attracted the waitress's attention and ordered a bottle of wine.

Meg was astonished by the ease with which they could talk, once all the pretense between them had been resolved. She told him about her bookstore and liked hearing about his body shop. They lingered over coffee and dessert, and not until it became apparent that the restaurant was about to close did they get up to leave.

"I enjoyed myself," Meg said as they strolled to the door.

"Don't sound so surprised."

"Frankly, I am."

He laughed. "I guess I am, too."

The valet brought her Ford Escort to the front of the restaurant and held open her door.

"Thank you for a lovely dinner," she said, suddenly feeling shy and awkward.

"The pleasure was all mine."

Neither of them made an effort to move. The valet

checked his watch and Meg glanced at him guiltily. Steve ignored him and eventually so did Meg.

"I guess this is goodbye," she said, wishing now that she hadn't made such a big issue about not being her daughter's pawn.

"Looks that way."

She lowered her eyes, fighting the enticement she read in his. "Thanks again."

Steve traced his finger along her jaw. His work-calloused fingertip felt warm against her skin. If they hadn't been standing under the lights of a fancy French restaurant with a valet looking on, Meg wondered if he would've kissed her. She wanted to think he might have.

On the drive home, she dismissed the idea as fanciful. It had been a long time since she'd been wined and dined, that was all. And an even longer time since she'd been kissed…

Sensation after sensation traveled across her face where he'd touched her. Smile after smile flirted with her mouth at the memory of his lips so close to hers. She wouldn't forget the date or the man anytime soon. That was for sure.

"Well, how'd it go?" Nancy demanded. His teenage sister met Steve at the door. Her eyes were wide with curiosity as she followed him inside.

Steve looked at his watch and frowned. "What are you still doing up?"

Nancy's face fell. "You asked me to wait for you, so we could talk."

Steve slid his fingers through his hair. "I did, didn't I?"

"You're much later than you thought you'd be."

He didn't respond, unwilling to let his sister know how much he'd enjoyed himself. "I'm furious with you for what you did," he said, forcing his voice to sound gruff with irritation.

"I don't blame you," she agreed readily enough.

"Haven't you got an exam to study for or something?" he asked, although he knew very well she didn't. Nancy attended the nearby University of Washington. She was staying with Steve for the summer, since their parents were now living in Montana.

"You liked her, didn't you?"

Nancy sounded much too smug to suit Steve.

"And no, I don't have any exams to study for, and you know it. They ended two weeks ago." Since then, she'd taken a summer job at the university library.

"So you've decided to stay in Seattle and make my life miserable."

"No, I've decided to stay in Seattle and see you married. Come on, Steve, you're thirty-eight! That's getting up there." She flopped down on the sofa and sat with her legs underneath her, as if she planned to plant herself right there until he announced his engagement.

The problem, Steve decided, was that Nancy was the product of parents who'd never expected a second child and had spoiled her senseless. He was partially to blame, as well, but he'd never thought she'd pull something like this.

"You work too hard," she said. "Loosen up and enjoy life a little."

"You're going to write Meg Remington a formal letter of apology." He refused to back down on this.

"Okay, I'll write her." All at once she was on her feet. "When are you seeing her again?"

"I'm not."

Nancy fell back onto the sofa. "Why not?"

Darned if Steve could give her an answer. He and Meg had made that decision early on in their conversation, and for the life of him he couldn't remember why.

"Because," he growled. "Now leave me alone."

Nancy threw back her head and laughed. "You like her. You really, really like her."

Meg sat in the back storeroom and rubbed her aching feet. The new shoes pinched her toes, but this was what she got for buying them half a size too small. They were on sale and she loved them, although the store had been out of size eights. Even knowing her feet would pay the penalty later, Meg had chosen to wear them today.

Laura stuck her head through the door and smiled when she saw her. "A beautiful bouquet of flowers just arrived for you," she said.

"For me?"

"That's what the envelope said."

"Who from?"

"I didn't read the card, if that's what you're asking, but Lindsey's here and she grabbed it and let out a holler. My guess is the flowers are from Steve."

"Steve." Pain or no pain, Meg was on her feet. She hobbled to the front of the store and found her fifteen-year-old daughter grinning triumphantly.

"Steve Conlan sent flowers," she crowed.

"So I see." Meg's fingers shook as she removed the card from the small envelope.

"He said, and I quote, 'You're one special woman, Meg Remington. Love, Steve.'"

The bouquet was huge, with at least ten different varieties of flowers all arranged in a white wicker basket. It must have cost him easily a hundred dollars.

"We agreed," she whispered.

"Agreed to what?" Lindsey prodded.

"That we weren't going to see each other again."

"Obviously he changed his mind," Lindsey said, as excited as if she'd just discovered a twenty-dollar bill in the bottom of her purse.

Unwilling to trust her daughter's assessment of the situation, Meg stared at her best friend.

"Don't look at me," Laura said.

"I'm sure you're wrong," Meg said to Lindsey, her heart still beating a little too fast.

"Why else would he send flowers?" Lindsey asked calmly.

"He wanted to say he was glad we met, that's all. I don't think we should make something out of this," she said. "It's just…a courtesy."

"Call him," Lindsey pleaded.

"I most certainly will not!"

"But, Mom, don't you see? Steve's saying he likes you,

but he doesn't want to pressure you into anything unless you like him, too."

"He is?" Whatever confidence she'd felt a moment earlier vanished like ice cream at a Fourth of July picnic.

"The next move is yours."

"Laura?"

"I wouldn't know," her fickle friend said. "I've been married to the same man for twenty-six years. All this intrigue is beyond me."

"I agree with your daughter," a shy voice said from the other side of the counter. "You should call him."

It was Meg's customer, Judith Wilson. Meg wasn't sure she should listen to the older woman who faithfully purchased romance novels twice a month. Judith was a real romantic and would undoubtedly read more into the gesture than Steve had intended.

"See?" Lindsey said excitedly. "The ball's in your court. Steve made his move and now he's waiting for yours."

Meg didn't know what to do.

"It's been three days," Lindsey reminded her. "He's had time to think over the situation, and so have you."

"Call him," Laura suggested. "If for nothing more than to thank him for the flowers."

"Yes, call him," Judith echoed, clutching her bag of books.

"It's the least you can do." Once more it was her daughter offering advice.

"All right," Meg said reluctantly. The flowers were gorgeous, and thanking him would be the proper thing to do.

"I'll get his work number for you," Lindsey volunteered, pulling the Yellow Pages from behind the cash register.

The kid had Steve's shop number faster than directory assistance could have located it.

"I'll use the phone in the back room," Meg said. She didn't need several pairs of ears listening in on her conversation.

She felt everyone's eyes on her as she hurried into the storeroom. Her hand actually shook as she punched out the telephone number.

"Emerald City," a gruff male voice answered.

"Hello, this is Meg Remington calling for Steve Conlan."

"Hold on a minute."

"Of course."

A moment later, Steve was on the line. "Meg?"

"Hello, Steve. I know you're busy, so I won't take up much of your time. I'm calling to thank you for the flowers."

A long pause followed her words. "Flowers? What flowers?"

Three

"You mean you don't know anything about these flowers?" Meg cried, her voice raised. Steve could see that he hadn't done a very good job of breaking the news, but he was as shocked as she was.

"If you didn't send them, who did?" Meg demanded.

It wasn't difficult to figure that one out. "I can make a wild guess," he said with heavy sarcasm. He jerked his fingers through his hair, then glanced at the wall clock. It was close to quitting time. "Can you meet me?"

"Why?"

Her blatant lack of enthusiasm irritated him. He'd been thinking about her for three days. Nancy was right—he liked Meg Remington. She was a bit eccentric and a little on the hysterical side, but he was willing to overlook that. During their time together, he'd been struck by her intelligence and her warmth. He'd wished more than once that they'd decided to ignore the way they'd been thrown together and continue to see each other. Apparently Meg suffered no such regrets and was pleased to be rid of him.

"Why do you want to meet?" she repeated, lowering her voice.

"We need to talk."

"Where?"

"How about a drink? Can you get away from the store in the next hour or so?"

She hesitated. "I'll try."

Steve mentioned a popular sports bar in Kent, and she agreed to meet him there at five-thirty. His spirits lifted considerably at the prospect of seeing her again. He must've been smiling as he hung up because his foreman, Gary Wilcox, cast him a puzzled look.

"I didn't know you had yourself a new girlfriend," Gary said. "When did this happen?"

"It hasn't." The last thing Steve needed was Gary feeding false information to his sister. Nancy and her outrageous ideas about marrying him off was enough of a problem, without Gary encouraging it.

"It hasn't happened *yet,* you mean," Gary said, making a notation in the appointment schedule.

Steve glanced over his shoulder, to be sure Gary wasn't making notes about the conversation he'd had with Meg. He was getting paranoid already. A woman did that to a man, made him jumpy and insecure; he knew that much from past experience.

An hour later Steve sat in the bar, facing a big-screen television with a frosty mug of beer in his hand. The table he'd chosen was in the far corner of the room, where he could easily watch the front door.

Meg walked in ten minutes after him. At least Steve thought it was Meg. The woman carried a tennis racket and wore one of those cute little pleated-skirt outfits. He hadn't realized Meg played tennis. He knew she didn't run and disliked exercise, but...

Steve squinted and stared, unsure. After all, he'd only seen her the one time, and in the slinky black dress she'd looked a whole lot different.

Meg solved his problem when she apparently recognized him. She walked across the room, and he noticed that she was limping. She slid into the chair beside him, then set the tennis racket on the table.

"Lindsey knows," she announced.

Steve's head went back to study her. "I beg your pardon?"

"My daughter figured it out."

"Figured what out?"

"That I was meeting you," she said in exasperated tones. "First, I called you from the back room at the store, so our conversation could be private."

"So?"

She glared at him. "Then I made up this ridiculous story about a tennis game I'd forgotten. I haven't played tennis in years and Lindsey knows that. She immediately had all these questions. She saw straight through me." She pulled the sweatband from her hair and stuffed it in her purse. "She's probably home right now laughing her head off. I can't do this.... I could never lie convincingly."

"Why didn't you just tell your daughter the truth?" He was puzzled by the need to lie at all.

Meg's look of consternation said that would've been impossible. "Well…because Lindsey would think the two of us meeting meant something."

"Why? You told her I didn't write those letters and e-mails, didn't you?"

"No."

"Why not?"

Meg played with the worn strings of the tennis racket as her eyes avoided his. "I should have…. I mean, this is crazy."

"You can say that again." He tried to sound nonchalant and wondered if he'd managed it. He didn't think so. He was actually rather amused by the whole setup. Her daughter and his sister. The girls were close in age and obviously spoke the same language.

"Lindsey's still got romantic ideas when it comes to men and marriage, but…" Meg paused and chanced a look at him. "She really stepped over the line with this stunt."

"What did you say about our date?"

Meg's hands returned to the tennis racket. "Not much."

Steve hadn't been willing to discuss the details of their evening together with Nancy, either. Nothing had surprised him more than discovering how attractive he'd found Meg Remington. It wasn't solely a sexual attraction, although she certainly appealed to him.

Whenever he'd thought about her in the past three days, he'd remember how they'd talked nonstop over wine and dessert. He remembered how absorbed she'd been in what he was saying; at one point she'd leaned forward and then realized her dress revealed a fair bit of cleavage. Red-faced, she'd pulled back and attempted to adjust her bodice.

Steve liked the way her eyes brightened when she spoke about her bookstore and her daughter, and the way she had of holding her breath when she was excited about something, as if she'd forgotten to breathe.

"Your sister—the one who wrote the letters—is the same one who sent the flowers?" Meg asked, breaking into his thoughts.

Steve nodded. "I'd bet on it."

Meg fiddled with the clasp of her purse and brought out a small card, which she handed him.

Steve raised his arm to attract the cocktail waitress's attention and indicate he wanted another beer for Meg.

"I shouldn't," she said, reaching for a pretzel. "If I come home with beer on my breath, Lindsey will know for sure I wasn't playing tennis."

"According to you, she's already figured it out."

She slid the bowl of pretzels closer and grabbed another handful. "That's true."

Steve opened the card that had come with the flowers and rolled his eyes. "This is from Nancy, all right," he muttered. "I'd never write anything this hokey."

The waitress came with another mug of beer and Steve paid for it. "Do you want more pretzels?" he asked Meg.

"Please." Then in a lower voice, she added, "This type of situation always makes me hungry."

She licked the salt from her fingertips. "Has my daughter, Lindsey, been in contact with you?"

"No, but then I wouldn't know, would I?"

Meg was holding the pretzel in front of her mouth. "Why wouldn't you?"

"Because Lindsey would be writing to Nancy."

Meg's head dropped in a gesture of defeat. "You're right. Much more of this craziness and heaven only knows what they could do to our lives."

"We need to take control," Steve said.

"I totally agree with you," was her response. She took a sip of her beer and set the mug down. "I shouldn't be drinking this on an empty stomach—it'll go straight to my head."

"The bar's got great sandwiches."

"Pretzels are fine." Apparently she'd realized that she was holding the bowl, and she shoved it back to the center of the table. "Sorry," she muttered.

"No problem."

He saw her wince and recalled that she'd been limping earlier. "Is there something wrong with your foot?"

"The shoes I wore to work were too tight," she said, speaking so quietly he had to strain to hear.

"Here," he said, reaching under the table for her feet and setting them on his lap.

"What are you doing?" she asked in a shocked voice.

"I thought I'd rub them for you."

"You'd do that?"

"Yes." It didn't seem so odd to him. The fact was, he hated to see her in pain. "Besides, we need to talk over how we're going to handle this situation. I have a feeling that we'll have to be in top mental form to deal with these kids."

"You're right." She closed her eyes and purred like a well-fed kitten when he removed her tennis shoes and kneaded her aching feet.

"Feel better?" he asked after a couple of minutes.

She nodded, her eyes still closed. "I think you should stop," she said, sounding completely unconvincing.

"Why?" He asked the question, but he stopped and bent down to pick up her shoes, which he'd placed on the floor.

"Thank you," Meg said. She looked around a little self-consciously as she slipped her shoes back on and tied the laces.

Feeling somewhat embarrassed by his uncharacteristic response to her, Steve cleared his throat and picked up his beer. "Do you have any ideas?" he asked.

She stared at him as if she didn't know what he was talking about, then straightened abruptly. "Oh, you mean for dealing with the kids. No, not really. What about you? Any suggestions?"

"Well, we're agreed that we've got to stop letting them run our lives."

"Exactly. We can't allow them to force us into a relationship."

He nodded. But if that was the case, he wondered, why did he experience the almost overwhelming desire to kiss her? All of a sudden, it bothered him that they were discussing strategies that would ensure the end of any contact between them.

He imagined leaning toward her, touching his lips to hers....

There's something wrong with this picture, Conlan, he said to himself, but he couldn't keep from studying her—and picturing their kiss.

He'd been wrong about her face, he decided. She was beautiful, with classic features, large eyes, a full mouth. He'd trailed his finger down the curve of her cheek the first time they'd met, and now he did so a second time, mentally.

She knew what he was thinking. Steve swore she did. The pulse in her throat hammered wildly and she looked away.

Steve did, too. He didn't know what was happening, didn't want to know. He reached for his beer and gulped down two deep swallows.

What on earth was he doing? Rubbing her feet, thinking about kissing her. He didn't need a woman messing up his life!

Especially a woman like Meg Remington.

"So you met Steve again," Laura said. They sat on a bench in Lincoln Park enjoying huge ice-cream cones. A ferry eased toward the dock at Fauntleroy.

"Who told you that?" Meg answered, deciding to play dumb.

"Lindsey, who else? You really didn't think you fooled her, did you?"

"No." Clearly she had no talent for subterfuge.

"So tell me how your meeting went."

Meg didn't answer. She couldn't. She wasn't sure what, if anything, she and Steve had accomplished during their meeting at the bar. They'd come up with a plan to dissuade his sister and her daughter, but the more hours that passed, the more ridiculous it seemed. And Meg's willingness, indeed her eagerness, to see Steve again was disturbing.

In retrospect she saw that it'd been a mistake for them to get together. All she could think about was how he'd lifted her legs onto his lap and rubbed the tired achiness away. There'd been a sudden explosion of awareness between them. A living, breathing, throbbing awareness.

Rarely had Meg wanted a man to kiss her more. Right in the middle of a sports bar, for heaven's sake! It was the craziest thing to happen to her in years. That of itself was distressing, but what happened afterward baffled her even more.

Melting ice cream dripped onto her hand and Meg hurriedly licked it away.

"Meg?" Laura said, studying her. "What's wrong?"

"Nothing," she said, laughing off her friend's concern. "What could possibly be wrong?"

"You haven't been yourself the last couple of days."

"Sure I have," she said, then deciding it was pointless to go on lying, she blurted out the truth. "I'm afraid I could really fall for this guy."

Laura laughed. "What's so awful about that?"

"For one thing, he isn't interested in me."

This time Laura eyed her suspiciously. "What makes you think that?"

"Several things."

Laura bit into her waffle cone. "Name one."

"Well, he wanted to meet so we could figure out a way to keep the kids from manipulating our lives."

"That sounds suspiciously like an excuse to see you again," Laura murmured.

"Trust me, it wasn't. Steve did everything but come right out and say he's not interested in me."

"You're sure about this?"

"Of course I am! There was ample opportunity for him to suggest we get to know each other better, and he didn't." She'd assumed Steve had experienced the same physical attraction she had, but maybe she'd been wrong.

Lindsey and Brenda had insisted she still had it. All Meg could say was that recent experience had proven otherwise. Whatever *it* was had long since deserted her.

"Did it occur to you that he might've been waiting for *you* to suggest something?" Laura asked.

"No," Meg told her frankly. Steve wasn't a man who took his cues from a woman. If he wanted something or someone, he'd make it known. If he wanted to continue to see her, he would've said so.

"There's got to be more than that."

"There is." Meg took a deep breath. "I was just getting ready to tell you. Steve came up with the idea originally, but I agreed."

"To what?"

Meg stood and found the closest garbage receptacle to dump what remained of her ice cream. "Before I tell you, remember I'd been drinking beer on an empty stomach." Okay, she'd had the pretzels.

"This doesn't sound promising," Laura said.

"It isn't." Drawing in another deep breath, she sat down on the park bench again. "We realized that the louder we protested and the more often we said we weren't attracted to each other, the less likely either Lindsey or Nancy will believe us."

"There's a problem with this scenario," Laura muttered.

"There is?"

"Yes. You *are* interested in Steve. Very interested." Laura gave her a look that said Meg hadn't fooled her.

Meg glanced away. "I don't want to confuse the issue with that."

"All right, go on," Laura said with a wave of her hand.

"Steve thinks the only possible way we have of convincing Lindsey that he's not the right person for me is if he starts dating me and—"

"See?" Laura said triumphantly. "He's interested. Don't you get it? This idea of his is just an excuse."

"I doubt it." Meg could see no reason for him to play games if he truly wanted a relationship with her. "You can come over this evening if you want and see for yourself."

"See what?"

"Steve's coming to meet Lindsey."

"To your house?"

"Yes."

Laura grinned widely. "R-e-a-l-l-y," she said, dragging out the word.

"Really. But it isn't what you think." Because if Laura did believe Steve wanted to pursue something with Meg, her friend was in for a major disappointment.

Meg got home an hour later. Lindsey had taken Steve's visit seriously. She'd cleaned the house, baked cookies and wore her best jeans. A dress would've been asking too much.

"Hello, sweetheart."

"Mom," Lindsey said, frowning at her watch. "Do you have any idea what time it is?"

"Yeah."

"Don't you think you should shower and change clothes? Steve will be here in an hour and a half."

"I know." She supposed she should reveal more enthusiasm, if only for show, but she couldn't make herself do it. This had been Steve's idea and she'd agreed, but she still wasn't convinced.

"I was thinking you should wear that sundress we bought last year with the pretty red-rose print," Lindsey suggested. "That and your white sandals." She studied her mother critically. "I wish you had one of those broad-brimmed sun hats. A pretty white one would be perfect. Very romantic."

"We'll just have to make do with the sombrero Grandpa bought you in Mexico," Meg teased.

"Mother," Lindsey cried, appalled. "That would look stupid!"

Meg sighed dramatically, for effect. "I don't know how I managed to dress myself all these years without you."

She thought—or hoped—that her daughter would laugh. Lindsey didn't. "That might be the reason you're still single. Have you considered that?"

This kid was no help when it came to boosting her confidence.

"You're a great mother," Lindsey said, redeeming herself somewhat, "but promise me you'll never go clothes-shopping without me again."

Rather than make rash pledges she had no intention of keeping, Meg hurried up the stairs and got into the shower. The hot water pulsating against her skin refreshed her and renewed her sense of humor. She could hardly wait to see Lindsey's face when she met Steve.

With a towel tucked around her, Meg wandered into her bedroom and examined the contents of her closet. In this case, Lindsey was right; the sundress was her best choice. She wore it, Meg told herself, because it looked good on her and *not* because Lindsey had suggested it.

Her daughter was waiting for her in the living room. The floral arrangement Steve, or rather Nancy, had sent was displayed in the middle of the coffee table.

Lindsey had polished the silver tea set until it gleamed. The previous time Meg had used it was when Pastor Delany came for a visit shortly after Meg's father died.

The doorbell chimed. Lindsey turned to her mother with a grin. "We're ready," she said, and gave her a thumbs-up sign.

Meg had assumed she knew what to expect, but when she opened the front door her mouth sagged open.

"Steve?" she whispered to the man dressed in a black leather jacket, tight blue jeans and a white T-shirt. "Is that you?"

He winked at her. "You expecting someone else?"

"N-no," she stammered.

"Invite me in," he said in a low voice. As she stepped

aside, he walked past her and placed his index finger under her chin, closing her mouth.

He stood in the archway between the entry and her living room, feet braced apart. "You must be Lindsey," he said gruffly. "I'm Steve."

"You're Steve?" Lindsey sounded uncharacteristically meek.

"Lindsey, this is Steve Conlan," Meg said, standing next to him.

Steve slid his arm around Meg's waist and planted a noisy kiss on her cheek. He glanced at Lindsey. "I understand you're the one who got us together. Thanks."

"You're welcome." Lindsey's eyes didn't so much as flicker. She certainly wasn't about to let them read her thoughts. "You, uh, don't look anything like your picture."

Steve refused to take his eyes off Meg. He squeezed her waist again. "The one I sent was taken a while back," he said. "Before I went to prison."

Lindsey gasped. "Prison?"

"Don't worry, sweetheart. It wasn't a violent crime."

"What…were you in for?" Lindsey asked, her voice shaking.

Steve rubbed the side of his jaw, shadowed by a dark growth of beard. "If you don't mind, I'd rather not say."

"Sit down, Steve," Meg said from between gritted teeth. Talk about overkill. Any more of this and everything would be ruined.

"Would you care for coffee?" Lindsey asked. Her young voice continued to tremble.

"You got a beer?"

"It's not a good idea to be drinking this early in the afternoon, is it?" Meg asked sweetly.

Steve sat down on the sofa, balancing his ankle on the opposite knee. He looked around as if he were casing the joint.

Meg moved to the silver service. "Coffee or tea?"

"Coffee, but add a little something that'll give it some kick."

Meg poured coffee for him and added a generous dollop of half-and-half. He frowned at the delicate bone china cup as though he wasn't sure how to hold it.

Lindsey sat down on the ottoman, her eyes huge. "I...you never said anything about prison."

"Don't like to mention it until people have a chance to meet me for themselves. Some of 'em tend to think the worst of a person when they hear he's had a felony conviction."

"A...felony." Lindsey snapped her mouth shut, inhaled deeply, then said in a subdued tone, "I see."

"The flowers are lovely." Meg fingered a rosebud from the bouquet.

Steve grinned. "My probation officer told me women like that sort of thing. Glad to know he was right." He sipped his coffee and made a slurping sound. "By the way, you'll be glad to hear I told him about you and me, and he did a background check on you and said it was fine for us to see each other."

"That's wonderful," Meg said with enthusiasm that wasn't *entirely* faked.

Steve set aside the delicate cup and leaned forward, his elbows on his knees. He stared at Lindsey and smiled. "Yup, I got to thank you," he said. "I realize your mother's upset with you placing that ad and everything. It's usually not a good idea to fool someone like that, but I wasn't being completely honest with you, either, so I guess we're even."

Lindsey nodded.

"Your mother's one special woman. There aren't a lot of females who'd be willing to overlook my past. Most women don't care that I've got a heart of gold. Your mama did. We sat down in that fancy restaurant and I took one look at her pretty face and I knew she was the woman for me." He rubbed the side of his unshaven jaw and laughed. "I do have to tell you, though, that when you suggested Chez Michelle, I was afraid Meg might be too high maintenance for someone like me."

"I'm sorry…" Lindsey floundered with the apology. "I didn't know."

"Don't you worry. Your mama was worth every penny of that fancy dinner. Just getting to know her and love her—why, a man couldn't ask for a prettier gal." He eyed her as if she were a Thanksgiving feast, then moistened his lips, implying it was all he could do to keep from grabbing her right then and there and kissing her.

"Steve…" Meg muttered.

"Sorry," he said, and seemed to pull himself together. "Earl Markham, my probation officer, says I've gotta be careful not to rush things. But I look at your beautiful eyes and I can't help myself."

"Yes, well..."

"You didn't tell me how good-looking your daughter is," he said, as though Meg had purposely been holding out on him.

"Lindsey's my pride and joy," Meg said, beaming her daughter a smile.

"I got plenty of friends who wouldn't mind meeting a good-looking girl like you." He winked at Lindsey, suggesting that all he needed was one word from her and he'd make the arrangements immediately.

"Absolutely not!" Meg said, forgetting this was just a game. "I won't have you introducing my daughter to your friends."

Steve's eyes widened with surprise and he held up his right hand, as if taking an oath. "Sorry, I didn't mean to offend. You don't want Lindsey dating any of my buddies, fine, I'll see it never happens."

"Good." Meg had to acknowledge that Steve was an excellent actor. He almost had *her* believing him. She suspected that was because he'd turned himself into the man she'd half expected to meet that night.

Steve smacked his lips. "I gotta tell you when I first saw Meg in that pretty black dress, my heart went all the way to the floor. She's the most beautiful woman I've seen since I was released." His eyes softened as his gaze fell on Meg.

"Released?" Lindsey squeaked.

"From prison," Steve clarified, his gaze immediately returning to Meg.

It would help considerably if he didn't look so sincere, Meg thought.

"Yes, well…" she said, standing. But once she was on her feet, she wasn't sure what to do.

"I'll bet you want me to take you on that motorcycle ride I been promising you," Steve said, downing the last of his coffee.

"Mom's going on a motorcycle with you?" Lindsey asked, swallowing visibly.

"I'd better change clothes," Meg said, eager to escape so she could speak to Steve alone.

"No need," Steve said. "You can ride sidesaddle if you want. I brought my Hog. There's plenty of room, although I gotta tell you, I been dreaming about you sitting behind me, wrapping your arms around my waist. You'll need to hold on tight, honey, real tight." His eyes didn't waver from hers, and the sexual innuendo was unmistakable.

"Yes, well…" Either the room had grown considerably warmer or Meg was in deep trouble.

Judging by the look of disgust Lindsey cast her, she could see it was the latter.

"I think I'll change into a pair of jeans, if it's all the same to you."

"Sure," Steve said, wiping the back of his hand across his mouth. "Just don't keep me waiting long, you hear?"

"I won't," she promised.

Meg rushed toward the stairs, anxious to get away.

Steve reached out to stop her. His hand closed over her shoulder and he brought her into his arms. She gasped in shock. Without giving her time to recover, he lowered his mouth to hers.

It was all for show, but that didn't keep her heart from fluttering wildly. Her stomach muscles tightened at the unexpectedness of his kiss.

Her lips parted and she slid her arms tightly around his narrow waist.

Steve groaned and Meg was afraid the hunger she felt in him was a reflection of her own. By the time he dragged his lips from hers they were both panting. Speechless, they stared at each other.

"I'll…I'll be right back," she managed to whisper. Then she raced up the stairs as if demons were in hot pursuit. On the way she caught a glimpse of Lindsey staring after her, open-mouthed.

Four

The minute they were alone outside, Meg hit Steve across his upper arm, hurting her hand in the process. Biting her lip, she shook her fingers several times, then clutched her aching hand protectively with the other.

"What was that for?" Steve demanded, glaring at her.

"You overdid it," she snapped, barely understanding her own outrage.

"I had to convince her I was unsuitable, didn't I?"

Meg bristled. "Yes, but you went above and beyond what we discussed. All that business about me being so beautiful," she muttered as she walked to the driveway where he'd parked the Harley-Davidson. She climbed onto the leather seat without thinking.

"I thought I did a great job," Steve argued. A smile raised the edges of his mouth.

"That's another thing," she said, unable to stop looking at him. "Was that kiss really necessary?"

"Yes," he said calmly, but Meg could tell that he didn't take kindly to her rebuke. "Lindsey needed to see me in action," he insisted.

"You frightened my daughter half out of her wits as it was. There was no need to…"

Steve's eyes widened, then softened into a smile. "You liked the kiss," he said flatly. "You liked it and that scared you."

"Don't be ridiculous! It…it was disgusting."

"No, it wasn't." His smile was cocky. He laughed, the timbre low and mildly threatening. "Maybe I should prove how wrong you are."

Meg shifted uncomfortably on the seat. "Let's get this over with," she said, feigning boredom. "You're going to take me out for an hour or so and then drive me back. Right? By the way, where did you get the motorcycle?"

He advanced a step toward her. "It's mine."

"Yours?" He was exactly the kind of man her mother had warned her about, and here she was flirting with danger. He moved a step closer and she held herself rigid.

"You don't know much about men, do you?" he asked, his voice low and husky.

"I was married for nearly six years," she informed him primly. He was close now, too close. She kept her spine stiff and her eyes straight ahead. If the motorcycle was his, it was reasonable to assume the leather jacket belonged to him as well. The persona he'd taken on, the criminal element, might not be too far from the truth.

"You haven't been with a man since, have you?"

She felt his breath against her flushed face. "I refuse to answer questions of a personal nature," she returned, her voice hoarse and low.

"You haven't," he said confidently. "Look at me, Meg."

"No. Let's get this ride over with."

"Look at me," he repeated.

She tried to resist, but the words were warm and hypnotic. Against her better judgment, she twisted toward him. "Yes?" she asked, her heart pounding so hard she thought it might leap right through her chest.

He wove his hands into her hair and tilted her head back so that she couldn't avoid staring up at him. His gaze bored relentlessly into hers.

"Admit it," he whispered. "You enjoyed the kiss." His eyes were compelling, she admitted reluctantly, resisting him every step.

"How like a man—everything's about ego," she said in an effort to make light of what had happened. "Even a silly little kiss."

Steve frowned.

There was a fluttery feeling in the pit of her stomach, the same feeling that had attacked her when he'd kissed her by the staircase. She felt vulnerable and helpless.

"It wasn't little and it wasn't silly. But it was what we both wanted," he said in a deceptively normal voice.

"You're crazy," she murmured, hurrying to assure him that he'd been wrong. Very wrong. She lowered her eyes, but this proved to be a tactical error. Before she realized what he intended, he was kissing her again.

Meg wanted to protest. If she'd fought him, struggled, he might have released her. But her one weak objection came in the form of a moan, and it appeared to encourage rather than dissuade him.

All at once it was important to get closer. A moment later she was kneeling on the leather cushion and Steve had slipped his arms around her middle. They didn't stay there long. He glided his hands along her back, urging her more tightly against him.

Meg didn't require much inducement. Her body willfully molded itself to his. Then, abruptly, her eyes fluttered open and with a determined effort she broke free. Steve's arms tightened before he relaxed and finally released her.

The look on his face was one of shock.

For her own part, Meg was having a difficult time breathing. Sensations swarmed through her. Unwanted sensations. Steve made her feel as if she'd never been kissed before, never been held or loved. Never been married or shared intimacies with a man.

She blinked, and Steve backed away. He frowned and raked his fingers through his hair, apparently sorting out his own troubled emotions.

"I suppose you expect me to admit I enjoyed that," she said with more than a hint of belligerence. These feelings frightened her. The fact that she'd reacted to him could easily be explained. Good grief, she was a normal woman— but this giddy, end-of-the-world sensation wasn't anything she'd ever experienced.

"You don't have to admit to a damned thing," he said. He climbed onto the Hog and revved the engine aggressively.

"Stop," she cried, shouting above the noise. She waved a hand to clear away the exhaust.

"What's wrong now?" he snapped, twisting around to look at her.

"Nothing…. Just go slow, all right?"

Separated by only a couple of inches, Meg felt him tense. "I'm not exactly in a slow mood."

"I guessed as much."

She didn't know what he intended as he expertly maneuvered the motorcycle out of her driveway. Mortified, Meg glanced up and down the street, wondering how many of her neighbors had witnessed the exchange between her and Steve. Fortunately Lindsey wasn't at the front window watching as Meg had half feared.

"Hang on," he shouted.

She placed her hands lightly on either side of his waist, hoping to keep the contact as impersonal as possible—until they turned the first corner. From that moment on, she wrapped her arms around him as tightly as she could.

Meg was grateful that he chose not to drive far. He stopped at a park less than a mile from her house. After he'd eased into a parking space, he switched off the engine and sat motionless for a couple of minutes.

"You okay?" he asked after a while.

"I'm fine. Great. That was…fun." She was astonished at her new talent for telling white lies. She was far from fine. Her insides were a mess, although that had almost nothing to do with the motorcycle ride. Her heart refused to settle down to a normal pace, and she couldn't stop thinking about their kisses. The first time had been traumatic, but it didn't compare to her nearly suffocating reaction to his second kiss.

Steve checked his watch. "We'll give it another five minutes and then I'll take you back to the house. That should give Lindsey enough time to worry about you without sending her into a panic."

"Perfect," she said brightly—a little too brightly.

"Then tomorrow afternoon I'll pick you up after work and you can do your thing with my sister."

Although he couldn't see her, she nodded. Meg only hoped her act for Nancy would be as convincing as Steve's had been with Lindsey.

"After that, we won't need to see each other again," Steve said. "As far as I'm concerned, it isn't a minute too soon."

Meg felt much the same way. She was just as eager to get him out of her life.

Wasn't she?

It hadn't been a good day. Steve would've liked to blame his foul mood on work-related problems, but everything at Emerald City Body Shop had run like clockwork. The one reason that presented itself was Meg Remington.

He'd known from the first night that getting involved with her would mean trouble. Sure enough, he was waist-deep in quicksand, and all because he hadn't wanted to hurt the woman's feelings.

Okay, that accounted for their dinner date, but afterward…what happened was no one's fault except his own. Donning his leather jacket and jeans and playing the role of the disgruntled ex-con had been fun. But then he had to go and do something stupid.

The stupid part was because of the kiss. He'd been a fool to force Meg to admit how good it had been. This was what he got for allowing his pride to stand in the way.

Well, Steve had learned his lesson. The next time he was tempted to kiss Meg, he'd go stand in the middle of the freeway. Man, oh man, she could kiss. Only she didn't seem to realize it. Much more of that kissing and he would've been renting a hotel room.

Not Meg, though. Oh, no. She acted as outraged as a nun. Apparently she'd forgotten that men and women did that sort of thing. Enjoyed it, too. Looked forward to doing it again.

The woman was insane, and the sooner he could extract her from his life, the better. He didn't need this. Who did?

One more night, he assured himself. He was taking Meg to meet Nancy this evening, and when they were finished, it would be over and they'd never have to see each other again. If she played her cards right. He'd done his part.

Despite his sour mood, Steve grinned. He'd never forget the look of shock and horror in Lindsey's eyes when he walked into the house. Her jaw had nearly hit the carpet when he put his arms around Meg's waist and announced that he was an ex-con. He wouldn't forget the look in Meg's eyes, either.

Steve laughed outright.

"Something funny?" Gary Wilcox asked.

Steve glared at his foreman. "Not a thing. Now get back to work."

At six o'clock, Steve pulled into the parking space in the alley behind Meg's bookstore. He didn't like the idea of sneaking around and going to her back door, but that was what Meg wanted and far be it from him to argue. He'd be well rid of the woman—at least that was what he kept trying to tell himself.

He knocked and waited a few minutes, growing impatient.

The door opened and a woman in black mesh nylons and the shortest miniskirt he'd seen in years stood in front of him. She vaguely resembled Tina Turner. She wore tons of makeup and she'd certainly had her hair done at the same salon as Tina.

"I'm here for Meg Remington," he said, annoyed that Meg had made such a fuss about his coming to the back door and then sent someone else to answer it.

"Steve," Meg whispered, "it's me."

"What the hell?" He jerked his head back and examined her more thoroughly. "We're meeting my sister," he reminded her stiffly, "not going to some costume party."

"I took my cue from you," she said. "Good grief! You arrived at my door looking like a Hell's Angel—what did you expect *me* to do?"

Steve rubbed his face. Darned if he knew anymore. All he wanted was to get this over with. "Fine. Let's get out of here."

"Just a minute. I need to change shoes."

She slipped out of a perfectly fine pair of flats and into

spiky high heels that added a good five inches to her height. Steve wondered how she'd manage to walk in those things. She might as well have been on stilts.

He led her around to his car and opened the door. He noticed that she sighed with what sounded like relief once she was inside the car.

"I didn't know what I was going to do if you brought that motorcycle again." She tugged down her miniskirt self-consciously.

"For the record, I don't often take it out."

She looked relieved, but why it should matter to her one way or the other, he had no idea.

"Just remember," he said, feeling obliged to caution her. "Nancy's a few years older than Lindsey. She won't be as easily fooled."

"I'll be careful about overkill," she mumbled, "unlike certain people I know."

The drive took an eternity, and it wasn't due to heavy traffic, either. In fact, when Steve looked at his watch he was surprised at what good time they'd made. What made the drive so troublesome—he hated to admit this—was Meg's legs. She'd crossed them, exposing plenty of smooth, shapely thigh. Her high heels dangled from the ends of her toes.

Steve appreciated women as a whole—some more than others, of course. He didn't focus on body parts. But it was torture to sit with Meg in the close confines of his car and keep his eyes off her legs. The woman looked incredible. If only she'd keep her mouth shut!

Nancy was standing on the porch when Steve pulled into the driveway.

"This is where your sister lives?" Meg asked.

"It's my home," Steve answered, certain she was about to find something wrong with it.

"Your home?" She sounded impressed. "It's very nice."

"Thanks." He turned off the engine. "Nancy's quite a bit younger than I am—a surprise for my mom and dad. She attends college at the University of Washington nine months out of the year. Our parents retired to Montana a couple of years back."

"I see. Does Nancy live with you?"

"Not on your life," he said, climbing out of the car. "She's in residence during the school year. She got a job here this summer and I agreed to let her stay with me a few months. A mistake I don't plan to repeat anytime soon."

Steve was watching for his sister's reaction when he helped Meg out of the car. To her credit, the nineteen-year-old didn't reveal much, but Steve knew her well enough to realize she was shocked by Meg's appearance.

"You must be Nancy," Meg said in a low, sultry voice.

"And you must be Meg," Nancy said, coming down the steps to greet her. "I've been dying to meet you."

"I hope I'm not a disappointment." This was said in a soft, cooing tone, as if she couldn't have tolerated disillusioning Steve's little sister. She clasped Steve's arm and he noticed for the first time that her nails—now two inches long—were painted a brilliant fire engine red.

Nancy held open the door and smiled in welcome. "Please, come inside."

Meg's high heels clattered against the tile entryway. Steve looked around, pleased to note that his sister had cleaned up the house a bit.

"Oh, Stevie," Meg whined, "you never told me what a beautiful home you have." She trailed one finger along the underside of his jaw. "But then, we haven't had time to discuss much of anything, have we?"

"Make yourself comfortable," Steve said and watched as Meg chose to sit on the sofa. She sat, crossing her legs with great ceremony. Then she patted the empty space beside her, silently requesting Steve to join her there. He glanced longingly at his favorite chair, but moved across the room and sat down next to Meg.

The minute he was comfortable, Meg placed her hand possessively on his knee and flexed her nails into his thigh. Inch by provocative inch she raked her nails up his leg until it was all Steve could do not to pop straight off the sofa. He caught her hand and stopped her from reaching what seemed to be her ultimate destination.

Her expression was mildly repentant when she looked at him, but Steve knew her well enough to know the action had been deliberate.

"I thought you might be hungry before Steve takes you to dinner, so I made a few hors d'oeuvres," Nancy said and excused herself.

"What are you doing?" Steve whispered the minute his sister was out of the room.

"Doing? What do you mean?" She had wide-eyed innocence down to an art.

"Never mind," he muttered as Nancy returned from the kitchen carrying a small silver platter.

"Those look wonderful," Meg said sweetly when his sister put the tray on the coffee table in front of them. "But I couldn't eat a thing."

To the best of his knowledge it was the first time his sister had cooked from the moment she'd moved in with him, and he wasn't about to let it go to waste. He chose a tiny wiener wrapped in some kind of crispy dough and tossed it in his mouth.

"You shouldn't have gone to all this trouble," Meg told his sister.

Nancy sat across the room from them, apparently at a complete loss for words.

"I suspect you're wondering about all these letters and e-mails I wrote," Meg said, getting the conversation going. "I hope you aren't unhappy with me."

"No, no, not at all," Nancy said, rushing the words together.

"It's just that I've come to know what people *really* want from me by the things they say." She turned, and with the tip of her index finger wiped a crumb from the corner of his mouth. Her tongue moistened her lips and Steve's insides turned to mush.

"I learned a long time ago what men want from a woman," Meg continued after a moment, "especially when I went to work for a phone sex line. Most of the guys are just looking for a woman to talk dirty to them."

"I see." Nancy folded her hands primly in her lap.

"There was the occasional guy who was looking for a good girl to shock, of course. I got very talented at acting horrified." She made a soft, gasping sound, then laughed demurely.

"Why…why would someone like you place an ad in Dateline?" Nancy asked, nervously brushing the hair from her face.

"Well, first," Meg said, holding his sister's gaze, "it's just about the only way someone like me can meet anyone decent. But it wasn't your brother who answered the ad, now, was it?"

"No, but—"

"Not that it matters," Meg said, cutting her off. "I was tired of my job and all those guys asking me to say those nasty things, and I didn't want to start working on my back again."

"On your…back," Nancy repeated.

"I'm sorry, sugar. I didn't mean to shock you. I've got a colorful past—but that doesn't mean I'm a bad girl. I've got a heart just brimming with love. All I need is the right man." Her gaze wandered to Steve and was long and deliberate. "Your brother's given me a reason to dream again," Meg said softly. "Lots of people think women like me don't have feelings, but they're wrong."

"I'm sure that's true," Nancy said tentatively.

"I knew I chose right when I found out your brother has his own business."

"He's struggled financially for years," Nancy was quick to tell her. "It's still touch and go. He lives from one month to the next." Nancy glared at him pointedly. "Don't you, Steve?"

"Not anymore. I'm more than solvent now," Steve tossed in for good measure, struggling not to laugh. He was enjoying this.

Meg tightened her arm around his. "I can see how well Stevie's doing for himself. He's wonderful," she said, refusing to look away. The adoration on her face embarrassed him.

"Why, Steve here could make enough money to keep me in the lifestyle to which I'd like to become accustomed." She laughed coyly.

"Ah…" It sounded to Steve as if his sister was close to hyperventilating.

"Of course, I wouldn't take anything from him without giving in return. That wouldn't be fair." She snuggled closer to his side and gave him a look so purely sexual Steve was convinced he'd embarrass them all.

"There are things I could teach your brother," Meg said in a husky voice full of sexual innuendo. She acted as though she was eager to get started right that moment and the only thing holding her back was propriety. Her breathing grew heavy—and if he didn't know better he'd think she actually *had* worked for one of those disreputable phone services.

Soon he was having a problem controlling his own breathing.

"Steve!" Nancy snapped.

He turned his attention back to his sister, staring at her blankly.

"Didn't you hear Meg?" she asked.

He shrugged. He knew the two women were talking, but he'd barely noticed their conversation.

"Meg's talking about moving in with you," Nancy said through clenched teeth.

"I don't mean to rush you, darling'," Meg whispered. Leaning forward, she licked his earlobe with the tip of her tongue.

Hot sensation shot down his spine.

Meg threw back her head and laughed softly, then whispered just loudly enough for Nancy to hear, "I have an incredibly talented tongue."

Nancy closed her eyes as if she couldn't bear to watch another minute of this. Frankly, Steve didn't know how much more he could take himself.

"I think it's time we left for dinner," he said. Otherwise he was going to start believing all the promises Meg was making. Heaven knew, he *wanted* to believe them. The demure bookseller had turned into something completely different. All traces of innocence had disappeared and in their place was the most sexually provocative female he'd ever met. Just being in the same room with her made his blood sizzle.

"You want to leave already?" Meg gave the impression that she was terribly disappointed.

"That's probably best," Nancy muttered, and then realizing what she'd said, hurried to add, "I mean, you two don't want to waste your evening with me, do you?" She frowned at Steve. "You won't be late, will you?"

"No."

"Unfortunately, I'm still working for the phone people," Meg said, "so I won't keep him too long, but I can't promise he'll have much kick left in him when I'm finished."

Apparently thinking herself exceptionally clever, Meg laughed at her own joke.

It wasn't until they were back in the car and on the freeway that Steve recognized how angry he was. It made no sense, but he wasn't exactly rational just then.

"Why are you so mad?" Meg asked about halfway back to the bookstore. They hadn't spoken a word from the time they'd left his house.

"Talk about overkill," he muttered.

"I thought I did a good job," she said.

"You came off like a—"

"I know. That's what I wanted. After meeting me, do you honestly think your sister's going to encourage our relationship?"

"No," he growled.

"I can guarantee you that Lindsey doesn't want me to see you, either. I thought that's what this whole scheme of yours was about."

"It sounded like a good idea at the time." He tightened his hands on the steering wheel. "It seemed like a surefire way to convince your daughter that I was the wrong man for you."

"And your sister that I was equally wrong for you."

Silence settled over them like nightfall. Neither of them seemed inclined to talk again.

Steve edged his car into the alley behind Meg's store and parked his car behind hers.

"I'm not so sure anymore," he said without looking at her.

"About what?"

"The two of us. Somewhere in the middle of all this, I

decided I kind of like you." It hadn't been easy to admit, and he hoped she appreciated what it had cost his pride. "It probably wouldn't have been as obvious if you hadn't made yourself out to be so cheap. That isn't you any more than the rebel without a cause is me."

He wished she'd say something. When she did speak, her voice was timid and small. "Then there was the kiss."

"Kisses," he corrected. "They were pretty great and we both know it," he said with confidence. He knew what his own reaction had been, and she hadn't fooled him with hers.

"Yes," she said softly.

"Especially the one on the motorcycle," he said, prompting her to continue.

"Especially the one on the motorcycle," she mimicked. "Honestly, Steve, you must've known."

His smile was full blown. "I did."

"I…I didn't do a very good job of disguising what I was feeling."

She hadn't, but he was in a gracious mood.

"How about dinner?" he suggested. He was eager to have the real Meg Remington back. Eager to experiment with a few more kisses—see if they were anything close to what his memory kept insisting they'd been.

She hesitated. "I want to, but I can't," she eventually said.

He bristled and turned in the driver's seat to face her. "Why not?"

"I promised Lindsey I'd be home by seven and it's nearly that now."

"Call her and tell her you're going out to dinner with me."

She dragged in a deep breath and seemed to hold it. "I can't do that, either."

"Why not?"

"After meeting you, I promised her we'd talk. She wanted to last evening, and we didn't.... That was my fault. You kissed me," she said, "and I didn't feel like a heart-to-heart with my daughter after that."

"And it's all my fault?"

"Yes," she insisted.

"Do you know what Lindsey wants to discuss?"

"Of course, I know. You. She doesn't want me seeing you again, which is exactly the point of the entire charade. Remember?"

"Yeah," Steve said, scowling.

"Are...are you telling me you've changed your mind?" she asked.

"Yes." He hated to be the one to say it first, but one of them had to. "What about you?"

"I think so."

Steve flattened his hand against the steering wheel. "I swear you're about the worst thing that's ever happened to my ego."

She laughed and rested her hand on his shoulder. The wig she had on tilted sideways and she righted it. "That does sound terrible, doesn't it?"

He smiled. "Yeah. The least you could do is show some enthusiasm."

"I haven't dated much in the last ten years. But if I was going to choose any man, it would be you."

"That's better," he said. He wanted to kiss her. He'd been thinking about it from the moment he'd picked her up.

"Only..." Meg said sadly.

"Only what?" he repeated, lowering his mouth to hers.

Their lips met and it was heaven, just the way he'd known it would be. By the time the kiss ended, Steve was leaning his head against the window of the car door, his eyes closed. It was even more wonderful than he'd remembered, and that seemed impossible.

Meg's head was on his chest, tucked beneath his chin.

"It's too late," she whispered.

"What's too late?"

"We've gone to all this trouble to convince Lindsey that you're all wrong for me."

"I know, but..."

"Do you think Nancy will believe this was all a silly joke?"

"No."

"I think we should end everything right here and now, don't you?" she asked.

Steve stiffened. "If that's what you want."

She moved away from him. "I guess it is," she said, with just a hint of regret.

Five

Lindsey was pacing the living room, waiting for Meg when she walked in the front door.

"Hi, honey," Meg said, trying to sound cheerful yet exhausted—since she'd led Lindsey to believe she was taking inventory at the bookstore and that was why she'd come home so late.

"It's way after seven!" her daughter cried, rushing toward her. "You weren't with Steve, were you?"

"Ah…" Meg wasn't willing to lie outright. Half truths and innuendos were about as far as she wanted to stretch this.

Lindsey closed her eyes and waved her hands vaguely. "Forget it. Don't answer that."

"Honey, what's wrong?" Meg asked as calmly as she could. Unfortunately, she didn't think she sounded all that reassuring. She'd left Steve only moments earlier and was already feeling some regret. After following through with this ridiculous charade, Steve wanted to change his mind and continue seeing Meg. She'd quickly put an end to *that* idea. Now she wasn't sure she'd made the right decision.

"Mom," Lindsey said, her dark eyes challenging, "we need to talk."

"Of course." Meg walked into the kitchen and took the china teapot from the hutch. "My mother always made tea when we had something to discuss." Somehow, the ritual of drinking tea together put everything in perspective. Meg missed those times with her mother.

Lindsey helped her assemble everything they needed and carried it into the dining room. Meg poured them each a cup, once the tea had steeped, and they sat across from each other at the polished mahogany table.

Meg waited, and when Lindsey wasn't immediately forthcoming she decided to get the conversation started. "You wanted to talk to me about Steve, right?"

Lindsey clasped the delicate china cup with one hand and lowered her gaze. "Do you really, really like him?" she asked anxiously.

Meg answered before she took time to censor the question. "Yes."

"But why? I mean, he's nothing like what I thought he'd be." She hesitated. "I suppose this is what Brenda and I get for pretending we were you," she mumbled. "Maybe if you'd read his stuff, you would've been able to tell what kind of guy he really is."

"Steve is actually a fine person." And he was. Or at least the Steve Meg knew.

Lindsey risked a glance at her. "You've said hundreds of times that you don't want me to judge others by outward appearances, but sometimes that's all there is."

"You're worried about me and Steve, aren't you?" Meg said gently.

Lindsey rubbed her finger along the edge of the teacup. "I realize now that what Brenda and I did was really stupid. We linked you up with a guy who has a prison record. We sure were easy to fool," Lindsey said with a scowl. "We're only fifteen years old!"

"But I like Steve," Meg felt obliged to tell her.

Lindsey looked as if she didn't know how to account for that. "I'm afraid he's going to hurt you."

"Steve wouldn't do that," Meg assured her, "but I understand your concern, honey, and I promise you I won't let the situation get out of hand."

Lindsey frowned, stiffened her shoulders and blurted out, "I don't want you to see him again."

"But…"

"I mean it, Mom. This guy is trouble."

Talk about role reversal!

"I want you to *promise* me you won't see Steve Conlan again."

"Lindsey…"

"This is important. You may not understand it now, but I promise you will in the future. There are plenty of other men, law-abiding citizens, who'd give their right arms to meet a woman like you."

Meg stared. She couldn't be hearing this. This sounded

exactly like something her mother had said back when Meg was in high school.

The intense look in Lindsey's eyes softened and she gestured weakly. "The time will come when you'll thank me for this."

"Really?" Meg couldn't resist raising her eyebrows.

"There'll be a boy in my life that you'll disapprove of and I won't understand why," Lindsey went on. "When that happens, I want you to remind me of now."

Meg shook her head—in bafflement and disbelief. "Are you telling me you'd break up with a boy simply because I didn't like him?"

"No," Lindsey said carefully. "But I'd consider it because I know how I feel about you seeing Steve, and I'd understand how you might feel about someone I was dating. Don't get me wrong," she hurried to add, "I don't dislike Steve…. He's kind of cute. It's just that I feel you could do a whole lot better."

"I'll think about it," Meg promised.

Lindsey nodded. "I can't ask for more than that."

Her daughter had behaved just as Meg had predicted. This had gone precisely according to plan. But Meg didn't feel good about it. If anything, she felt more depressed following their conversation than before.

She didn't have any talent when it came to relationships, Meg decided, as she finished putting away the dinner dishes later that evening. Steve had come right out and told her he'd had a change of heart, and she'd bungled everything. Instead of admitting that she felt the same way he did, she'd trampled all over his ego.

Meg turned to the kitchen phone, tempted to call him. It couldn't end like this, with such confusion, such uncertainty about what she really wanted. What *they* wanted.

Never had an evening passed more slowly. It seemed to take Lindsey hours to go to bed, and by then Meg was yawning herself.

As soon as Meg could be reasonably sure that her daughter was asleep, she tiptoed toward the kitchen phone and dialed Steve's number, her heart pounding. Finally she heard his groggy voice.

"Steve?" she whispered. "Thank goodness it's you. I didn't know what I was going to do if Nancy answered."

"Meg? Is that you?" He sounded surprised to hear from her, and none too pleased.

She bristled. "How many other women do you have phoning you at eleven o'clock at night?"

He didn't respond right away, and when he spoke his voice definitely lacked welcome. "I thought you said it wasn't a good idea for us to see each other."

"I…I don't know what I want."

"Do you expect me to make your decisions for you?"

"Of course not." This wasn't going well. In fact, it was going very badly. She probably should've waited until she'd had time to figure this out a little more clearly.

"Is there a reason you called?" he asked gruffly.

"Yes," she said, sorry now that she'd phoned him. "I wanted to apologize for being abrupt earlier. I…can see now that I shouldn't have called."

Having said that, she carefully replaced the receiver. For a long moment she stared at the phone, feeling like an idiot.

She'd turned away to head up the stairs when the phone rang, jolting her. Quickly she grabbed it before the noise could wake Lindsey.

"Hello," she whispered.

"Meet me." It was Steve.

"I can't leave Lindsey."

"Why not? She's in bed, isn't she?"

"Yes, but…"

"Write her a note. Tell her you're going to the grocery store."

How reasonable he made it sound—as if she usually did her shopping in the middle of the night.

"She won't even know you're gone," Steve said.

Meg closed her eyes. They'd been together only a few hours earlier, and yet it felt as if they'd been apart for weeks.

Her stomach twisted. Then—before she could change her mind—she blurted out, "All right, but I can't stay long."

"Fair enough."

They agreed to meet in the Albertson's parking lot. The huge store was open twenty-four hours a day. Meg had been shopping there for years. The note she left Lindsey said she'd gone to pick up some milk—that classic excuse—but it was exactly what she intended to do.

She sat in her car until she saw Steve pull into the nearly empty lot. Uncertain she was doing the right thing, she got out and waited for him.

Steve parked in the spot next to hers. They stood facing each other for a moment, neither speaking.

"I can't believe we're doing this," she said.

It appeared she wasn't the only one with doubts. Steve's face was blank, emotionless. "Me neither."

They walked into the store together and reached for grocery carts. Meg's had a squeaky wheel. The sound echoed through the cavernous store.

The deli was closed, but Steve was able to get them each a cup of coffee from the friendly night manager. They parked their empty carts and sat at a small white table in the deli section. Neither seemed inclined to speak.

She felt encouraged that Steve had phoned her back, but she suspected he regretted it now.

"You know what you said earlier?" she began.

"I said lots of things earlier. Which particular thing are you referring to?"

Meg guessed his sarcasm was warranted. After all, she'd wounded his ego, and he wasn't giving her the chance to do it again. "About the two of us, you know, dating."

"You said Lindsey wouldn't like it."

"She doesn't," Meg said. "She asked me not to see you again."

His gaze pinned hers. "Did you agree?"

"Not…entirely."

His eyes narrowed with a frown. "You'd better explain."

"Well, as you've already surmised, Lindsey isn't keen on me seeing you. Which is exactly the reason you stopped by the house and did your biker routine, right? Well, it worked. She's worried that you're the wrong man for me." It would've helped if he hadn't bragged about his prison record and mentioned his parole officer's name. But now didn't seem to be the time to bring that up.

"Did you or did you not promise her you wouldn't see me again?"

"Neither." Meg sipped from the disposable cup and grimaced at the taste of burned coffee.

"Then what *did* you say to her?"

Meg lifted one shoulder in a shrug. "That I'd think about it."

"Have you?"

Propping her elbows on the table's edge, Meg swirled the black liquid around the cup and avoided looking at Steve. "I called you, didn't I?"

"I still haven't figured out why."

That was the problem: she hadn't, either. Not really. "I guess it's because you have a point about seeing each other again."

"Oh, yeah?" He gave her a cocky grin.

Her anger flared. "Would you stop it?"

"Stop what?" he asked innocently.

"The next thing I know, you're going to ask me how much I enjoyed kissing you."

Steve smiled for the first time. "It wouldn't hurt to know."

"All right, since it means so much to you, I'll admit it. No man's ever kissed me the way you do. It scares me— but at the same time I wish it could go on forever." Having admitted this much, she supposed she might as well say it all. "My marriage left me wondering if I was…if I was capable of those kinds of feelings…." She paused and lowered her eyes. "I was afraid I was, you know, frigid," she said in a choked whisper.

She stared down at her coffee, then took a sip, followed by several more, as if the vile stuff were the antidote to some dreaded illness.

The last thing she expected her small confession to provoke in Steve was a laugh. "You're joking!"

She shook her head forcefully. "Don't laugh. Please."

His hand reached for hers and their fingers entwined. "I wasn't laughing at you, Meg," he said gently. "You're one of the most sensual women I've ever met. Trust me, if you're frigid—and there's a word I haven't heard in years—then I'm a monk."

Meg looked up and offered him a fragile smile. It astonished her that this man who'd known her for only a few days could chase away the doubts that had hounded her through the years after her divorce.

He cleared his throat. "I, uh, don't think you should look at me like that."

"Like what?"

"Like you want me to kiss you."

Her eyes drifted shut. "Maybe I do.... That's what makes everything so complicated. I'm really attracted to you. I haven't felt like this before—not ever, not even with my ex-husband, and like I said, that scares me."

He stood up, still holding Meg's hand, and tugged her to her feet.

"Where are we going?" she asked.

"Someplace private," he said, scanning the store. He led

her through the frozen food section, past the bakery and into a small alcove where the wine was kept. With her back to the domestic beer, he brought her into his arms and covered her mouth with his.

Their kiss was rough with need, but she wasn't sure whose need was greater. Meg could feel Steve's heart racing as hard as her own. She supposed she should've pulled away, ended the kiss, stepped out of his arms. But Meg didn't want that.

Steve yawned. He was *so* tired. With good reason. It'd been almost three before he'd gone to bed and four before he'd been able to fall asleep. His alarm had gone off at six.

He arrived at the shop and made a pot of coffee. He mumbled a greeting when Gary got in.

"I hope you're in a better mood than you were yesterday," his foreman told him. "What's wrong with you, anyway?"

Steve checked over the job orders for the day. "Women," he muttered in explanation and apology.

"I should've guessed. What's going on?"

"You don't want to hear this," he said and headed for the garage.

"Sure I do," Gary said, following him. "I don't suppose this has anything to do with Nancy, does it?"

Steve glared at him. "What do you know about my sister?"

"Not much," Gary said and held up both hands. "Just what you said about her fixing you up with some woman. It's none of my business, but you and this woman seem to be hitting it off just fine."

Steve continued to glare at him. "What makes you say that?"

Gary laughed. "I haven't seen you this miserable in years. Which probably means you've fallen for her. Why don't you put yourself out of your misery? Shoot yourself and be done with it."

Frowning, Steve turned away. The kid was a smartass, although now that Steve thought about it, Gary might have come up with the perfect solution.

It was noon before Steve had a chance to go into his office. He made sure no one was looking, then closed the door and reached for the phone.

"Book Ends, Laura speaking," a woman said in a friendly voice.

"Is Meg available?" he asked, sounding as businesslike as possible.

"May I ask who's calling?"

Steve hesitated. "Steve Conlan."

"One minute, please."

It took longer than that for Meg to get on the line. "Steve, hi." She seemed tired but happy to hear from him. That helped.

"How are you?" he asked, struggling to hold back a yawn.

"Dead on my feet. I'm not as young as I used to be."

"Does Lindsey know you slipped out of the house last night?"

"No, but I should never have stayed out that late."

Steve didn't have any argument there. They'd left the Albertson's store when a stock boy stumbled upon them in the wine section, embarrassing Meg no end—although Steve had rather enjoyed the way her blush had brightened her cheeks.

With no other idea of where to take her at that hour, Steve had driven down to Alki Point in west Seattle, where they sat on the beach and talked.

They hadn't discussed anything of earth-shattering importance, but he discovered that they had a great deal in common. Mostly, he discovered that he liked Meg. He was already well aware of what Meg, the sensuous and beautiful woman, was capable of doing to him physically. Last night, he learned about Meg, the person.

They hadn't kissed again. Steve was convinced they both knew how dangerous kissing had become. It wouldn't take much for their kisses to lead to more…a *lot* more. And when that happened, he didn't plan to have it take place on a public beach.

He didn't know where the time had gone, but when he'd looked at his watch he'd been shocked. Meg, too. It was after three in the morning. They'd rushed their farewells without making arrangements to see each other again.

"When can we get together?" he asked.

"I don't know…."

Was this how it was going to be? Would they have to start over each and every time they met? "Would you rather we didn't meet again?" he asked.

"No," she said immediately.

"We've got to make some decisions," he said, angry

with himself for not saying anything about it on that moonlit beach. They'd discussed so many different things, from politics to movies to lifelong dreams, yet hadn't talked about their own relationship.

"I know."

"Would tonight work?" he asked. "Same time?"

She hesitated and he gritted his teeth with impatience.

"Okay." The longing in her voice reassured him.

"Fine," he said, relieved. "I'll pick you up at your house at eleven."

"I have to go now."

"Yeah. Me, too."

Steve replaced the receiver and glanced up to find Nancy standing in his office doorway, her arms folded in disapproval.

"Was that Meg?" she demanded.

"That's none of your business," Steve said sharply.

"We need to talk about her and I'm tired of you putting me off."

"I'm not discussing Meg Remington with you."

"How could you date someone like her?" Nancy asked, her face wrinkled in disgust.

"Might I remind you that you were the one who introduced us?"

"Yes, but she deceived me. Steve, be serious! Can you honestly imagine introducing her to Mom and Dad?"

"Yes," he answered calmly.

Nancy threw her arms in the air. "This is your problem. You're thinking with your you know what."

"Nancy!"

"It's true!"

"Stay out of my business. Understand?"

"But…"

"I make my own decisions," Steve said forcefully.

"And your own mistakes," Nancy muttered, walking out of the room.

"We're both crazy," Meg said, sitting next to Steve in his car. She sipped from a can of cold soda, enjoying the sweet taste of it.

"Candidates for the loony bin," he agreed.

"I wasn't sure I'd be able to get away," Meg confessed. "Brenda's spending the night with Lindsey, and those two are going to be up half the night."

"Did you tell them you were leaving the house?"

"No," she said, "but I left them a note. Just in case… Although I'm hoping they won't come downstairs. Oh, and this time I should remember to bring home some milk."

"I was thinking Lindsey and I should have another meeting," Steve began. "Only this time I want you to bring her to the shop. I'll show her around and explain that the whole biker, ex-con routine was a joke." He waited, then looked at Meg. "What do you think?"

"I'm afraid hell hath no fury like a teenager fooled."

"That's what I was afraid you were going to say." Steve finished his drink and placed his arm around her shoulder. "One thing's for sure. I'm through with sneaking around in the middle of the night."

Meg covered her mouth as she yawned. "I'm too old for this."

"You and me both."

Meg finished her soda, too, and leaned back against Steve, his chest supporting her back. She didn't dare close her eyes for fear she'd fall asleep.

"Nancy isn't any too happy about me seeing you, either."

"I'll talk to her, explain everything." Except that, like Lindsey, Steve's sister probably wouldn't be too pleased.

"It's settled, then," Steve said. "I'll talk to Lindsey and you'll talk to Nancy. Neither one of them is going to enjoy being the butt of a joke, but it wasn't like we planned this. Besides, it serves them right for manipulating us like they did."

"You'd think they'd be pleased," Meg inserted. "Their plan worked—not the way they wanted, mind you, but we're seeing each other and that's the whole point. Right?"

Steve chuckled and stroked her hair. "Right."

"I wish it wasn't like this," Meg whispered.

Steve kissed the top of her head. "So do I."

Meg smiled, twisting in his arms so they faced each other.

Steve's hands lingered on her face. His mouth was so close she could feel his breath against her cheek. A shiver of awareness skittered down her spine.

Meg closed her eyes and lifted her mouth to Steve's. He hesitated for a fraction of a second, as if he had second thoughts about what might happen next.

His kiss was warm and gentle. But his gentleness didn't last long. There was a hunger in Steve, a hunger in Meg that flared to life like a fire stoked.

"Meg…"

"I know…I know."

"Tomorrow," he said and drew in a deep, even breath.

"Tomorrow," she repeated, but she had no idea what she was agreeing to. She opened her eyes and leaned back. "What about tomorrow?"

"We'll talk to Lindsey and Nancy."

"Okay."

Fifteen minutes later, Steve dropped her off at the house.

It wasn't until he drove away that she realized she'd left her purse in his car. Her purse with the key to her house…

"Damn," she muttered, hurrying into the backyard, hoping Lindsey had forgotten to lock the sliding glass door. She hadn't; it was locked tight.

No help for it—she searched until she found the spare key, hidden under one of the flowerpots on her porch. It'd been there for so many years she wasn't sure it would work.

Luckily it did. As quietly as she could, Meg slipped into the house.

She climbed the stairs and tiptoed into her room. She undressed without turning on the light and was in bed minutes later.

The neighbor's German shepherd barked, obviously from inside their house, and Lindsey looked up from painting her toenails. "There it is again," she said.

"I heard it, too," Brenda said.

"Wolf doesn't bark without a reason."

Ever curious, Brenda walked over to the bedroom

window and peered into the yard below. After a moment, she whirled around. "There's someone in your backyard," she whispered, wide-eyed.

"This isn't the time for jokes," Lindsey said, continuing to paint her toenails a bright shade of pink. "We were discussing my mother, remember?"

Brenda didn't move away from the window. "There *is* someone there."

"Who?"

"It's a man…. Oh, my goodness, come and look."

The panic in her friend's voice made Lindsey catapult to a standing position. Walking on her heels to keep her freshly painted toenails off the carpet, she hobbled toward the window.

Brenda was right; she *did* see someone in the yard. "Turn the lights off," she hissed.

Lindsey's heart lodged in her throat as she recognized the dark form. "It's Steve Conlan!" She saw him clearly in the moonlight; he wasn't even making any attempt to hide.

"What's that in his hand?"

Lindsey focused her attention on the object Steve was carrying. It looked like a purse. Gasping, she twisted away from the window and placed her back against the wall. She gestured wildly toward the phone.

"What's wrong?" Brenda cried. "Are you having an asthma attack?"

Lindsey shook her head. "He broke in to the house and stole my mother's purse." Brenda handed her the phone and Lindsey dialed 911 as fast as her nervous fingers would let her.

She barely gave the operator time to answer. "There's a man in our backyard," she whispered frantically. "He took my mother's purse."

The emergency operator seemed to have a thousand questions she wanted Lindsey to answer. Lindsey did the best she could.

"He's a convicted felon.... I can give you the name of his probation officer if you want. Just hurry!" she pleaded.

"Officers have been dispatched."

"Please, please hurry." Lindsey was afraid that unless the police arrived within the next minute Steve would make a clean getaway.

Steve debated whether he should leave Meg's purse on the front porch. It would be easy enough to tuck it inside the mailbox, but then she might not find it until much later the next day.

He walked around the house to the backyard, thinking there might be someplace he could put it where she'd find it in the morning.

There wasn't.

The only thing he'd managed to do was rouse the neighbor's dog. He would've rung the doorbell and given her the silly thing if there'd been any lights on, but apparently she'd gone to bed. He wasn't especially eager to confront Lindsey, either. Not yet.

He still hadn't made up his mind, when he heard a noise from behind him.

"Police! Freeze!"

Was this a joke? Maybe not—whoever it was sounded serious. He froze.

"Put the purse down and turn around slowly."

Once more Steve did as instructed. With his arms raised, he turned to find two police officers with their weapons drawn and pointed at him.

"Looks like we caught ourselves a burglar," one of them said, switching on a huge flashlight.

"Caught him redhanded," the other agreed.

Six

"If you'd let me explain," Steve said, squinting against the light at the two officers. A dog barked ferociously in the next-door neighbor's yard. A man in pajamas had let the dog out and joined the audience.

"Do you always carry a woman's purse?"

"It belongs to—"

"My mother."

Although Steve couldn't see her face, he recognized the righteous tones as belonging to Meg's daughter. Lindsey and her friend stood beside the two officers and looked as if they'd gladly provide the rope for a hanging.

"Wolf." The neighbour silenced the German shepherd, but made no move to go inside.

"My name's Steve Conlan," Steve said, striving to come across as sane and reasonable. This was, after all, merely a misunderstanding.

"I wouldn't believe him if I were you," Lindsey advised

the officers. "It might not be his real name." Then in lower tones she added, "He has a criminal record. I happen to know for a fact that he's a convicted felon."

"I'm not a felon," Steve growled. "And it *is* my real name. Officers, if you'd give me the opportunity to—"

"His parole officer's name is Earl Markham." Lindsey cut him off, her voice indignant. "He told me himself!"

"I know Earl Markham," the younger of the two police-men said. "And he is a parole officer."

"I know him, too," Steve barked impatiently. "We went to high school together."

"Yeah, right."

The scorn in Lindsey's voice reminded Steve of Meg when she was furious with him. Like mother, like daugh-ter, it seemed.

"If you'd let me explain." Steve tried again, struggling to stay calm. It wasn't easy with two guns aimed at him and a man in pajamas clutching the collar of a huge dog— thank goodness for the fence. Not to mention a couple of teenage girls accusing him of who knew what.

"Don't listen to him," the other girl was saying. "He lies! He had us believing all kinds of things, and all because he thought we were Lindsey's mother."

A short silence followed her announcement. "Say that again?" the older officer muttered. "How well do you know this man?"

"My name's Steve Conlan." Steve tried yet again.

"Which may or may not be his real name." This, too, came from Lindsey's friend.

"If you'll let me get my wallet, I'll prove who I am," Steve assured them. He made an effort to sound vaguely amused by the whole situation. He lowered one arm and started to move his hand toward his back pocket.

"Keep your hands up where I can see them," the older cop snapped.

"What's going on?" The voice drifted down from the upstairs area of the house. A sweetly feminine, slightly groggy voice.

Steve glanced up, and to his great relief saw Meg's face framed in the second-floor window.

"Meg," Steve shouted, grateful that she'd finally heard the commotion. "Tell these men who I am, so they can put their weapons away."

"Steve?" she cried, shocked. "What are you doing at my house?"

"Do you know this man?" the cop asked, tilting his head back and shouting up at Meg.

"Ma'am, would you mind stepping outside?" the second officer asked. He mumbled something Steve couldn't hear under his breath.

"I'll be right down," Meg told them, and Steve watched her turn away from the window.

"Have you been sneaking around seeing my mother?"

"Lindsey, it's not like it seems," Steve said, experiencing a twinge of guilt at the way he'd misled the girl. He'd planned to talk to Meg's daughter soon, but he hadn't intended to do it in front of the police.

"I'd be more interested to find out why he has your mother's purse, if I were you," the second teenager said.

"I already know why he's got Mom's purse," Lindsey said loudly. "He stole it."

"No, I didn't!" Steve rolled his eyes. "I was trying to return it."

"You have my purse?" This was from Meg. "Oh, hello, Mr. Robinson. Hi, Wolf. I think everything's under control here." Man and dog went back inside a moment later.

"My purse!" she said again.

Steve relaxed and lowered his arms. "You left it in my car," he said.

"Thank goodness you found it." Meg, at least, displayed the appropriate amount of appreciation. "I didn't know when I'd get it back."

Now that the flashlight wasn't blinding him and the officers had returned the guns to their holsters, Steve saw Meg for the first time. In fact, he couldn't take his eyes off her. She'd thrown a flimsy cotton robe over her baby-doll pajamas but despite that, they revealed a length of sleek, smooth thigh whenever she moved. The top was low-cut and the robe gaped open and... Meg grabbed the lapels and held them together with both hands. It didn't help much.

Steve was afraid he wasn't the only one who'd noticed Meg's attire. Both officers looked approvingly in her direction. Steve was about to ask the younger of the two to wipe the grin off his face, but he held his breath and counted backward from ten.

He got to five. "Lindsey, go get your mother a coat."

"I don't have to take orders from you," the girl snapped.

Meg blinked and seemed to realize that despite the robe, such as it was, her nightwear left little to the imagination.

In an apparent effort to deflect a shouting match, one officer asked Lindsey a few questions, while the other engaged Steve and Meg in conversation.

"You know this man?" he asked Meg.

"Yes, of course. His name's Steve Conlan."

"Steve Conlan." The officer made note of it on a small pad. "That's what he said earlier."

Steve pulled out his wallet and flipped it open, silently thrusting it out. The cop glanced at it and nodded.

"He didn't steal my purse, either," Meg went on.

Steve cast the other man an I-told-you-so look, but said nothing.

"You went out with Steve behind my back?" Lindsey cried, peering around the second policeman. Her eyes narrowed. "I can't *believe* you'd do something like that— after our talk and everything."

Meg cast her a guilty look. "We'll discuss this later."

But Lindsey wasn't going to be so easily dissuaded. "After our talk, I really, really thought I was getting through to you. Now I see how wrong I was."

"If you'd give me a chance to explain…" Steve began, wanting to avoid an argument between Meg and her daughter.

Static from the police officer's walkie-talkie was followed by a muffled voice. The two men were obviously being dispatched to another location.

"Everything okay here?" the policeman asked Meg.

"It's fine."

"Young lady?"

Lindsey folded her arms and pointed her nose toward the night sky. "All I can say is that my mother's a serious disappointment to me."

"I'm afraid I can't help you there."

"I didn't think you could," she said, shaking her head. "I thought better of her than this—sneaking out at night to see a man of…of low moral fiber."

"Lindsey!"

"Why don't we all go inside and discuss this," Steve suggested. He felt more than a little ridiculous standing in Meg's yard, and he was eager to clear the air between Lindsey and him.

"I have nothing to say to either of you," Lindsey said. She marched into the house, with Brenda scurrying behind.

Steve watched them stomp off in single file and released a deep breath. He was about to apologize for having made such a mess of things, when Meg whirled around to face him.

"I can't believe you!"

Steve ran his fingers through his hair. Meg didn't seem to grasp that this ordeal hadn't exactly been a pleasure for him, either.

"I apologize, Meg." He did feel bad about all the trouble he'd caused, but he'd only been trying to help. When he'd found her purse, returning it had seemed the best thing to do. He didn't want her wondering where it was, and he'd honestly thought he could do it without ending up in jail.

"How dare you tell my daughter to get me a coat."

Steve's head jerked up. His throat tightened with the strength of his anger. "I nearly got myself arrested—thanks to your daughter, I might add—and *you're* upset because I objected to you traipsing around in front of the neighborhood half-naked?"

Meg opened her mouth and then closed it.

"Okay," he amended, "you are wearing a robe, although it's not much of one. Neither of those cops could take their eyes off you. I supposed you enjoyed the attention."

"Don't be ridiculous! I came downstairs as fast as I could, in order to help you."

"You call parading in front of those men like that *helping* me? All I needed was for you to identify me so I could leave. That's all." His words grew louder. He was close to losing his cool and he knew it.

"I think you'd better go," Meg said, pointing in the direction of the street. Steve noticed with satisfaction that her finger shook.

"I'm out of here," he told her, "and not a minute too soon. You might have appreciated the embarrassment I endured trying to do you a favor, but I can see you don't. Which is fine by me."

"Like *you* didn't embarrass *me?*" she shouted.

"You weren't the one who had a gun pointed at you and a kid claiming you were a menace to society."

"Lindsey was only repeating what you'd told her." Meg pushed the hair away from her face, using both hands. "This isn't working."

"Wrong," he said sharply. "It's working all too well. You make me crazy, and I don't like it."

"But…"

"If I'm going to get arrested, I want it to be for someone who's willing to acknowledge the trouble I've gone through for her." Certain he was making no sense whatsoever, Steve stalked over to his car and drove away.

Meg squared her shoulders and drew her flimsy robe more tightly around her as she opened the screen door and walked back inside. The exhaust from Steve's car lingered in the yard, reminding her how angry he'd been when he left.

She was angry, too. And confused.

It didn't help to find Lindsey and Brenda sitting in the darkened living room waiting for her.

"You should both be in bed," Meg told them.

"We want to talk to you first," Lindsey announced, her hands folded on her knees.

"Not tonight," she said shortly. "I'm tired and upset."

"You!" Lindsey cried. "Brenda and I are exhausted, but that doesn't matter. What does is that you broke your word."

"I didn't promise not to see Steve again," Meg told her. She'd been careful about that.

Meg went back to the door and stood in front of the screen, half hoping Steve would return—not knowing what she'd say or do if he did.

"You've been sneaking out of the house to see him, haven't you?"

Meg lifted one shoulder in a shrug.

"You have!" Lindsey was outraged. "When?"

Meg lifted the other shoulder.

"Can't I trust you anymore?"

"Lindsey, Steve's not exactly what he said he was."

"I'll just bet," she muttered. "He's got you fooled, hasn't he? You'd believe anything he says because that's what you *want* to believe. You're so crazy about this guy you can't even see what's right in front of your face."

If she'd been a little less upset herself, Meg might've been willing to set the record straight then and there. "We want to talk to you," Meg told her daughter. "Steve and I, together, and explain everything."

"Never!"

"Mrs. Remington, don't let him fool you," Brenda threw in dramatically.

"Let's not worry about this now," she said as defeat settled over her. "It's late and I have to be at the store early in the morning."

Lindsey stood, her hands clenched at her sides. "I want you to promise me you won't see him again."

"Lindsey, please."

"If you don't, Mom, I'll never be able to trust you again."

"It's time we had a little talk," Nancy said, bringing a steaming cup of coffee to the breakfast table. After the night he'd had, the last thing Steve wanted was a tête-à-tête with his troublesome younger sister.

"No, thanks."

Nancy left the table, taking the coffee with her.

"Hey, I want the coffee."

"Oh." She brought it back and slipped into the chair across from him. "Something's bothering you."

"Nothing gets past you, does it?" He almost scalded his mouth in his eagerness to get some caffeine into his system.

"Can you tell me what's wrong?" She stared at him with big brown eyes that suggested she could solve all his problems, if only he'd let her.

"No."

"It has to do with that Meg, doesn't it?"

Steve mumbled a noncommittal reply. He didn't care to discuss Meg Remington just then. What he'd told Meg was the simple truth—she made him crazy. No woman had ever affected him as powerfully as she did. After the way they'd parted, he doubted they'd see each other again, and damn it all, that wasn't what he wanted.

"She's not the woman for you," Nancy said, her eyes solemn.

"Nancy," he said in a low voice, "don't say any more. Okay?"

She closed her eyes, shaking her head. "You're falling in love with her."

"No, I'm not," he muttered. Cradling the mug in both hands, he tried the coffee again, sipping from the edge to avoid burning his mouth.

"Thou protest too much," she told him, with a sanctimonious sigh. "I'm afraid you've made it necessary for me to take matters into my own hands. Someone's got to look out for your best interests."

Steve lowered the mug and glared at his sister. "What did you do *this* time?"

"Nothing yet. There's this woman, a widow I met on campus, and I'd like you to get to know her. She's nothing like Meg, but as far as I'm concerned…"

"No!" He wasn't listening to another word. The last time his sister had roped him into her schemes he'd met a crazy woman with an even crazier daughter. No more.

"But Steve…"

"You heard me." The chair made a scraping sound against the tile floor as he stood. "I won't be home for dinner."

Nancy stood, too. "When will you be back?"

Steve regarded her suspiciously. "I don't know. Why?"

"Because the least you can do is meet Sandy."

Steve gritted his teeth. "You invited her to the house?"

"Don't worry—I didn't mention you. I wanted the two of you to meet casually. She's nervous about dating again, and I was afraid if I told her about my big, bad brother she'd run in the opposite direction."

"That's what I'm going to do. If you want to work on anyone's love life, you might try your own."

"All right, all right," Nancy said, sounding defeated. "Just stay away from Meg, okay? The woman's bad news."

Steve's laugh was humorless. "You're telling me?"

A week passed. Steve refused to dwell on his confrontation with Meg. He didn't call her and she didn't phone him, either.

He hated to end it all, but he didn't see any other option.

He missed her, though. He tried to tell himself otherwise. Tried to convince himself a man has his pride. Tried not to think about her.

And failed.

Early one afternoon, Nancy came by the shop with a friend. They were on their way to a movie, or so Nancy claimed.

Nancy smiled a little-sister smile and cheerfully asked Steve if he'd give Sandy an estimate on repairing her fender.

Sandy was petite. Cute. A little fragile.

It didn't take Steve long to figure out that this Sandy was the same one Nancy had wanted him to meet. The widow. The woman who'd save him from Meg's clutches.

"Pleased to meet you," Steve said, wiping his greasy hands on the pink cloth he had tucked in his hip pocket.

Nancy smiled innocently, looking pleased with herself.

"I'll have a written estimate for you by the time you two get back here."

"You don't have to work late again, do you?" Nancy asked, not even attempting to be coy.

Steve could already see what was coming. His conniving sister was about to wrangle a dinner invitation out of him. One that meant he'd be stuck entertaining Sandy.

"I'm afraid I'm tied up this evening," he said stiffly.

"Oh, darn. I was hoping you could take Sandy and me to dinner."

"Sorry," he said. "Now, if you'll excuse me…"

"It was a pleasure to meet you, Mr. Conlan."

"The pleasure was mine," he said and turned away.

Unfortunately, it didn't end with Sandy. His sister had several other friends with dented fenders or cracked windshields. They all seemed to need estimates in the days that followed.

"The next time a woman comes in and asks for me, I'm unavailable," he told his crew. Steve made sure that on her next visit Nancy would know he didn't have time for her matchmaking games. He told her as much when she stopped by—alone—a couple of days later.

"I was only trying to help."

"Thanks, but no thanks." He sat at his desk, making his way through the piles of paperwork stacked in front of him.

Nancy expelled a sigh. "You aren't seeing Meg again, are you?"

His hand tightened around the pen. "That's none of your business."

"Yes, it is! A woman like that could ruin your life."

In some ways she already had, but Nancy wouldn't understand. Whenever he met another woman, Steve found himself comparing her to Meg. Invariably everyone else fell short. Far short. He was miserable without her.

Nancy left, and Steve leaned back in his chair, studying the phone. All it would take was one call. He wouldn't have to mention the incident with the police. He could even make a joke of it, maybe buy her a pair of flannel pajamas. The kind that went from her neck to her feet. They'd both laugh, say how sorry they were and put an end to this stalemate.

Then he'd take her in his arms, hold her and kiss her. This was the part he dwelled on most. The reconciliation.

"Steve." Gary Wilcox stuck his head in the office door. Steve jerked his attention away from the phone.

"There's someone here to see you. A woman."

Impatience made Steve's blood boil. "What did I say earlier? I gave specific instructions to tell any of my sister's friends that I'm unavailable."

"But—"

"Is that so hard to understand?"

"Nope," Gary said without emotion. "I don't have a problem doing that, if it's what you really want, but I kinda had the feeling this one's special."

Knowing his foreman had cast an appreciative eye at the widow, Steve suspected it was Sandy who'd dropped by unannounced. "You talk to her."

"Me?"

"Yeah, you."

"What am I supposed to say?"

Steve rubbed a hand down his tired face. Did he have to do everything himself? "I don't know, just say whatever seems appropriate. I promise you Nancy won't be sending any more eligible women to the shop."

"Nancy didn't send this one."

The pen slipped from Steve's hands and rolled across the desk. "Who did?"

"She didn't say. All I got was her name. Meg Remington. I seem to recall hearing it mentioned a time or two—generally when you were upset."

Steve pushed back his chair and slowly stood. His heart reacted with a swift, furious pace. "Meg's here?"

"That's what I've been trying to tell you for the last five minutes."

Steve sank back into the chair. "Send her in."

A mischievous grin danced across Gary's mouth. "That's what I thought you'd say."

Steve stood, then sat back down and busied himself with things on his desk. He wanted Meg to think he was busy. The minute she walked into the room, he'd set everything aside.

A full five minutes passed and still she didn't show up. Steve came out of his office and ran into Gary, who frowned and shook his head. "She's gone."

"Gone?"

Gary nodded. "The only thing I can figure out is that she must've overheard you say you weren't available and left."

Steve muttered a four-letter word and hurried out. He wasn't sure where he'd find her, but he wasn't going to let her walk out of his life.

She wasn't at the bookstore and he didn't see her car at home. He tried the grocery store, too, for good measure. Without success.

It wasn't until nearly seven that he drove to her house again. That he was willing to confront her daughter was a sign of how desperate he'd become.

He stood on her front porch and rang the doorbell. Waiting for someone to answer, he buried his hands deep in his pockets. A preventive action, he realized, to keep from reaching for her the instant she appeared.

"Just a minute," he heard her call.

Then the door opened and Meg was standing there.

His gaze drifted over her. He'd planned to play it cool, casually mention that he was in the neighborhood and heard she'd stopped by the office. Their eyes met, held, and Steve forgot about hiding his feelings. She wore a pretty pale blue summer dress.

"Hello, Steve."

"Hello."

The screen door stood between them.

They continued to stare at each other.

"Can I come in?" he asked. Pride be damned. It'd been cold comfort in the past two weeks. If he had to apologize, or grovel or beg forgiveness, then so be it. He wanted her back in his life.

"Of course." She unlatched the door and pushed it open.

Steve stepped inside. He could barely breathe, never mind think. Pulling her into his arms didn't seem appropriate, but that was all he wanted to do.

"Where's Lindsey?" he managed to ask.

Meg's voice was breathy and uneven. "She's out for the evening."

He needed to touch her. Reaching up, he cupped her cheek in his rough palm. Slowly, Meg closed her eyes and leaned her head into his hand.

"I had to come here," he whispered.

"I'm so sorry. About everything."

"Me, too."

Unable to wait a second longer, Steve folded her in his arms and brought her mouth to his. Gentleness was beyond him, his hunger as great as any he'd ever known.

Meg grabbed his shirt as if she needed an anchor, something to secure her during the wild, sensual storm. He backed her against the door.

Meg gasped, and Steve moved a few inches away. With his hands framing her cheeks, he studied her beautiful face. Her shoulders were heaving, and he realized his own breathing was just as labored.

He rubbed the pad of his thumb across her moist, swollen lips. The action was unhurried—an apology for his roughness, his eagerness.

She moaned softly and he kissed her again. Gently. With restraint. Her arms were around his neck, and Steve had never tasted a sweeter kiss.

"I was going to call," he told her, burying his face in the slope of her neck. "A thousand times I told myself I'd call. Every minute apart from you was torture."

"I wanted to call you, too."

"I'm glad…."

"You were right," Meg confessed. "I should've been wearing something more…discreet."

"I was jealous, pure and simple." He felt her smile against the side of his face and smiled, too.

"I would've been jealous if the situation had been reversed."

"Don't worry. I didn't date a single one of the women Nancy arranged for me to meet."

Meg jerked back. "What women?"

"Ah…it's not important."

"It is to me."

He knew it would've been to him, as well, so he explained. "Nancy felt it was necessary to save me from a loose woman, so she introduced me to some of her friends."

"And you refused to go out with them." Meg sounded pleased.

"All I want to do is talk to Lindsey. Get things straightened out."

"Me, too. But we can't right now."

"So I see."

"Hold me," she said, nestling in his arms. "I don't want you to leave for a long, long time."

Steve planted tiny kisses along the side of her neck, marking his way back to her lips. "When will Lindsey be back?" he whispered.

"She's spending the night at Brenda's."

His hold tightened. "Meg," he said, then kissed her with a hunger he couldn't deny. "I want to make love to you. There's a lot we have to discuss before we make that kind of commitment, but we have an opportunity to do that now, don't we?"

"Mmm."

He kissed her again, pacing himself. "Thank God you dropped in at the office. I don't know how long it would've taken me to come to my senses otherwise."

"The office?" Meg repeated, breaking away from him. "I was never at your office."

Seven

"It doesn't matter if you were at my office or not," Steve said, kissing Meg again. Slowly. Thoroughly.

She couldn't manage even a token resistance, although her mind whirled with questions.

She was starved for the taste of him. Starved for his touch. Starved for *him*. The loneliness had been suffocating. Before she'd met Steve, her life had seemed just fine. Then within a matter of weeks she'd realized how empty everything was without him.

"I've missed you so much," she told him between deep kisses.

"Me, too."

"You should've phoned," she whispered.

"You, too."

"I know."

"I'm crazy about you."

She was so tempted to throw caution to the wind and

make love with this man who excited her so much. Who made her feel alive.

If ever the moment was right it was now, with Lindsey gone until morning.

But…

The questions returned. There'd only been one man in her life, her ex-husband, Lindsey's father, and by the time they'd divorced Meg had felt like a failure as a wife. Inadequate. Unresponsive.

"Steve…Steve." Her fingers were in Steve's hair as his mouth roamed over her throat. "Stop, please."

He went still, his lips pressed against the hollow of her throat. "You want me to stop? Now?"

"Please…for just a minute. Did you say you thought I'd been to your office?" She wanted that confusion cleared up first.

"It's what Gary told me." He raised his head, eyes clouded with passion. "It doesn't matter—I'm here now. I've missed you so much. I can't believe either of us let this go on so long."

"But it does matter," she argued. "Because I wasn't there."

Steve shut his eyes and seemed to be fighting something in himself. Finally, he straightened and eased away from her.

"I'm glad you're here," she whispered. "I've missed you, too. It's just that before we…" She felt as though her face was on fire. How she wished she was more experienced, more sophisticated. "You know."

"Make love," he finished for her.

"Yes… We should come to some sort of understanding. It's like you said—we should talk first."

Steve took her by the hand. He led her into the living room and chose the big overstuffed chair that was her favorite.

He sat and, reaching up, pulled her onto his lap. "So let's talk."

"Okay," she said, hating the way her voice trembled.

"First I want to clear something up. You say you *didn't* stop by my office this afternoon?"

"No. I was at the store until after six."

"I didn't see you there."

"I was in the back room, processing orders." Because she was afraid he'd think she was lying in order to save face, she added, "You can check with Laura if you want."

Steve frowned. "I believe you. Why wouldn't I?" He studied her. "But that isn't why you stopped us just now, is it?"

Meg lowered her gaze. "No," she whispered.

"I didn't think so. Are you going to tell me?"

"Tell you what?" Steve's arm went around her waist. It felt good to be this close to him.

"I suspect your reluctance has to do with your marriage."

"My marriage?"

"It doesn't take a detective to figure out that your ex-husband hurt you badly."

"No divorce is easy," Meg admitted, "but I'm not an emotional cripple, if that's what you mean."

"It isn't." He drew her even closer and kissed her

again. She kissed him back, offering him her heart, her soul, her body…

"I can't seem to keep my hands off you," he murmured. "I wanted to talk to you about your marriage. Instead, I'm a second away from ravishing you."

And she was a second away from letting him.

"It was a friendly divorce," Meg insisted, returning to the subject he'd introduced. It wasn't a comfortable one— but it was safer than touching and kissing and where that would lead.

Steve eyed her suspiciously. "How friendly?" he asked.

"We parted amicably. It was a mutual decision."

"What caused the divorce?"

Meg closed her eyes and sighed. "He had a girlfriend," she said, trying not to reveal her bitterness. For years she'd kept the feelings of hurt and betrayal buried deep.

In the beginning, that had been for Lindsey's sake. Later, she was afraid to face the anger for fear of what it would do to her. "Dave didn't love me anymore," she said, in an unemotional voice. As if it didn't matter. As if it had never mattered.

"What about Lindsey? He abandoned her, too?"

"He knew I'd always be there for her, and I will. He lives in California now."

"What about his commitment to you and his daughter? That wasn't important to him?"

"I don't know—you'd need to ask Dave about that."

"How long did this business with the girlfriend go on before he told you about her?"

"I don't know," she said again. She had her suspicions, plenty of them, but none she was willing to discuss with Steve. "I do know that when Dave got around to telling me he wanted a divorce, she was pregnant."

"In other words, you felt there was nothing you could do but step aside?"

"I had no problem doing that." Maybe if she'd loved Dave more, she would've been willing to fight for him. But by the time Dave told her about Brittany, she wanted out of the marriage. Just plain out.

"So you got divorced."

"Yes, with no fuss at all. He gave me what I wanted."

"And what was that?"

"He was willing to let me raise Lindsey." She shook her head. "It's not what you're thinking."

"And what am I thinking?"

She placed the back of her hand against her forehead and gave him a forlorn look, like the heroine of a silent movie. "That the divorce traumatized me."

"I wasn't thinking that at all," he assured her. "Your marriage had already taken care of that."

Meg dropped her hand, then raised it again to brush away her tears. How well Steve understood.

"It wasn't enough that your husband had an affair. When he walked out on you and Lindsey, he made sure you blamed yourself for his infidelity, didn't he?" She didn't respond, and he asked her a second time, his voice gentle. "Didn't he?"

Meg jerked her head away for fear he'd read the truth in her eyes. "It's over now…. It was all a long time ago."

"But it isn't over. If it was, we'd be upstairs making love instead of sitting here talking. You haven't been able to trust another man since Dave."

"No," she whispered, her head lowered.

"Oh, baby," he said tenderly, gathering her in his arms. "I'm so sorry."

She blinked rapidly in an effort to forestall more tears. "I trust you," she told him, and she knew instinctively that Steve would never betray his wife or walk away from his family.

"You do trust me," he said, "otherwise you wouldn't have let me get this close to you. Just be warned. I intend to get a whole lot closer, and soon."

With anyone else Meg would have felt threatened, but with Steve it felt like a promise. A promise she wanted him to fulfill.

"It's better that we wait to make love," he surprised her by adding.

"It is?" Her head shot up.

"I want to clear the air with Lindsey first," he told her. "Get things settled between us. I'd much rather be her friend than her foe."

"And I'd like to be Nancy's friend, too," Meg said.

He smiled. "Those girls don't know what they started— or where it's going to end."

"Exactly where are we going?" Lindsey asked, staring out the car window.

"I already told you." Meg was losing patience with her daughter.

"To see Steve at work?"

"Yes."

"Work release, you mean."

"Lindsey!" Meg said emphatically. She'd never known her to be this difficult. "Steve has his own business. We both thought if you could see him at work, you'd know that what he told you about being an ex-con was all a farce."

Lindsey remained sullen for several minutes, then asked, "Why'd he say all those things if they weren't true?"

Her daughter had a valid point, but they'd gone over this same ground a dozen times. "We wanted you to dislike him."

Unfortunately Steve's plan had worked all too well. And Meg had obviously done an equally good job with Nancy, because his sister didn't want him continuing to see her, either. What a mess they'd created.

"Why wouldn't you and Steve want me to like him?" Lindsey asked.

"I've already explained, and I don't feel like repeating the story yet again," Meg said. "Suffice it to say I'm not especially proud of our behavior."

Lindsey pouted, but didn't ask any more questions.

Meg pulled into the parking lot at Steve's business and watched as Lindsey took in everything—the well-established body shop, the customers, the neat surroundings.

There were three large bays all filled with vehicles in various states of disrepair. Men dressed in blue-striped coveralls worked on the cars.

"They *all* look like they came straight from a prison yard," Lindsey mumbled under her breath.

"Lindsey," Meg pleaded, wanting this meeting to go well. "At least give Steve a chance."

"I did once, and according to you he lied."

Once more, Meg had no argument. "Just listen to him, okay?"

"All right, but I'm not making any promises."

The shop smelled of paint and grease; the scents weren't unpleasant. There was a small waiting area with a coffeepot, paper cups and several outdated magazines.

"Hello," Meg said to the man standing behind the counter. "I'm Meg Remington. Steve is expecting me."

The man studied her. "*You're* Meg Remington?" he asked.

"Yes."

"You don't look like the Meg Remington who was in here last week."

"I beg your pardon?"

"Never mind, Gary," Steve said, walking out from the office. He smiled warmly when he saw Meg. Lindsey sat in the waiting area, reading a two-year-old issue of *Car and Driver* as if it contained the answers to life's questions.

"Hello, Lindsey," Steve said.

"Hello," she returned in starched tones.

"Would you and your mother care to come into my office?"

"Will we be safe?"

A hint of a smile cracked Steve's mouth, but otherwise he didn't let on that her question had amused him. "I don't think there'll be a problem."

"All right, fine, since you insist." She set aside the magazine and stood.

Steve ushered them into the spotlessly clean office and gestured at the two chairs on the other side of his desk. "Please, have a seat."

They did, with Lindsey perched stiffly on the edge of hers.

"Would you like something to drink?" he asked.

"No, thanks."

Meg didn't think she'd ever seen Lindsey less friendly. It wasn't like her to behave like this. Presumably she thought she was protecting her mother.

"I have a confession to make," Steve said, after an awkward moment. He leaned back in his chair.

"Shouldn't you be telling this to the police?" Lindsey asked.

"Not this time." His eyes connected with Meg's. She tried to tell him how sorry she was, but nothing she'd said had changed Lindsey's attitude.

"I did something I regret," Steve continued undaunted. "I lied to you. And as often happens when people lie, it came back to haunt me."

"I'm afraid I was a party to this falsehood myself," Meg added.

"How do you know it's really a lie?" Lindsey demanded of Meg. "Steve could actually be a convicted criminal. He might be sitting behind that desk, but how do we know if what he says is true?"

Meg rolled her eyes.

"Who are you *really,* Steve Conlan?" Lindsey leaned forward, planting both hands on the edge of his desk.

"I'm exactly who I appear to be. I'm thirty-eight years old. Unmarried. I own this shop and have ten full-time employees."

"Can you prove it?"

"Of course."

A knock sounded on the door.

"Come in," Steve called.

The man who'd greeted her when she first arrived stuck his head inside the door. He smiled apologetically. "Sorry to interrupt, but Sandy Janick's on the phone."

Steve frowned. "Are we working on Sandy's vehicle?" he wanted to know. "I don't remember seeing a work order."

"No, she's that friend your sister was trying to set you up with. Remember?"

"Tell her I'll call her back," Steve said without hesitating.

Meg bristled. He'd admitted that his sister had been playing matchmaker. So Nancy had set him up with another woman. Probably one without a troublesome teenager and a bunch of emotional garbage she was dragging around from a previous marriage. Meg tried to swallow the lump forming in her throat.

"Gary," Steve said, stopping the other man from leaving. "Would you kindly tell Lindsey who owns this shop?"

"Sure," the other man said with a grin. "Mostly the IRS."

"I'm serious," Steve said impatiently.

Gary chuckled. "Last I heard it was Walter Milton at

Key Bank. Oops, there goes the phone again." He was gone an instant later.

"Walter Milton," Lindsey said skeptically. "So you really *don't* own this business."

"Walter Milton's my banker and a good friend."

"So is Earl Markham, your parole officer," Lindsey snapped. "A high school friend, correct?" She shook her head. "I'm afraid I can't believe you, Mr. Conlan. If you were trying to get me to change my mind about you seeing my mother, it didn't work." Then turning to Meg, she said, "I wouldn't trust him if I were you. He's got a look about him…."

"What look?" Meg and Steve asked simultaneously.

"You know—a criminal look. I'm sure I've seen his face before, and my guess is that it was in some post office."

Meg ground her teeth with frustration. "Lindsey, would you please stop being so difficult?"

"I don't think it's a good idea for you to date a man who lies."

"You're right," Steve surprised them both by saying. "I should never have made up that ridiculous story about being a felon. I've learned my lesson and I won't pull that stunt again. All I'm asking is that you give me a second chance to prove myself."

"I don't think so."

Meg resisted throwing her arms in the air.

"You know what really bothers me?" Lindsey went on. "That you'd involve my mother in this stupid scam of yours. That's really low."

"I don't blame you for being angry with me," Steve said, before Meg could respond. "But don't be upset with your mother—it was my idea, not hers."

"My mother wouldn't stoop to anything that underhanded on her own."

Meg's eyes met Steve's and she wanted to weep with frustration.

"I was hoping you'd find it in your heart to forgive me," Steve said contritely, returning his attention to Lindsey. "I'd like us to be friends."

"Even if we were, that doesn't mean I approve of you seeing my mother."

"Lindsey," Meg began. "I—"

"Mom, we can't trust this guy," Lindsey interrupted. "We know how willing he is to lie. And what about that phone call just now?" She pointed at Steve. "Another woman calls and he can hardly wait to get back to her. You saw the expression on his face."

"Don't be ridiculous," Steve snapped. "I'm crazy about your mother. I wouldn't hurt her for the world."

"Yeah, whatever. That's what they all say." Lindsey had perfected the world-weary tone so beloved of teenagers everywhere.

"I've had enough, Lindsey," Meg said sternly. "I think you'd better go wait in the car."

Lindsey leapt eagerly out of her chair and rushed from the office, leaving Steve and Meg alone.

"I'm sorry," she whispered, standing.

"I'll try to talk to her again." Steve walked around the

desk and pulled her into his arms. "All she needs is a little time. Eventually she'll learn to trust me." He raised her hand to his mouth and kissed the knuckles. "But one thing's for sure…."

"What's that?"

"I'm through with sneaking around meeting you. I'm taking you to dinner tonight and I'm coming to the front door. Lindsey will just have to accept that we're dating. In fact, I'll ask her if she'd like to join us."

"She won't," Meg said with certainty.

"I'm still going to ask. She may not like me now, but in time I'll win her heart, just the way I intend to win her mother's."

What Steve didn't seem to understand was that he'd already won hers.

At seven that night, Meg was humming softly to herself and dabbing perfume on her wrists. Steve was due any minute.

The telephone rang, but Meg didn't bother to answer. There was no point. The call was almost guaranteed to be for Lindsey. She heard the girl racing at breakneck speed for the phone, as if reaching it before the second ring was some kind of personal goal.

"Mom!" Lindsey screeched from the kitchen downstairs, reaching her in the master bath.

"I'll be right there," she called back, checking her reflection in the bathroom mirror one last time.

Lindsey yelled something else that Meg couldn't hear.

"Who is it?" Meg asked, coming out of her bedroom and hurrying downstairs.

"I already told you it's Steve," Lindsey said indifferently as she passed her leaving the kitchen.

Meg glanced at her watch and reached for the phone. "Hello."

"Hi," he said, sounding discouraged. "I ran into a problem and it looks like I'm going to be late."

"What kind of problem?" It was already later than her normal dinnertime, and Meg was hungry.

"I'm not sure yet. Sandy Janick phoned and apparently she's got a flat tire...."

"Listen," Meg said with feigned cheerfulness, "why don't we cancel dinner for this evening? It sounds like you've got your hands full."

"Yes, but..."

"I'm hungry right now. It's no big deal—we'll have dinner another night."

Steve hesitated. "You're sure?"

"Positive." She was trembling so badly it was difficult to remain standing. Steve and Sandy. She suspected Nancy had arranged the flat tire, but if Steve couldn't see through that, then it was obvious he didn't want to. "It's not a problem," Meg insisted.

"I'll give you a call tomorrow."

"Sure.... That would be great." She barely heard the rest of the conversation. He kept talking and Meg hoped she made the appropriate responses. She must have, because a couple of minutes later he hung up.

Closing her eyes, Meg exhaled and replaced the receiver.

"Mom?"

Meg turned to face her daughter.

"Is everything okay?"

She nodded, unable to chase away the burning pain that attacked the pit of her stomach and radiated out.

"Then how come you're so pale?"

"I'm fine, honey. Steve and I won't be going out to dinner after all." She tried to sound as if nothing was amiss, but her entire world seemed to be collapsing around her. "Why don't we get a pizza? Do you want to call? Order whatever you want. Okay?"

She was overreacting and knew it. If Steve was doing something underhanded, he wouldn't tell her he was meeting Sandy Janick. He'd do the same things Dave had done. He'd lie and cheat.

"I'm going to change my clothes," Meg said, heading blindly for the stairs.

She half expected Lindsey to follow her and announce that she'd been right all along, that Steve wasn't to be trusted. But to Meg's astonishment, her daughter said nothing.

"I knew if anyone could help Sandy with her flat tire it would be you," Nancy said, smiling benevolently at her older brother.

Steve glanced at his watch, frustrated and angry with his sister—and himself. She'd done it again. She'd manipulated him into doing something he didn't want to do.

Instead of spending the evening with Meg, he'd been trapped into helping these two out of a fix.

Leave it to his sister. Not only had Nancy and Sandy managed to get a flat, but they'd been on the Mercer Island floating bridge in the middle of rush-hour traffic. Steve had to arrange for a tow truck and then meet them at his shop. From there, they'd all ended up back at the house, and Sandy had made it clear that she was looking for a little male companionship. There was a time Steve would've jumped at the chance to console the attractive widow. But no longer.

"I can't tell you how much I appreciate your help," Sandy told him now. "Thank you so much."

"You're welcome." He looked pointedly at his watch. It was just after nine, still early enough to steal away and visit Meg. Lindsey would disapprove, but that couldn't be avoided.

The girl was proving to be more of a problem than Steve had expected. She was downright stubborn and unwilling to give him the slightest bit of credit. Well, she was dealing with a pro, and Steve wasn't about to give up on either of the Remington women. Not without a fight.

"You're leaving?" Nancy asked as Steve marched to the front door.

"Yes," he said. "Is that a problem?"

"I guess not." His sister wore a downtrodden look, as if he'd disappointed her.

"I have to be going, too," Sandy Janick said. "Again, thank you."

Steve walked her to the door and said a polite goodbye, hoping it really *was* goodbye. He wished her well, but wasn't interested in becoming her knight in shining armor. Not when there was another damsel whose interest he coveted.

He closed the door as he went to retrieve his car keys from the hall table and grab his jacket.

Nancy got up and followed him as he prepared to leave. "Where are you going?" she asked.

Steve glared at his sister. "What makes you think it's any of your business?"

"Because I have a feeling that you're off to see that… that floozy."

"*Floozy?* What on earth have you been reading?" Shaking his head, he muttered, "Meg isn't a floozy or a woman of ill repute or a hussy or any other silly term you want to call her. She's a single mother and a businesswoman. She owns a bookstore. She—"

"That's not what she told me."

"Listen. I'm thirty-eight years old and I won't have my little sister running my love life. Now, I helped you and your friend, but I had to break a dinner date with Meg to do it."

"Then I'm glad Sandy got that flat tire," she said defiantly.

Steve had had enough. "Stay out of my life, Nancy. I'm warning you."

His sister raised her head dramatically, as if she'd come to some momentous decision. "I'm afraid I can't do that. I'm really sorry, Steve."

"What do you mean, you *can't?*"

"I can't stand idly by and watch the brother I've always loved and admired make a complete fool of himself. Especially over a woman like *that*."

Steve's patience was gone. Vanished. But before he could say a word, Nancy threw herself in front of him.

"I won't let you do this!" she said, stretching her arms across the door.

The phone rang just then, and Steve knew he'd been saved by the bell. Nancy flew across the room to answer it.

Hoping to make a clean getaway, Steve opened the door and dashed outside. As he'd suspected, Nancy tore out after him.

"It's for you," she called from the front porch.

Steve was already in his car and he wasn't going to be waylaid by his sister a second time.

"Tell whoever it is I'll call back."

"It's a woman."

"What's her name?"

"Lindsey," she called at the top of her voice. "And she wants to talk to you."

Eight

The last person Steve expected to hear from was Meg's standoffish teenage daughter. He climbed out of his car and ran up the porch steps. He walked directly past his sister and without saying a word went straight to the phone.

"Lindsey? What's the problem?" he asked. He was in no mood for games and he wanted her to know it.

"Are you alone?" Lindsey asked him.

Steve noticed that her voice was lower than usual. He assumed that meant Meg wasn't aware of her daughter's call.

"My sister's here," he answered. Nancy stood with her arms folded, frowning at him with unconcealed disapproval.

"Anyone else?" Lindsey asked, then added snidely, "Especially someone named Sandy."

It sounded as if Lindsey was jealous on her mother's behalf, which was ridiculous. The kid would be glad of an excuse to get rid of him. "No. Sandy left a few minutes ago."

"So you *were* with her," she accused.

In light of the confrontation he'd just had with his sister, Steve's hold on his patience was already strained. "Is there a reason for your call?" he asked bluntly.

"Of course," Lindsey muttered with an undignified huff. "I want to know what you said that upset my mother."

"What I said?" Steve didn't understand.

"After you called, she told me to order pizza for dinner and then she said I could have anything on it I wanted. She knows I like anchovies and she can't stand 'em. Then," Lindsey said, after a short pause, "the pizza came and she looked at me like she didn't have a clue where it came from. Something's wrong and I want you to tell me what it is."

"I have no idea."

"Mom's just not herself." Another pause, a longer one this time. "You'd better come over and talk to her."

An invitation from the veritable dragon of a daughter herself? This was a stroke of luck. "You sure you can trust me?" he couldn't resist asking.

"Not really," she said with feeling. "But I don't think I have a choice. My mom likes you although I can't figure out why."

The kid was a definite hazard to his ego, but Steve decided to let the comment pass.

"You think your mother's upset because I broke our dinner date?" he asked. "Well, I've got news for you—she's the one who called it off. She said it was no big deal."

"And you believed her?"

"Shouldn't I?"

Steve could picture the girl rolling her eyes. "Either you aren't as smart as you look, or you've been in prison for so long you don't know anything about women."

Steve didn't find either possibility flattering. "All I did was phone to tell her I was going to be late. What's so awful about that?"

"You were late because you were meeting another woman!"

"Wrong," Steve protested. "I was *helping* another woman. Actually two women, one of whom was my sister."

"Don't you get it? My dad left my mother because of another woman. He made up all these lies about where he was and what he was doing so he could be with her."

"And you're worried that your mother assumes I'm doing the same thing? Lindsey, isn't that a bit of a stretch?"

"Yes…no. I don't know," she said. "All I know is you canceled—"

"*She* canceled."

"Your dinner date because you were meeting another woman—"

"Helping another woman and my sister."

"Whatever. All I know is that Mom hasn't been the same since, and if you care about her the way you keep saying…"

"I do."

"Then I suggest you get over here, and fast." The line was abruptly disconnected.

Steve stared at the receiver, then replaced it, shaking his head as he did.

"What's wrong with Meg?" Nancy asked.

Steve shrugged. "Darned if I know. No one ever told me falling in love was so complicated." Having said that, he marched out the door.

Nancy ran after him. "You're in love with her?"

"I sure am."

A huge smile lit up his sister's face. Steve stood next to his car, wondering if he was seeing things. A smile was the last reaction he would've expected from Nancy.

He muttered to himself on the short drive to Meg's house. He didn't stop muttering—about women and daughters and sisters—until he rang the doorbell.

The door was opened two seconds later by Lindsey. "It took you long enough," she said.

"Lindsey, who is it?" Meg asked, stepping out from the kitchen. She'd apparently been putting away dishes, because she had a plate and a coffee mug in her hand. "Steve," she whispered, "what are you doing here?"

"Have you had dinner yet?"

"Not really," Lindsey answered for her mother. "She nibbled on a slice of pizza, but that was only so I wouldn't bug her. I ordered her favorite kind, too." She paused and grimaced. "Vegetarian. Even though *I* like anchovies and pepperoni."

"Weren't you hungry?" Steve asked, silencing Lindsey with a look.

Meg raised one shoulder in a shrug. "Not really. What about you? Did you get anything to eat?"

"Nope."

"There's leftover pizza if you're interested."

"I'm interested," he said, moving toward her. Lindsey was right—Meg seemed upset.

"You're not going to *eat,* are you?" Lindsey demanded.

"Why not?" Steve asked.

The girl sighed loudly. "What my mother needs here is reassurance. If you had a romantic thought in that empty space between your ears, you'd take her in your arms and…and kiss her."

All Steve could do was stand there and stare. This was the same annoying girl who'd been a source of constant irritation from the moment they'd met. Something had changed, and he didn't know what or why.

"Lindsey?" Meg obviously had the same questions as Steve.

"What?" Lindsey asked. "Oh, you want to know why I changed my mind. Well, I've been thinking. If Steve really meant what he said about being friends, then I guess I'm willing to meet him halfway." This was said as if it had come at great personal sacrifice. She turned to Steve. "Actually, I can't see any way around it. It's clear to me that my mother's fallen in love with you."

"Lindsey!"

Steve enjoyed the way Meg's blush colored her pale cheeks.

"And it's equally clear to me that Steve feels the same, especially if he was willing to put up with all my insults. Frankly, I can't see fighting it any longer. What's the point? And really, I can't keep a constant eye on you two. I do have my own life."

Lindsey's change of heart was welcome news to Steve. The kid held the all-important key to Meg's heart. He'd never win her love, if he didn't gain Lindsey's approval first.

"Don't get the idea I *like* any of this," Lindsey added—to salvage her pride, he guessed. "But I can learn to live with it."

"Great," Steve said, offering her his hand. "Let's shake on it."

Lindsey studied his hand as if she wasn't sure she wanted to touch him. But once she did, her shake was firm and confident.

"You're nothing like you were supposed to be," she muttered under her breath.

"I apologize for being such a disappointment," he said out of the corner of his mouth.

"Can't do anything about that now. Mom's crazy about you."

"I think she's pretty terrific, too."

Lindsey sighed. "So I noticed."

"What are you two talking about?" Meg asked.

"Nothing," Lindsey answered with exaggerated innocence. She looked at Steve and winked.

He returned her wink, pleased to be on solid ground with the girl. "Did someone say something about pizza?"

"I did," Meg told him. "Come into the kitchen and I'll microwave the leftovers."

"Mother," Lindsey groaned. "I thought I could count on you to be a little more romantic. Or do I have to do everything myself?"

"What did I do wrong now?"

"Couldn't you make Steve something special?"

Meg took a moment to think this over. "I've got chicken I could make into a salad. If he doesn't like that, there's always peanut-butter-and-jelly sandwiches."

"I'd rather have the pizza," Steve interjected. He didn't want Meg wasting her time preparing a meal, all in the name of some romantic fantasy. He wanted her to talk—and to listen.

Before Lindsey could protest, Steve followed Meg into the kitchen. "Do you know what that was about?"

Meg smiled and opened the refrigerator. "Nope." She took out the pizza box and set it on the counter.

Steve climbed onto the stool. "So what happened earlier?" he asked.

Meg hesitated, separating a piece of the pizza. "I suppose Lindsey called you?"

"Yes, but I was already on my way over here."

He saw that she avoided his eyes, as she made busywork of setting two huge slices of pizza on a plate and heating them in the microwave. "After your phone call, I had kind of a panic attack."

"About?" he prompted.

"You… Us."

"And?"

"And I worked it out myself. I felt pretty foolish afterward. I realized you aren't the same kind of man Dave was…is. If you call to say you're helping another woman, then that's exactly what you're doing."

"You thought I was seeing someone else?" Lindsey had implied as much, but he hadn't taken it seriously.

"I feel silly now," she said, setting the sizzling pizza slices in front of him. She propped her elbows on the counter and rested her chin in her palms. "It was as if the craziness of my marriage was back. You see, at one time I tried to believe Dave. He'd make up the most outrageous stories to account for the huge periods of time he was away from home, and like a naive idiot, I'd believe him." She paused. "I guess because I wanted to. But Dave's not my problem anymore."

"A leopard doesn't change his spots," Steve said, finishing off the first slice. "If Dave cheated on you, he'll cheat on his present wife, too. It stands to reason."

"I know. From what Lindsey said after her last visit to California, Dave's marriage is on shaky ground. I'm sorry for him and for his wife."

Steve offered Meg the second slice, which she declined. He'd just taken a bite when the low strains of soulful violin music drifted toward them. Steve glanced at Meg and she shrugged, perplexed.

Lindsey appeared in the kitchen, looking thoroughly disgusted. "You two need my help, don't you?"

"Help?" Steve repeated. "With what?"

"Romance." She walked into the room and took Steve's hand and then her mother's. She led them both into the living room. The furniture had been pushed to one side and the lights turned down low. Two crystal glasses and a bottle of red wine sat on the coffee table, ready to be put to good use.

"Now, I'll disappear into my room for a while," she said, "and you two can do all the things I've read about in novels."

Steve and Meg stared blankly at each other.

"Don't tell me you need help with that, too!"

"We can take it from here," Steve was quick to assure her.

"I should hope so," Lindsey muttered. With an air of superiority she headed up the stairs.

The music was sultry. Inviting. Once Lindsey was out of sight, Steve held his arms open to Meg. "Shall we dance?"

Steve could've sworn she blushed, very prettily, too, before she slipped into his embrace. He brought her close and sighed, reveling in the feel of her.

"I'm not very good at dancing," she murmured.

"Hey, don't worry. All we have to do is shift our feet a little." He laid his cheek next to hers.

He'd never had the time or the patience for romance. Or so he'd believed. Then he'd met Meg and his organized, safe, secure world had been turned upside down. Nothing had been the same since, and Steve suspected it never would be again.

Even Gary Wilcox seemed to recognize the difference between Steve's attitude toward Meg and his attitude to the other women he'd dated over the years. Steve didn't know how his foreman had figured it out, but he had. Of course, inviting Meg and Lindsey to the shop might have given Gary a clue. The idea of letting Lindsey see him at work had been an excuse; in reality he'd been trying to impress Meg, show her how successful he was. Prove to her that he was worthy of her attention.

Steve had always kept his personal life separate from the business. His personal life—that was a joke. He'd worked for years, dedicating his life to building a thriving business. He'd been successful, but that success had come at a price. There was very little room in his life for love.

But there was room for Meg and Lindsey.

Meg's lithe body moved with the music provocatively, seductively, against his. He wanted to hold her even tighter, kiss her, caress her…

They stopped moving, the pretense of dancing more than he could sustain. "I want you so badly," he whispered.

Meg sighed and raised her head so their eyes met in the dim light. "I want you, too. It frightens me how much…"

He ran his fingers up through her hair and held his breath as he slowly lowered his mouth to hers. "Oh, Meg." He kissed her over and over, unable to get enough of her.

The sound of a throat being cleared suddenly penetrated his brain.

Lindsey. Again.

Steve groaned inwardly. Slowly, reluctantly, he loosened his grip on Meg and eased his body away from hers.

She resisted. "Don't stop."

"Lindsey's back," he whispered.

Meg buried her face in his sweater.

"Hello, again," Lindsey said cheerfully from the stairs. "It looks like I returned in the nick of time." She pranced down the steps, walked over to the wine bottle and sadly shook her head. "You didn't even open the wine."

"We didn't get a chance," Steve muttered.

"I gave you twenty minutes," she said. "From what I can see, that was about five minutes longer than I should've waited. You're a fast worker."

"Lindsey," Meg said, in what was obviously meant to be her sternest voice. Unfortunately, the effect was more tentative than severe.

"I know I'm making a pest of myself—and I apologize, I really do. But we've been talking about this stuff in my sex-ed. class, and there's a case to be made for abstinence."

"What's that got to do with your mother and me?" Steve made the mistake of asking.

"You don't really want me to answer that, do you?" Lindsey asked. "Mom's flustered enough as it is."

"I guess not."

"We could discuss safe sex, if you want."

Steve watched in fascination as Meg's face turned a deep shade of red. "Lindsey!" This time her mother's voice was loud and clear. "You're embarrassing me."

"Sorry, Mom, but I figured we should raise the subject now instead of later." She dropped down on the sofa, then reached for the wine bottle and examined the label. "It's a good month, too. September. Brenda's uncle bought it for us. He said it wasn't a great wine, but it'd get the job done."

Steve's hand gripped Meg's shoulder. "It was, uh, thoughtful of you."

"Thanks." She smiled broadly. "But we were going for the romantic element."

"Now," Steve said, "would you mind if your mother and

I talked? By ourselves? We didn't get much of a chance to do that earlier."

"I suppose that'd be all right—only I need to know something first." She set the wine bottle down and looked intently at Steve. "Are you going to marry my mother?"

Meg made a small mewling noise that suggested she was mortified beyond words. She sank onto the ottoman and covered her face with both hands.

"Well, are you?" Lindsey pressed, ignoring her mother entirely.

Steve couldn't very well say he hadn't been thinking along those lines. There'd been little else on his mind for the past few days. He loved Meg. When he wasn't with her, it felt as if something was missing from his life. From his heart.

Steve had never imagined himself with a ready-made family, but he couldn't see himself without Meg and Lindsey. Not now.

"I believe that's a subject your mother and I need to discuss privately, but since you asked I'll tell you."

Lindsey got to her feet and Meg dropped her hands and looked up at him.

"You're going to marry us, aren't you." Lindsey's words were more statement than question. A satisfied smile lit up her face. "You're really going to do it."

"If your mother will have me."

"She will, trust me," Lindsey answered, looking gleeful. "I've known my mother forever and I've never seen her this gaga over a man."

"I can do my own talking, thank you very much," Meg said. "This is the most humiliating moment of my life—thanks to you, Lindsey Marie Remington." She stood, hands on her hips. "Go to your room and we'll talk when I've finished begging Steve to forgive you."

"What did I do that was so terrible?" Lindsey muttered.

Meg pointed to the stairs.

It looked as though Lindsey was about to argue; apparently she thought better of it. Her shoulders slumped forward and she moved slowly toward the stairs.

"I was just helping," she said under her breath.

"We'll talk about that later, young lady."

Lindsey's blue eyes met Steve's as she passed him. "I know I'm in trouble when she calls me *young lady.* She's mad. Be careful what you say. Don't ruin everything now."

"I'll try my best," Steve promised.

Meg waited until her daughter had reached the top of the stairs before she spoke. "I can't begin to tell you how sorry I am about that." Although her voice was calm, Steve wasn't fooled. Meg was angry, just as Lindsey had said.

"I'll have Lindsey apologize after I've had a chance to cool down," Meg was saying. "I don't dare speak to her now." She paced the carpet. "I want you to know I absolve you from everything that was said."

Steve rubbed his jaw. "Absolve me from what, precisely?"

"I want it understood, here and now, that I don't expect you to marry me."

"But I like the idea."

"I don't," she flared. "Not when my daughter practically

ordered you to propose. Now," she said with a deep breath, "I think it might be best if you left."

Steve tried to protest, but Meg ushered him to the door and he could see that this wasn't the time to reason with her.

"I've never been so mortified in my life," Meg told Laura. She counted the change and put it in the cash register. The store was due to open in ten minutes and she felt far from ready to deal with customers.

"But he said he wanted to marry you, didn't he?"

"It was a pity proposal. Good grief, what else could he say?"

Laura restocked the front display with the latest bestsellers. "Steve doesn't look like the kind of guy who'd propose if he didn't mean it."

"He didn't mean it."

"What makes you so sure?"

Meg wanted to find a hole, crawl inside and hide for the rest of her natural life. No one seemed to appreciate the extent of her humiliation. Steve certainly hadn't. He'd tried to conceal it from her, but he'd viewed the incident with Lindsey as one big joke.

She hadn't intended to mention it to anyone. Laura knew because she'd sensed something was wrong with Meg, and in a moment of weakness, Meg had blurted out the entire episode.

"Have you talked to Lindsey about what she did?" Laura asked.

"In my current frame of mind," Meg told her, "I thought

it better not to try. I'll talk to her when I can do so without screaming or weeping in frustration."

"What I don't understand," Laura said, hugging a book to her chest, "is what happened to bring about such a reversal in her attitude to Steve. The last time we talked, you were pulling out your hair because she refused to believe he wasn't a convicted felon."

"I don't know what's going on with her. I just don't get it."

"You've got to admit, this romance between you and Steve has taken some unexpected twists and turns," Laura said. "First, you didn't even *want* to meet him, then once you did you agreed not to see each other again. It would've ended there if not for the flowers."

"Which didn't even come from Steve. He was just glad to be done with me."

"That's not the way I remember it."

"I doubt I'll ever see him again," Meg said, slamming the cash drawer shut.

"Now you're being ridiculous," Laura said.

"I wouldn't blame him. No man in his right mind would want to get tangled up with Lindsey and me."

"I'm sure that's not true."

Laura sounded so definite about that. Meg desperately wanted to believe her, but she knew better. When she closed the shop at six that evening, she still hadn't heard from Steve, which convinced Meg that he was relieved to be free of her.

Lindsey was sitting in the living room reading when

Meg got home from work. "Hi," she said, taking a huge bite out of a big red Delicious apple.

Meg set aside her purse and slipped off her shoes. The tiles in the entryway felt cool against her aching feet.

"You're not mad at me anymore, are you?" Lindsey asked. She got off the sofa and moved into the kitchen, where Meg was pouring herself a glass of iced tea.

"You embarrassed me."

"Steve wasn't embarrassed," Lindsey said. "I don't understand why you're so upset."

"How would you feel if I called up Dale Kotz and told him you wanted to go to the ninth-grade dance with him? He'd probably agree, because he likes you, but you'd never know if Dale would've asked you himself."

"Oh." Lindsey didn't say anything for several minutes.

"But it's more than that, Lindsey. I was mortified to the very marrow of my bones. I felt like you pressured Steve into proposing."

Lindsey sat in one of the kitchen chairs. "Would you believe me if I told you I was sorry?"

"Yes, but it doesn't change what happened."

"You are still angry, aren't you?"

"No," Meg said, opening the refrigerator and taking out lettuce for a salad. "I'm not angry anymore, just incredibly embarrassed and hurt."

"I didn't mean to hurt you, Mom," Lindsey said in a low voice. "I was only trying to help."

"I know, honey, but you didn't. You made everything much, much worse."

Lindsey hung her head. "I feel just awful."

Meg didn't feel much better herself. She sat down at the table, next to her daughter, and patted Lindsey's hand.

Lindsey managed a weak smile, then fell into her mother's arms and hid her face against Meg's shoulder. "Men are so dumb sometimes," she murmured. "Brenda says love is like a game of connect the dots. Only with men, you have to make the dots and then draw the lines. They don't get it."

Meg stroked her daughter's hair.

"Do you love him, Mom?"

Meg smiled for the first time that day. "Yeah, I think I do. I certainly didn't plan on falling in love with him, that's for sure. It just sort of…happened."

"I don't think he expected to fall in love with you, either."

The doorbell chimed, and horrified that she might be caught crying, Lindsey broke away from her mother and hurriedly brushed the tears from her face.

"I'll get it," Meg said. She padded barefoot into the hallway and opened the door.

Steve stood on the other side, holding a dozen long-stemmed roses. He grinned. "Hello," he said, handing her the flowers. "I thought we'd try this marriage-proposal thing again, only this time we'll do it my way—not Lindsey's."

Nine

"Marriage proposal?" Meg repeated, staring down at the roses in her arms. "Really, Steve, there's no need to do this." Her throat was closing up on her; she could barely speak and she couldn't meet his eyes.

"I know exactly what I'm doing," Steve said.

"Is it Brenda?" Lindsey called from the kitchen.

"No, it's Steve."

"Steve!" Lindsey cried excitedly. "This is great. Maybe I didn't ruin everything after all."

"Hello, Meg," Steve said softly.

"Hi." She still couldn't look him in the eye.

"I'd like to talk to you."

"I...I was hoping we could do that," Meg told him. "They're lovely, thank you."

She handed Lindsey the flowers. "Would you take care of these for me?" she asked her daughter. "Steve and I are going to talk and we'd appreciate some privacy. Okay?"

"Sure, Mom."

Lindsey disappeared into the kitchen and Meg sat down on the sofa. Steve sat beside her and took her hand. She wished he wasn't so close. The man had a way of muddling her most organized thoughts.

"Before you say anything, I have a couple of things I'd like to talk to you about," she began. She freed her hand from his and clasped her knees. "I've been doing a lot of thinking and…and I've come to a few conclusions."

"About what?"

"Us," she said. Dragging in a deep breath, she continued. "Laura reminded me this afternoon that our relationship has taken some unexpected twists and turns. Neither one of us wanted to meet the other—we were thrown into an impossible situation.

"We wouldn't have seen each other again if it wasn't for the flowers your sister sent me. From the moment we met, we've had two other people dictating our lives."

"To some extent that's true," Steve agreed, "but we wouldn't have allowed any of this to happen if we hadn't been attracted to each other from the beginning."

"Maybe," she admitted slowly.

"What do you mean, maybe?" Steve asked.

"I think we both need some time apart to decide what we really want."

"No way!" he said. "I've had thirty-eight years to look for what I want and I've found it. I'd like to make you and Lindsey a permanent part of my life."

"Ah, yes. Lindsey," Meg said. "As you might have

noticed, she's fifteen going on thirty. I have a feeling this is what the rest of the teen years are going to be like."

"So you could use a gentle hand to help you steer her in the right direction." Steve leapt to his feet and jerked his fingers through his hair. "Listen, if you're trying to suggest you'd rather not marry me, just say so."

Meg straightened, keeping her back stiff. For a moment she couldn't speak. "That's what I'm saying," she finally managed.

Steve froze, and it was clear to Meg that he was in shock. "I see," he said after a long pause. "Then what do you want from me?"

Meg closed her eyes. "Maybe it'd be best if we—"

"Don't say it, Meg," he warned in low tones, "because we'll both know it's a lie."

"Maybe it'd be best if we—" she felt she had to say the words "—didn't see each other for a while."

Steve's smile was filled with sarcasm. "Let me tell you something, Meg Remington, because someone obviously needs to. Your husband walked out on you and your daughter. It happens. It wasn't the first time a man deserted his family for another woman and it won't be the last. But you've spent the past ten years building a wall around you and Lindsey.

"No one else was allowed in until Lindsey took matters into her own hands. Now that I'm here, you don't know what to do. You started to care for me and now you're scared to death."

"Steve…"

"Your safe, secure world is being threatened by another

man. Do you think I don't know you love me?" he demanded. "You're crazy about me. I feel the same way about you, and to be fair, you've done a damned good job of shaking up my world, too.

"If you want it to end here and now, okay, but at least be honest about it. You're pushing me away because you're afraid of knocking down those walls of yours. You're afraid to trust another man with your heart."

"You seem to have me all figured out," she said, trying—without much success—to sound sarcastic. To sound as if her emotions were unaffected by his words.

"You want me to leave without giving you this diamond burning a hole in my pocket, then fine. But don't think it's over, because it isn't. I don't give up that easily." He stalked out of the room and paused at her front door. "Don't get a false sense of security. I'll be back and next time I'm bringing reinforcements." The door closed with a bang.

"Mom," Lindsey asked, slipping into the room and sitting down next to Meg. "What happened?"

Meg struggled not to weep. "I…got cold feet."

"But you told me you were in love with Steve."

"I am," she whispered.

"Then why'd you send him away?"

Meg released her breath. "Because I'm an idiot."

"Then stop him," Lindsey said urgently.

"I can't…. It's too late."

"No, it isn't," Lindsey argued and rushed out the front door. A part of Meg wanted to stop her daughter. Meg's pride had taken enough of a beating in the past few days. But her heart, her treacherous heart, knew that the battle had already been lost. She was in love with Steve Conlan.

A minute later Lindsey burst into the house, breathing hard. Panting, she said between giant gulps of air, "Steve says...if you want to talk to him...you're going to have to come outside...yourself."

Meg clasped her hands together. "Where is he?"

"Sitting in his truck. Hurry, Mom! I don't think...he'll wait much longer."

With her heart pounding, Meg walked onto the porch and leaned against the column. Steve's truck was parked at the curb.

He turned his head when he saw her. His eyes were cold. Unfriendly. Unwelcoming.

Meg bit her lip and met his gaze squarely. It took every ounce of resolve she had to move off the porch and take a few steps toward him. She paused halfway across the freshly mowed lawn.

Steve rolled down the window. "What?" he demanded.

She blinked, her heart racing.

"Lindsey said you had something you wanted to tell me," he muttered.

Meg should've known better than to let Lindsey do her talking for her. She opened her mouth, but her throat was clogged with tears. She tried to swallow, refusing to cry in front of him.

"Say it!"

"I...don't know if I can."

"Either you say it or I'm leaving." He turned away from her and started the engine.

"Mom, we're going to lose him," Lindsey cried from the porch. "Don't let him go...."

"I...love you," she whispered.

Steve switched off the engine. "Did you say something?"

"I love you, Steve Conlan. I'm scared out of my wits. You're right—I have built a wall around us. I don't want to lose you. It's just that I'm...afraid." Her voice caught on the last word.

His eyes held hers and after a moment, he smiled. "That wasn't so difficult, now, was it?"

"Yes, it was," she countered. "It was incredibly hard." He didn't seem to realize she was standing on her front lawn with half the neighborhood looking on as she told him how much she loved him.

"You're going to marry me, Meg Remington."

She sniffled. "Probably."

He got out of his truck, slammed the door and with three long strides eliminated the distance between them. "Will you or will you not marry me?"

"I will," she said, laughing and crying at the same time, then she ran to meet him halfway.

"That's what I thought." Steve hauled her into his arms and buried her in his embrace. He grabbed her about the waist and whirled her around, then half carried her back into the house.

Once inside, he kicked the door shut and and they leaned against it, kissing frantically.

Lindsey cleared her throat behind them. "I hate to interrupt, but I have a few important questions."

Steve hid his face in Meg's neck and mumbled something she couldn't hear, which was no doubt for the best.

"Okay, kiddo, what do you want to know?" Steve asked when he'd regrouped.

"We're getting married?" Lindsey asked. Meg liked the way she'd included herself.

"Yup," Steve assured her. "We're going to be a family."

Lindsey let out a holler that could be heard three blocks away.

"Where will we live? Your house or ours?"

Steve looked at Meg. "Do you care?"

She shook her head.

"We'll live wherever you want," Steve told the girl. "I imagine staying close to your friends is important, so we'll take that into consideration."

"Great." Lindsey beamed him a smile. "What about adding to the family? Mom's willing, I think."

Once more Steve looked at Meg, and laughing, she nodded. "Oh, yes," she murmured, "there'll be several additions to this family."

Steve's eyes grew intense, and Meg knew he was thinking the same thing she was. She wanted his babies as much as she wanted this man. She loved him, desired him, anticipating all they could discover together, all they could learn from each other.

"One last thing," Lindsey said.

It was hard to pull her eyes away from Steve, but she

wanted to include Lindsey in these important decisions. "Yes, honey?"

"It's just that I'd rather you didn't go shopping for your wedding dress alone. You're really good at lots of things, but frankly, Mom, you don't have any fashion sense."

As it turned out, Lindsey, Brenda and Steve's sister, Nancy, were all involved in the process of choosing the all-important wedding dress. Steve, naturally, wasn't allowed within a hundred feet of Meg and her dress until the day of the ceremony.

The wedding took place three months later, with family and friends gathered around. Lindsey proudly served as her mother's maid of honor.

Steve endured all the formality because he knew it mattered to Meg and to Lindsey. Nancy and his mother seemed to enjoy making plans for the wedding, too. All that was required of him was to show up and say "I do," which suited Steve just fine.

In his view, this fuss over weddings was for women. Men considered it a necessary evil. Or so he believed until his wedding day. When he saw Meg walk down the aisle, the emotion that throbbed in his chest came as a complete and utter surprise.

He'd known he loved her—he must, to put up with all the craziness that had befallen their courtship. But he hadn't realized how deep that love went. Not until he saw Meg so solemn and so beautiful. His bride. She stole his breath as he gazed at her.

The reception was a blur. Every time he looked at Meg he found it difficult to believe that this beautiful, vibrant woman was his wife. His thoughts were a jumbled, confused mess as he greeted those he needed to greet and thanked those he needed to thank.

It seemed half a lifetime before he was alone with his wife. He'd booked the honeymoon suite at a hotel close to Sea-Tac airport. The following morning they were flying to Hawaii for two weeks. Meg had never seen the islands. Steve suspected he didn't need a tropical playground to discover paradise. He would find that in her arms.

"My husband." Meg said the word shyly as Steve fumbled with the key card to unlock their suite. "I like the way it sounds."

"So do I, but not quite as much as I like the sound of wife." With the door open, he swept Meg into his arms and carried her into the room.

He hadn't taken two steps before they started to kiss.

Meg tasted of wedding cake and champagne, of passion and love. She wound her arms around his neck and enticed him to kiss her again. Steve didn't need much of an invitation.

At the unbridled desire he read in her eyes, Steve moaned and carried her to the bed. After he'd set her feet on the floor, he kissed her again, slowly, with all the pent-up desire inside him.

He reached behind her for the zipper of her dress. "I haven't made any secret of how much I want to make love to you."

"That's true," she whispered, kissing his jaw. "Thank you for agreeing to wait. It meant a lot to me to start our marriage this way."

He slipped the sleeve down her arm and kissed the ivory perfection of one shoulder. Then he kissed the other, his lips blazing a trail up the side of her neck to the hollow of her throat.

"You make my knees go weak," she told him in a low voice.

"Mine are, too."

Together they collapsed on the bed. Steve kissed her and loosened his tie. With their lips joined, Meg's fingers worked at his shirt, undressing him.

Soon they were lost in each other, loving each other, immersed in a world of their own. A world from which they didn't emerge until the summer sun had been replaced by a glittering moon and a sky full of stars.

Back at the reception, Lindsey sat with Steve's sister, Nancy, and licked the icing off their fingertips. "Do you suppose they'll ever figure it out?"

Nancy sipped champagne from a crystal flute. "I doubt either of them is thinking about much right now—except each other."

"We made some real mistakes, though."

"We?" Nancy said, eyeing Lindsey.

"Okay, me. I'll admit I nearly ruined everything by pushing the marriage issue. How was I to know my mother would take it so personally? Jeez, she just about had a heart attack, and all because I suggested Steve marry her."

"It worked out, though," Nancy said, looking pleased with herself. "And I made a few blunders of my own. Getting my friend to go to the shop and say she was Meg wasn't the smartest thing I've ever done. Steve was bound to find out sooner or later that it wasn't Meg."

"But we had to do something," Lindsey insisted. "They were both being so stubborn. One of them had to give in. Besides, your ploy worked."

"Better than the flowers I sent."

Lindsey sampled another bite of wedding cake. "You know what was the hardest part?"

"I know what it was for me. I had one heck of a time keeping a straight face when your mother came to the house dressed in a Tina Turner wig and five-inch heels. Oh, Lindsey, if you could've seen her."

"Steve was pretty funny himself, with his leather jacket and that bad-boy smirk."

"Neither one of them's any good at acting," Nancy said, still grinning.

"Not like us."

"Not like us," Nancy agreed.

* * * * *

*Mark your calendar! If you enjoyed
MARRIED IN SEATTLE, you'll want to read these
upcoming books by Debbie Macomber.*

*In February, watch for the long-awaited re-release of
Debbie's popular MIDNIGHT SONS, VOLUME 1,
which includes BRIDES FOR BROTHERS and
THE MARRIAGE RISK.*

*March brings THE MATCHMAKERS, first published in
1985 and now part of Harlequin's 60th Anniversary
collection.*

*Then, in April, her acclaimed novel, TWENTY WISHES,
will be out in paperback for the first time.*

*And…in May, her brand-new hardcover,
SUMMER ON BLOSSOM STREET,
will hit the bookstore shelves.*

Don't miss a single one!

Available wherever books are sold.

#1 *NEW YORK TIMES* BESTSELLING AUTHOR

DEBBIE
MACOMBER

Jason Manning is content with his life as a bachelor, a slob
and a sports fan. Then he's introduced to Charlotte Weston,
and Jason's feelings start to change once he gets to know his
Bride on the Loose.

With a broken engagement behind him, James Wilkens spent
New Year's Eve in Las Vegas...where he met Summer Lawton.
They made a date to meet in Vegas *Same Time, Next Year.*
Except it turns out to be more than a date—it's a wedding!

The Manning Grooms

Debbie Macomber has "earned her place
as one of today's most beloved authors."
—*New York Times* bestselling author Susan Wiggs

*Available the first week of December 2008
wherever paperbacks are sold!*

www.MIRABooks.com

MIRA®

MDM2602

#1 *New York Times* Bestselling Author

DEBBIE MACOMBER

Dear Reader,

I have something to confide in you. I think my husband, Dave, might be having an affair. I found an earring in his pocket, and it's not mine.

You see, he's a pastor. And a good man. I can't believe he's guilty of anything, but why won't he tell me where he's been when he comes home so late?

Reader, I'd love to hear what you think. So come on in and join me for a cup of tea.

Emily Flemming

8 Sandpiper Way

On sale August 26, 2008!

MDM2578

REQUEST YOUR FREE BOOKS!

2 FREE NOVELS
FROM THE ROMANCE/SUSPENSE
COLLECTION PLUS 2 FREE GIFTS!

YES! Please send me 2 FREE novels from the Romance/Suspense Collection and my 2 FREE gifts (gifts are worth about $10). After receiving them, if I don't wish to receive any more books, I can return the shipping statement marked "cancel." If I don't cancel, I will receive 4 brand-new novels every month and be billed just $5.49 per book in the U.S. or $5.99 per book in Canada, plus 25¢ shipping and handling per book plus applicable taxes, if any*. That's a savings of at least 20% off the cover price! I understand that accepting the 2 free books and gifts places me under no obligation to buy anything. I can always return a shipment and cancel at any time. Even if I never buy another book from the Reader Service, the two free books and gifts are mine to keep forever.

185 MDN EF5Y   385 MDN EF6C

Name	(PLEASE PRINT)
Address	Apt. #
City	State/Prov.	Zip/Postal Code

Signature (if under 18, a parent or guardian must sign)

Mail to **The Reader Service:**
IN U.S.A.: P.O. Box 1867, Buffalo, NY 14240-1867
IN CANADA: P.O. Box 609, Fort Erie, Ontario L2A 5X3

Not valid to current subscribers to the Romance Collection,
the Suspense Collection or the Romance/Suspense Collection.

Want to try two free books from another line?
Call 1-800-873-8635 or visit www.morefreebooks.com.

* Terms and prices subject to change without notice. N.Y. residents add applicable sales tax. Canadian residents will be charged applicable provincial taxes and GST. Offer not valid in Quebec. This offer is limited to one order per household. All orders subject to approval. Credit or debit balances in a customer's account(s) may be offset by any other outstanding balance owed by or to the customer. Please allow 4 to 6 weeks for delivery. Offer available while quantities last.

Your Privacy: Harlequin is committed to protecting your privacy. Our Privacy Policy is available online at www.eHarlequin.com or upon request from the Reader Service. From time to time we make our lists of customers available to reputable third parties who may have a product or service of interest to you. If you would prefer we not share your name and address, please check here. ☐

BOB08R

THE HARLEQUIN FAMOUS FIRSTS COLLECTION™

ENJOY SOME OF THE VERY FIRST
HARLEQUIN BOOKS WRITTEN BY
BESTSELLING AUTHORS OF TODAY!

**Read
#1 *New York Times*
bestselling author
Debbie Macomber's
very first
Harlequin book,
*The Matchmakers***

Newly single mom Dori Robertson has no interest in being
in a relationship. So when her son advertises for a new
dad, she is mortified. Former football player and single dad
Gavin Parker proposes a plan to Dori: they'll pretend to
date so that their matchmaking kids lay off. The plan goes
awry when Dori and Gavin start falling for one another...
but are they ready to face love again?

Available March 2009 wherever books are sold.

**Look for all 12 books in the
Harlequin Famous Firsts Collection
available March, June and September.**

www.eHarlequin.com

FFDM0308

DEBBIE MACOMBER

66974	MOON OVER WATER	___ $6.99 U.S.	___ $8.50 CAN.
32535	BACK ON BLOSSOM STREET	___ $7.99 U.S.	___ $7.99 CAN.
32569	ALWAYS DAKOTA	___ $7.99 U.S.	___ $7.99 CAN.
32474	THE MANNING BRIDES	___ $7.99 U.S.	___ $7.99 CAN.
32578	8 SANDPIPER WAY	___ $7.99 U.S.	___ $7.99 CAN.
66929	204 ROSEWOOD LANE	___ $7.50 U.S.	___ $8.99 CAN.
32160	THE SHOP ON BLOSSOM STREET	___ $7.50 U.S.	___ $8.99 CAN.
32295	A GOOD YARN	___ $7.99 U.S.	___ $9.50 CAN.
32334	6 RAINIER DRIVE	___ $7.99 U.S.	___ $9.50 CAN.
32208	50 HARBOR STREET	___ $7.50 U.S.	___ $8.99 CAN.
32350	THE MANNING SISTERS	___ $7.99 U.S.	___ $9.50 CAN.
32506	CHRISTMAS WISHES	___ $7.99 U.S.	___ $9.50 CAN.
32485	74 SEASIDE AVENUE	___ $7.99 U.S.	___ $9.50 CAN.
32511	DAKOTA BORN	___ $7.99 U.S.	___ $9.50 CAN.
32444	SUSANNAH'S GARDEN	___ $7.99 U.S.	___ $9.50 CAN.
32393	DAKOTA HOME	___ $7.99 U.S.	___ $9.50 CAN.
32369	READY FOR LOVE	___ $7.50 U.S.	___ $8.99 CAN.
32366	BE MY VALENTINE	___ $7.99 U.S.	___ $9.50 CAN.
32362	COUNTRY BRIDES	___ $7.99 U.S.	___ $9.50 CAN.
32110	ON A SNOWY NIGHT	___ $6.99 U.S.	___ $8.50 CAN.
32073	44 CRANBERRY POINT	___ $7.50 U.S.	___ $8.99 CAN.
32028	CHANGING HABITS	___ $7.50 U.S.	___ $8.99 CAN.
66674	BETWEEN FRIENDS	___ $7.50 U.S.	___ $8.99 CAN.
66930	A GIFT TO LAST	___ $6.99 U.S.	___ $8.50 CAN.
66891	THURSDAYS AT EIGHT	___ $7.50 U.S.	___ $8.99 CAN.
66830	16 LIGHTHOUSE ROAD	___ $6.99 U.S.	___ $8.50 CAN.
66719	311 PELICAN COURT	___ $7.50 U.S.	___ $8.99 CAN.
66434	MONTANA	___ $6.99 U.S.	___ $7.99 CAN.
66260	THIS MATTER OF MARRIAGE	___ $6.99 U.S.	___ $7.99 CAN.

(limited quantities available)

TOTAL AMOUNT	$ _____
POSTAGE & HANDLING	$ _____
($1.00 FOR 1 BOOK, 50¢ for each additional)	
APPLICABLE TAXES*	$ _____
TOTAL PAYABLE	$ _____

(check or money order—please do not send cash)

To order, complete this form and send it, along with a check or money order for the total above, payable to MIRA Books, to: **In the U.S.:** 3010 Walden Avenue, P.O. Box 9077, Buffalo, NY 14269-9077; **In Canada:** P.O. Box 636, Fort Erie, Ontario, L2A 5X3.

Name: _____

Address: _____ City: _____

State/Prov.: _____ Zip/Postal Code: _____

Account Number (if applicable): _____

075 CSAS

*New York residents remit applicable sales taxes.
*Canadian residents remit applicable GST and provincial taxes.

MIRA®

www.MiRABooks.com

MDM0109BL